Omens of Death

Nicholas Rhea

Nicholas Rhea has asserted his rights under the Copyright, Design and Patents Act, 1988, to be identified as the author of this work.

ISBN: 978-1-911445-09-8

First published in 1996 by Constable and Company Ltd.

This edition published in 2015 by Endeavour Press Ltd.

Printed and bound in Great Britain by Clays Ltd, St Ives plc.

Table of Contents

Chapter 1

When Detective Inspector Montague Pluke noticed the solitary crow upon the roof of No. 15 Padgett Grove, he realised it was an omen of death. Resembling the sky, the bird was black, sombre and threatening. It was a sultry Wednesday morning with a threat of thunder and although the clouds were silent and brooding, the bird was croaking raucously. It was a melancholy moment for Montague Pluke.

With some apprehension, he paused at the end of the Grove to view the modest two-bedroomed bungalow. Detached, with a red pantile roof and built of local stone, it boasted tidy gardens, a greenhouse and a single garage. Second from the far end and situated on the right, it had a green front door — a healthy colour, he mused, the colour of the countryside. Some might consider green to be unlucky; that was probably why green was so rarely used on our postage stamps. Montague contemplated that whenever we'd had green postage stamps, the country had experienced great social unrest.

He made a determined effort to ignore the significance of colours of postage stamps and concentrated upon the crow. It was perched upon the home of the Crowthers. They were nice people who had recently retired to live quiet and unobtrusive lives in Crickledale.

Cyril had been an agricultural engineer specialising in combine harvesters, while May had worked for forty-five years as a clerk in a building society. She had served faithfully, with no thoughts of promotion, neither had she sought additional responsibility. She was a steady sort of person, just like Cyril in fact. The Crowthers lived in mutual shared contentment and, being well-mannered people with well-ordered lives, were considered ideal residents for a small town like Crickledale.

Detective Inspector Montague Pluke was well acquainted with them because he knew most of the people in Crickledale. He knew their backgrounds too, and their social habits, even though they were not the sort of people to come to the notice of the police in a derogatory manner. The same could also be said about other residents of Padgett Grove, thus the neighbourhood had been locally established as desirable. It was the type of vicinage where you could confidently buy a house without worrying too much about the sort of neighbours you would acquire. The residents took the *Daily Telegraph*, didn't join trade unions, never ate fish and chips in public or repaired their cars in the street.

As he studied the scene before him, Montague Pluke appreciated that the Padgett Grove area was very similar to that in which he lived, although it must be said that the Pluke household stood in a street of 'olde', more substantial properties, genteel homes with a Georgian pedigree. None the less, each was a contented community replete with decent law-abiding citizens who held coffee mornings for charity and didn't have gnomes or model windmills in their gardens.

But even if the residents of Padgett Grove had never caused professional concern to the constabulary, the presence of that crow did create some anxiety in the meditative mind of Montague Pluke. It remained cawing on the roof and adopted an almost defiant attitude as he re-established his stride and continued his walk to work. In Montague's opinion, its presence could not be ignored — its message was strikingly clear. It heralded a death within that house. An added factor was that today was not the most providential of weekdays. Wednesday, like Wednesday's child, was often full of woe.

That unwelcome combination of portents dominated Montague's

morning walk to the office and produced a mood of impending doom, albeit with just a glimmer of excitement. That glimmer could never be mentioned to anyone else because it was based on the fact that, as the officer in charge of the CID at Crickledale Sub-Divisional Police Station, he had never solved a murder and never arrested a killer.

The death, when it happened, could mean work for him and his department. It was that possibility which had provoked those mixed feelings, because it was his ambition, before he retired from the Force to seek neglected or forgotten horse troughs, to detect a noteworthy murder. Before that day came, therefore, he wanted his name prominently placed in the annals of great and famous criminal investigations and the presence of that crow offered just a little hope of that. Throughout his service he had wanted to be a great detective, but all the glamorous investigations and high-profile inquiries had been the responsibility of someone else.

As he pondered the presence of that crow, therefore, he mused that it would be very nice to solve just one murder enquiry before he retired to enjoy his pension, but as his years of service carried him ever closer to retirement, the opportunities for professional glory were dwindling by the day.

Montague did appreciate that the natural peace of Crickledale had been a contributory factor to his lack of success in having a murder to solve. In fact, there had never been a murder in the town. Crickledale was a murder-free zone. But if one did occur, he would be in charge of the investigation. That would be his duty and it meant he would be able to display his latent detective acumen. He knew the theory of criminal investigation very well indeed, because he had attended lots of courses about techniques and procedures, so perhaps the forthcoming death would enable him to put his years of acquired knowledge to some practical use?

In considering these matters, he did remind himself that not every death is a murder. A crow on a roof merely foretold a death and not necessarily a murder; after all, a crow could not be expected to distinguish between suspicious deaths and natural causes. It was a well-known fact that most deaths were not suspicious, even if they were sudden and unexpected.

But in spite of his ruminations, he knew that the Crowther household could expect a funeral very shortly, probably before the week was out. As Montague Pluke contemplated that scenario, he realised it would not be very pleasant having to deal with the unexpected death of one's acquaintances, although actually to arrest the *murderer* of one's acquaintances would indeed be meritorious. Apart from any job satisfaction that would result, it would add to the high esteem in which he was already held in the town.

For generations, the Plukes had enjoyed positions of influence in Crickledale — Josiah Pluke (1803-81) had established the King's Head as a premier coaching inn, while Beaumont Pluke (1832-1914) had been the town's first head constable. There had been a long line of eminent Plukes in Crickledale and records showed that Sir Wylyngton Pluke had occupied the Manor House in 1422, although a Wortham Pluke (1349-93) had been a wandering minstrel. Montague was not totally sure of the social status of a wandering minstrel at that time, but it did suggest that one branch of the family was musical. His favourite ancestor was Justus Pluke (1553-1609) who achieved national distinction for his futuristic design of carved animals' heads upon the inlets to stone horse troughs.

On that Wednesday morning, however, illustrious ancestors were far from Montague's mind as he continued his thoughtful way to work. The police station, a former mansion with original beams and fireplaces, was located on an elevated site near the church. The handsome building was highly suitable for the accommodation of a Pluke, but this one served as offices for the other police of Crickledale as well.

As he continued his walk along Cornmill Lane, he tried to recollect the last time he had encountered either of the Crowthers. He hadn't seen Cyril for some time, although May's presence could be noticed most days; she'd be working in her garden, doing the shopping, visiting friends, working with her voluntary groups, helping those in need, or pottering across to the church to put fresh flowers on the altar.

He'd seen her a couple of weeks since and she'd looked fairly fit, but by Crickledale standards that was quite a long time ago. In such a small town, people saw one another on a much more regular basis. So had Cyril been ill recently? Perhaps he was in hospital? Montague hoped neither would be the victim of the grim reaper, but you couldn't tamper with fate. That crow had forecast a death, so perhaps they had friends or family staying at the house? That was a possibility, he mused, realising that neither of the Crowthers was compelled to be the victim.

In considering the fate of the Crowthers, Montague Pluke felt proud of his detailed professional knowledge of the town and its people. It was a knowledge acquired over many years without the slightest hint of direct prying, but in this case he was secure in the knowledge that he could regard the Crowthers as friends. Or to be precise, the Pluke-Crowther relationship was as close to friendship as the life of a police officer would permit. Police officers, especially senior ones, had to be circumspect in their choice of friends and social acquaintances. They had to be above criticism; they had to set a good example to the rest of society.

The Pluke-Crowther relationship arose because May Crowther was on the Church Flower Rota and shared watering duties with Millicent — Mrs Pluke. They were on the same Local History Society committee and were members of many other clubs and societies; they even shared tea-making duties at the Over-Sixties Club. Not that either Millicent or Montague was over sixty — but both of them did work very hard for those citizens who were less fortunate than themselves. The Plukes and the Crowthers were good neighbours to lots of people.

As Montague walked on, the crow remained in position. It bowed up and down as it croaked defiantly on the ridge of Cyril's and May's bungalow, its bedraggled plumage resembling a dismal undertaker in baggy trousers and a loose jacket. It was quite alone too. In vain, Montague searched the skies, the chimney pots and the nearby roofs for a second crow. The presence of two crows meant that something happy was about to occur, such as a wedding or even a birth, therefore two crows on that roof at the same time would have presented a totally different message to the world. But the menacing creature was utterly alone and Montague knew that he was powerless to prevent the drama which was about to engulf the Crowther household.

It was no good chasing it away or pretending he hadn't seen it. The crow had landed and its message was beyond dispute. As a consequence, it was with a feeling of impending gloom, coupled with just a little personal anticipation, that Montague continued his walk towards the police station. Bidding his smiling but frequently automatic good-mornings to people on his left and right, and doffing his panama to the ladies, he did consider returning to the Grove for words of advice with the Crowthers.

He could urge them — or their guests — to take great care in their daily routine, especially when crossing the road or fixing plugs on electrical appliances, but realised his well-meaning action would unsettle and disturb them. No one liked being told that any carelessness on his or her part could be fatal. Worse still, it would be a waste of time. Any such intervention would be fruitless. Nothing could halt the inevitable. Death was imminent at No. 15 Padgett Grove, Crickledale.

*

When Montague left the house for his walk to work, Millicent settled down to her routine. After making the bed and washing the pots she would consult her diary to check her daily appointments. Hadn't Amelia Fender hinted at something strange happening at the Crowthers' bungalow? But the Coffee Club meeting was tomorrow, Thursday. So who else was likely to be that well informed?

Chapter 2

For Detective Inspector Montague Pluke, the daily walk from his own fine period town house to the equally fine period police station took precisely twenty minutes — that's if he wasn't interrupted. He preferred to walk because it provided a period of modest exercise and enabled him to breathe the fresh air of each new day. In addition, his morning stroll offered some quiet moments during which to consider his plans for the day between greeting and meeting the people he encountered.

Among the regulars upon his route was Moses Nettlewren, the weighty and cheerful magistrates' clerk whom he always passed near the post office. He was a large but smartly dressed man, a veritable compendium of court procedures, whose shoes always shone with much spitting and polishing as he walked towards his modest office in the court-house building. There was the Crowthers' neighbour, the sepulchral George Dunwoody, a part-time taxi driver who had several other part-time jobs and was always on the move around the town, day and night. Montague saw him most mornings because he had a daily pick-up just outside the town hall, a lady going to work at the hospital.

He always saw Mrs Carstairs too; she was a lady with purple hair who ran Help the Aged and who repeatedly asked him for old clothes; there were the two sickly-looking Minskip children, who waited for the school bus near the Methodist chapel, and the whistling window cleaner whose name was Jasper and whose ladder he studiously avoided. Sometimes he encountered the mayor, Councillor Seymour Farrell, outside the Town Hall or that delicious young woman who ran the off-licence.

Montague liked his morning walk, which carried him over the cobbled areas, through the grassy patch near the Town Hall and along the quieter roads via Tannery Lane up to the police station on its elevated site. Being a man of substance in the small town, however, meant he had to utter his daily greetings to all with aplomb and without prejudice; he spoke to the street cleaner in the same manner as he did to the mayor or the magistrates' clerk. He was very aware that people of prominence had certain responsibilities and he was not afraid to set a good example to the townsfolk. Montague, conducting himself in an exemplary manner, was aware that his wife, Millicent, was likewise prominent in the community — she was secretary of the Women's Institute, (Crickledale being not too large to support a WI), the Parochial Church Council, the Church Flower Group, the Local History Society, Meals on Wheels, President of the Ladies Luncheon Club *and* chairwoman of the Town Hall Entertainments Committee. Mrs Dunwoody seemed to be secretary or treasurer of all the groups that Millicent was not. But Millicent was also a member of several other organisations of importance to the town's social standing, consequently Montague's off-duty conduct was equally important.

For a leading citizen such as himself to omit bidding good-morning to even a distant relation of one of Millicent's ladies would be social suicide, followed by a good deal of tut-tutting over scones and teacups. To the ladies of Crickledale such social graces mattered almost as much as their choice of hats, and such was their esteem of Montague that he had been invited to be guest speaker at many of their events. He regarded that as a measure of his own standing in the town.

Practically every group or society in Crickledale had been treated to one of his talks about the history of horse troughs. From time to time, however, certain forward-thinking ladies felt that

Montague, with his unrivalled knowledge of the underbelly of life in Crickledale, should be asked to speak about the unlawful, sexy or spurious nature of life in the town. They had often felt that he could offer them a glimpse into an unknown and intriguing world, but Montague, anxious to keep his social life quite distinct from his professional duties, had steadfastly resisted. He preferred to show his collection of photographs and slides about historic horse troughs, especially those depicting the heads of carved animals, those being an integral part of the Pluke family history. There was such a trough outside Crickledale Town Hall.

After all, in his private life he was Mr Montague Pluke, author of a pamphlet about 'The Horse Troughs of Crickledale and District since the 16th Century — fully illustrated by the author'. There was a copy in the local library. As he had so often said, bearing in mind the work of Justus Pluke, his illustrious ancestor, 'Horse troughs are in the blood of the Plukes.' His lifetime dedication to horse troughs was a wonderful antidote to the demands of his job and he believed that these forgotten watering places, the filling stations of a bygone era, were a vital part of local history. He felt the townspeople should be made aware of the past glories which were literally upon their doorsteps and constantly failed to understand the lack of interest he sometimes encountered.

For Montague Pluke, therefore, that morning walk, and all that occurred within its short duration, was as vital as the fresh air he breathed. A daily confirmation of his status in the community, it was also a means of starting the day in a happy and confident frame of mind, an opportunity to avoid any bad fortune that might be lurking and an opportunity to consolidate any manifestation of good luck that presented itself. It was, in addition, a splendid means of reinforcing his vital professional role in helping to keep the Queen's Peace in Crickledale.

There was some crime in Crickledale of course, but it was kept to a very modest level in comparison with other towns of comparable size. Besides, it wasn't every town with a population of less than four thousand that had a detective inspector walking through its market place and along its main thoroughfares every morning. During his business-like walk, he always used the left of the street, the most fortuitous side, and one of his delights was to hear the bells of the parish church as he progressed. Their musical sound was a sure sign of impending good fortune for the coming day. Usually, they began to chime as he passed the chemist's, a welcome sound because Whistling Jasper up his ladder was invariably cleaning the first-floor windows at that time. Once, when passing the time of day with that delightful Miss Berryford from the fruit shop, he'd actually walked under Jasper's ladder, but no bad luck had befallen him. He ascribed that to the ringing of the church bells and the fact he had made the sign of the cross with his first and second fingers the moment he had realised his lapse.

For the people of Crickledale, a peaceful, historic and pretty limestone-built market town on the edge of the North York Moors, Detective Inspector Montague Pluke was a regular and reassuring sight. His distinctive appearance formed a part of their daily routine as the town quickened with the beginning of each new day. Indeed, many residents reckoned they could set their clocks and watches by his progress through the streets. He would leave home at 8.30 a.m. prompt and arrive at his office at 8.50 a.m. precisely, passing the same shops, pubs, bus stops, pillar boxes and lamp posts at exactly the same time each morning. He always bade a respectful good-morning and raised his panama to those he encountered, irrespective of social status, and he would even pat their dogs or say hello to babies in prams.

At the start of each working day in Crickledale, Mr Pluke's distinctive panama hat, with its sky-blue band, could be seen weaving its way through the morning crowds, bobbing among the headscarves and bare heads like a cork on a rippling pond and frequently being lifted high by Mr Pluke's right hand. The hat was perhaps very slightly too small for his head because it seemed to perch precariously on top, so that his hair stuck out at awkward angles, rather like the untidy thatch of a neglected cottage. Some purists considered his hair rather too long for a senior police officer, for when Montague removed his hat he did reveal a head of very thick, dark-grey hair. Many balding Crickledonians were slightly envious, perhaps wondering if he used a secret potion gleaned from the Pluke family records, or whether he washed his hair in the water of horse troughs.

Whatever his secret, he had an astonishingly good head of hair for a man in late middle-age. However, some acute observers of the social scene considered his hair-style was not the most modern, nor was it flattering to his distinctive and strong face, but Millicent was confident that her tonsorial skills were just as professional as those of any of the local barbers. Besides, she felt that a man of Montague's status should not have to queue for haircuts alongside farm labourers, butchers' boys and lorry drivers. One never knew what one might catch from combs which had scraped the heads of some of the people who haunted Crickledale's masculine hair salons.

The face beneath the Pluke hair and hat wore heavy black-rimmed spectacles over thoughtful grey eyes. The eyebrows were lush and dark to match the colour of his hair, while Montague's teeth were his own, very white and well kept. A somewhat prominent nose protruded above a mouth which rarely smiled, while a clean-shaven, determined jaw-line hung beneath his long, rather narrow face which always seemed pink with good health, a tribute to his daily exercise.

Montague favoured expensive brown brogue shoes, enhanced with light beige-coloured spats which were a family heirloom. His great-grandfather, grandfather and father had all worn these self-same spats. Montague, however, had no children — he and Millicent didn't indulge in the sort of behaviour that begat families — and so the destiny of the Pluke spats was a constant source of worry to him. He had often considered leaving them to Crickledale Folk Museum as it did have a small 'Clothes of a Bygone Era' section.

The rest of his clothing was of interest too — he always wore a very old and worn beige-coloured Burberry check-patterned overcoat. Some experts said it was the very first coat ever made by Burberry and should be in a museum, but Mr Pluke denied that, saying it was a coaching coat which had belonged to an ancestor. It had a fitted cape about the shoulders, a large collar, wrist flaps and huge pockets. In one of the pockets he carried his lunch — a cheese sandwich and an apple. He had lunch at his desk, so that Millicent could undertake her many social engagements without the worry of ministering to his needs at midday.

The famous Pluke greatcoat was rather large for Montague, but he wore it because it was a family heirloom. Like the spats, it had belonged to his great-grandfather, grandfather and father, all of whom had been rather tall gentlemen of generous width. Great-grandfather had been a coachman and had worn this coat during journeys aboard the 'Highflyer', but time had taken its toll. Now the wrist flaps were invariably undone because they lacked the necessary buttons; all the edges — hems, tips of sleeves, epaulettes, pockets — were worn and tattered, and the coat had what some described as a 'lived-in' appearance. Newcomers to the town had often commented in private that they thought he bought his clothes from Oxfam, whereas the local people knew the impressive history of the Pluke greatcoat. It had even survived two coach crashes and one fire. He thought he might leave it, like the spats, to the Folk Museum because he had sometimes visualised a full-size wax model of himself in the coat and spats after his death.

His trousers, always in need of a crease, had deep turn-ups and were very similar in colour to his greatcoat, a beige check design.

The fact that they rode at half-mast meant they did reveal the full glory of his spats, which concealed his socks — a good thing, perhaps, because he favoured socks in unsympathetic colours like pink, white or yellow. Montague wore the same clothes winter and summer alike, consequently few who observed him away from the office knew what kind of jacket he preferred when out of doors, because that old greatcoat enveloped his upper torso.

His shirts were on view, however, or at least the upper portion of the breast and collars were. They were clean, neat and tidy, thanks to Millicent's loving care and he always wore a dicky bow of sky-blue, his lucky colour. He liked to sport a white collar with his many coloured shirts — but so few shops sold collar studs these days. He sometimes congratulated himself upon his foresight in accumulating a large stock of them.

His jacket was the same colour as his trousers, rather like a faded Macmillan tartan with some wrong colours added. All his external jacket pockets had buttoned flaps, with pleats to allow the material to expand in direct proportion to the objects stuffed within. His breast pocket was always bulging with fountain pens and propelling pencils, and he sported a pocket watch and chain which he kept in a shiny waistcoat of chestnut hue. By no stretch of anyone's imagination, therefore, could Montague Pluke be described as well-dressed or even tidy, but he was distinctive. Although he considered himself an adequately attired gentleman, Millicent had, in her younger days, attempted to dissuade him from wearing his old coat and spats, but he had rejected her pleas. He'd been emphatic that his distinctive mode of dress was part of the renowned Pluke family history — his father, grandfather and great-grandfather had worn these very clothes and he, being the last of the Plukes, was determined to uphold the family tradition until his dying day. Millicent had sometimes said he would be buried in his old greatcoat, probably in a horse trough-shaped coffin. There were times when he thought this a good idea.

Over the years, though, Millicent had come to accept that the Pluke menfolk were eccentric dressers. That character trait had extended into Montague's early days as a uniformed constable. To the chagrin of his superiors, he was always untidy, with tunic buttons missing or undone, and pink or yellow socks showing below his uniform trousers which were too short. And none of his supervisory officers would agree that spats looked right with police uniform. Regular expressions of concern to the then Police Constable Pluke had failed to make any impression, so the Chief Constable had transferred Montague to the CID, the plain-clothes branch of the Service.

Montague, on the other hand, considered his transfer had been a recognition of his criminal investigative skills, but for his superiors it signified intense relief from jokes about the bespatted constable, while no one could say there was anything plain about that particular plain-clothes constable. But for Montague, being a detective meant he could personalise his attire while working for the good of society.

Side-shuffling Montague into the CID had been a wonderful piece of personnel management, although his subsequent progress had not been spectacular.

But he had been lucky. Due to amalgamations of Force boundaries, there had been a vacancy for a detective sergeant and he had been the sitting tenant. He was the only available detective constable who had passed his exams, so he had won promotion. Likewise, his promotion to detective inspector arose because none of the detective sergeants had passed their promotion exams at the time of that particular vacancy. His somewhat rapid and spectacular rise through the ranks led Montague to believe that he was a very successful detective. After all, one of his triumphs had been the arrest of a gang of teenage tearaways who were stealing cricket balls from unattended pavilions. It was a feat which had won him an invitation to Crickledale Cricket Club's annual dinner as the guest of honour, when he had delivered a memorable talk about horse troughs in cricket fields.

It was the prevailing air of tranquillity and lack of serious crime in Crickledale that had allowed Montague Pluke to indulge in his off-duty passion of researching the history of stone horse troughs. That he was the acknowledged expert was not in doubt — he had catalogued and photographed every one which had come to his notice. To facilitate his research, he always carried a pocket camera and a notebook; many horse troughs would have vanished for ever had Montague not rediscovered them and recorded them for posterity. That had become his life's work. Even during his morning walk to work he had identified a lost trough. He'd discovered it built into a wall of the Town Hall, having been placed there many years ago. It had been almost invisible among the surrounding stonework, but it had not escaped the trained eye of Montague Pluke — it was now catalogued.

It was amazing how few people knew that the wall of the Town Hall contained an entire horse trough laid on its side and used as a giant building stone. At his instigation, a replica had been built outside and it was now a feature of the town centre. As he passed it each morning, he experienced a glow of Pluke pride.

Upon arrival at the police station that Wednesday, he entered with his right foot first (one always entered buildings with the right foot first) but instead of going to his own office, he diverted into the Control Room.

'Good-morning, Detective Inspector Pluke,' beamed Sergeant Cockfield (pronounced Cofield), the officer in charge of the tiny Control Room.

'Good-morning, Sergeant. A quick answer if you please, as I am heading for my office. Have we had a report of any sudden, unexplained or suspicious deaths since I left the office last night?'

'No, sir,' responded Cockfield pronounced Cofield.

'Thank you, Sergeant,' said Montague, departing without further comment. As he made his way upstairs to his own office, he wondered when the death would occur. That it would happen was never in doubt, so would it be tomorrow? And when it did occur, would it be murder?

*

Millicent, having dusted and then set off the washing machine containing Montague's socks and some other woollies, rang Amelia Fender. 'Amelia, will you be at the Coffee Club tomorrow?'

'Oooh, yes, I will, Millicent, yes, most definitely. See you there perhaps?'

'Yes, I just wondered if you'd heard any more about the happenings at the Crowthers' bungalow? They are away, you know, on holiday.'

'Oooh, yes … I'll tell you tomorrow, keep you in suspense till then, eh? Naughty of me …'

Chapter 3

The following morning, a mild, damp Thursday, Montague observed there was no crow upon the roof of the Crowthers' bungalow.

Unfortunately, that did not undo the omen of yesterday and even though he had since learned from Millicent that the Crowthers were on holiday, Montague continued to worry about the crow's message. Had they, or one of them, been involved in an accident? There had been no plane crashes, coaches overturning on mountain roads, express trains colliding or ocean liners sinking at sea, but one of the Crowthers could, he supposed, have had a less spectacular mishap. Fallen off the Alps perhaps? Drowned in Lake Ontario?

Chattering last night, as she always did after her day's activities, Millicent had said she thought relations were using the bungalow during the Crowthers' absence, so had something nasty happened to one of them? His curiosity aroused and his detective acumen at its sharpest, Montague decided to make a short diversion during this morning's walk to work. He would make a swift visit to the bungalow. In the event of an occupant responding to his knock, he would pretend he wanted to discuss the Church Flower Rota on behalf of Millicent. But there was no reply. From the garden he could peer into the lounge and there were signs of human presence — a clutch of coffee mugs on the hearth although the fire was dead, a tea towel draped over the mirror above the hearth, some shoes near a chair, perhaps cast off by someone curling up his or her legs ... and; peering through the kitchen window, there were some unwashed pots in the sink and more on the table.

Without a doubt, people were living here and they did not keep it as clean or as tidy as the Crowthers. Thus it seemed that Millicent's information was correct. No doubt the place would be tidied up before the Crowthers returned, but whoever was staying here must have gone out early. The place seemed deserted and there was no vehicle on the drive. He tried to look into the bedroom, but the lace curtains obscured his view, although the main curtains were open, a further sign of absence.

As he walked away, curtains fluttered in several neighbouring properties and for a fleeting moment he wondered if he should bring some constables to break into the bungalow, just to determine whether or not a corpse was reclining there. But he had no evidence to justify that kind of drastic action, so he decided against it.

Montague walked away, taking in deep breaths of the balmy morning air, and arrived at his office five minutes after his usual time. He had missed bidding his 'good-mornings' to his regulars — but there had been a few additional greetings, plus with a good deal of speculation that something important must have happened because Mr Pluke was late. Only a matter of some magnitude would cause him to be delayed on his morning walk.

Upon arrival at the police station he was perspiring slightly due to the mildness of the morning and noted that yesterday's threatened thunderstorm had not materialised, although there had been a slight shower overnight. It had freshened the atmosphere, but the threat of thunder remained. The swallows and house martins were flying low too, a sure sign of further rain. The sky was dark and moody — something nasty was brewing.

Upon reaching the office door and in keeping with his practice, he stepped over the threshold by leading with his right foot. Next, he hung his panama on the hat-stand inside the door, performed a rapid obeisance to the sun as it shone through his office window and settled at his desk. The office cleaner had dusted earlier this morning, as she did every morning, but she never replaced things quite as he liked them. He spent a moment or two rearranging his desk, edging the blotter a fraction to the right, the coaster for his coffee mug even a little further to the right, the plastic model of a stone horse trough (which contained his paper clips) a vestige further to the left and the pen rack six inches closer. The front edges of his in-tray and out-tray, on the extreme left and right corners of his desk, needed alignment because they lacked the necessary balance — the in-tray was at least quarter of an inch further forward than the out-tray. He corrected that deficiency and smiled at the neatness of the work surface before him. When he had completed all these adjustments, he was ready.

On his blotter lay the morning's correspondence, much of it comprising internal circulars and memoranda, although the letters which had come by post had been opened by his secretary, Mrs Plumpton, and arranged for his arrival. The papers were held in place by a paperweight which was in fact a witchstone. This was a circular stone with a hole through the centre, one he'd found on the moors during one of his trough-hunting expeditions. He'd kept it because it would bring good fortune to him during his working days.

Known to some as a hagstone, this one, in its earlier life, would have been suspended in a house or cattle shed to keep evil spirits at bay and to ensure the good health of man and beast alike. Now, at Montague's insistence, Mrs Plumpton always made sure she placed it upon each day's correspondence to prevent the papers blowing away when the place was draughty, which sometimes happened when Mr Pluke opened the windows. Aware of his slightly delayed arrival, Mrs Plumpton came into his office bearing a mug of steaming coffee and placed it on the coaster.

'Good-morning, Mr Pluke.' Her chubby face crinkled with a smile as she welcomed him.

Rounded and jolly as a freshly made jelly, she loved her work in

Crickledale CID. It was undemanding but interesting.

'Ah, good-morning, Mrs Plumpton. I fear storms are on the way. I sense a bout of thunder and rain before too long, the martins are flying low.' And he returned her smile, taking care never to appear to be too familiar with her. One's high reputation could soon be scuppered by too-friendly overtures and he was aware that Mrs Plumpton had once had a crush on a superintendent. 'Thanks for the coffee. Anything of import in the post?'

Montague liked the word 'import'. It was almost as good as contravallation or pedagogic, although his favourite was rumpus. It was such an expressive word, was rumpus.

'Nothing urgent, Mr Pluke.' Her spacious and flowing mauve dress of gossamer-like fabric quivered and floated with her movements, performing a wonderful job of hiding the more protuberant of her ample fleshy bits. He'd often wondered what was concealed within her bounteous garments, but always tried to dismiss any erotic thoughts. As a detective inspector in a very responsible post, he had to remain aloof from that sort of thing.

'I've taken some of the routine stuff away. I'll deal with the replies and bring them in for signature as usual.'

'Well done. Now, is Detective Sergeant Wain in yet?'

'Yes, he's in his office. Shall I call him?'

'Ask him to see me in about ten minutes' time with the crime reports.' Montague beamed. 'We will then discuss the day's routine.'

'Yes, all right, Mr Pluke.' And she left.

When she had gone, Montague rang the station's small Control Room and spoke to Sergeant Cockfield (pronounced Cofield). 'Detective Inspector Pluke speaking, Sergeant. Is everything quiet this morning?'

'Yes, sir,' responded the voice. 'All quiet this morning. Nothing of major importance for your lads, sir, nothing since Sergeant Wain called in.'

'No murders? Unexplained or sudden deaths? Suicides? Fatal accidents?'

'No, sir. Just like yesterday. Not a whisper.'

'Fine. Well, keep me informed if anything does occur, Sergeant.'

'Yes, of course, sir,' replied Sergeant Cockfield pronounced Cofield., wondering if Pluke had received some kind of foreknowledge.

He'd asked those questions yesterday as if he'd been anticipating something and had done the same thing months ago. On that earlier occasion, he'd worried about an impending death, thinking he might have a murder to deal with, because an apple had stayed suspended on a tree right through the winter and had remained well into the spring. The peculiar thing was that the owner of tree had collapsed and died in the street a few days before the apple fell off. It had not been a murder, but it had been a sudden death which had shocked the town. And Pluke's anticipation had been uncanny. Now he appeared to be repeating that exercise.

'You haven't been seeing apples hanging on trees in the spring again, have you?' the sergeant added with good humour.

'No, Sergeant, but on the way to the office yesterday morning I did see a crow perched on the roof of a bungalow. That heralds a death very soon, I should say.' And Pluke replaced the phone.

A knock on the door announced the arrival of Detective Sergeant Wain who was Montague's able deputy. Well over six feet tall (two metres or so), he was a thirty-two-year-old career police officer, ambitious, smart and efficient. A head of curly black hair and more than a hint of unshaven whiskers upon a tanned facial skin, appeared around the open door as Wain asked, 'All right to come in now, sir?'

'Yes, sit down, Wayne.'

Montague felt he could call Wayne by his first name because it sounded exactly the same as his surname. Montague Pluke was very particular in the way he addressed others, especially his colleagues whether of superior or subordinate rank. He seldom used forenames — he disliked Dave for David or Steve for Stephen. The Force was full of Daves, Steves, Kevs and the like. There were times he wondered whether there was a policeman anywhere in the United Kingdom who was called David — the newspapers always featured constables called Dave. There were lots of Daves in the Fire Brigade too.

But so far as Sergeant Wain was concerned, his father had worshipped the antics and films of cowboy actor John Wayne, and had given his son a double-barrelled name which had been a source of embarrassment throughout his life. At school, it was said of Wayne Wain that it 'never wains but it pours,' while little girls would chant, 'Wayne Wain go away, come again another day.' Now, of course, the little waindrop had blossomed into a handsome, lovable hunk of a man with film star looks and an attraction which was magnetic to women of all shapes, ages and sizes. Nobody really cared about his silly name. And Detective Sergeant Wayne Wain was determined not to let it hinder his progress — his ambition was not restricted to the laying of willing women; he wanted to become a senior detective. If he was honest, he intended to become *the* most senior detective in his police force: detective superintendent no less, or even deputy chief constable with special responsibility for criminal investigation.

Always smartly dressed and never afraid of long and hard work, he recognised his first step would arise from the promotion, sideways shuffle, or retirement of Detective Inspector Pluke. If or when he went, Wayne would surely fill the vacancy. Keen to show his mettle, so that his quarterly appraisals were always of the finest standard, Wayne settled opposite his boss and waited for him to speak.

'How are things, Wayne?'

'Quiet just now, sir.' Wayne wore a beautifully cut dark-grey suit, a pink shirt and a red tie.

'Any overnight crime?' asked Pluke.

'A few thefts from motor vehicles, a burglary at the Co-op with a few fags and spirits stolen. I have despatched teams to investigate them. Chummy smashed the windows of several parked cars — same team, I reckon. Radios nicked and a couple of overcoats gone. Little chance of tracing the villains unless we catch them with the stuff. Travelling criminals I think, from Teesside or the north-east. SOCO went to the Co-op but there were no prints. A quick and professional job, sir, probably outsiders as well. Otherwise it's deadly quiet.'

'Not enough to cause concern over our crime figures, then? But it could be the calm before the storm.'

'Storm, sir? Are we expecting trouble?'

'There is thunder on the way, Wayne, but I refer to our duties. I have a feeling we shall shortly be told of a death.' He spoke solemnly and Wayne realised that Montague had experienced another omen. So far as his boss' superstitious beliefs were concerned, though, Wayne, knowing upon which side his promotional bread was buttered, did not openly ridicule them. Sometimes in private, however, he thought they were rather out-of-date. None the less, he had to acknowledge that there were times when Montague had unknowingly provided a clue to the winner of more than one horse race.

Montague had sometimes uttered, albeit unwittingly, the names of lucky colours and lucky numbers. On one occasion, when seeing six magpies together just before Thunderclap ran at Beverley with odds of 50-1, Montague had chanted 'Six is for gold'. Upon hearing these words, Wayne had put £5 on Thunderclap which was No. 6; the horse had romped past the winning post several lengths ahead of the field and Wayne had walked home with a handsome profit. Because he had had several good wins based on Pluke's prognostications, Wayne did not mock his boss' quirks; after that first win, he had repeated his success during meetings at Ayr, Uttoxeter, Newmarket and Pontefract. Although Montague had not produced anything remotely likely to win the National Lottery, Wayne did take care always to listen to the words of wisdom which occasionally dripped from Montague's mouth.

'There are times your intuition is remarkable, sir.' Wayne smiled. 'I'll await the day with interest.'

And Pluke was right once more.

Even though the thunder never materialised, there was a death.

Shortly before 11.30 a.m. that Thursday, Sergeant Cockfield pronounced Cofield rang Montague's office. 'Sir,' he said quietly. 'I don't know how you anticipate these things, but there's a report of a body.'

'In Padgett Grove, is it?' asked Pluke with a hint of anticipation in his voice as he pondered the fate of the occupants of the Crowthers' home.

'No, sir, at the Druids' Circle. A young woman. Nude. The man who found the body is there, I told him to await your arrival. He will show you the body.'

'Really? A young woman? How odd it should be at the Circle! Suspicious death, is it?' There was a note of hope in Pluke's voice. It seemed the Crowthers had been spared.

'Yes, sir,' said Sergeant Cockfield pronounced Cofield. 'This one does look very suspicious.'

'Does it really?' Pluke's heart began to pound as he anticipated a moment of forthcoming triumph. 'Sadly, it means someone has lost a dear one. It's Thursday for losses, Sergeant. All right, I'll go straight away and I will take Detective Sergeant Wain. We'll use his car.'

And as Detective Inspector Montague Pluke prepared for what appeared to become the first murder investigation over which he had command, and the first in the history of Crickledale, he muttered a line from Shakespeare: 'Murder cannot be hid long', and then added *sotto voce*: 'And neither can murderers.'

*

After seeing Montague off to work that Thursday, Millicent went about her domestic duties with her usual thoroughness before getting ready for the Coffee Club. She and her friends met regularly at the Coffee Pot for coffee and biscuits, and Millicent was so thrilled that Amelia Fender had something exciting to tell them about happenings at May Crowther's house.

Chapter 4

When going about his mobile constabulary duties, Detective Inspector Montague Pluke favoured an official driver. Other persons of stature did likewise. Her Majesty the Queen, the Lord-Lieutenant of the County, the Chairman of the County Council and the Chief Constable each had an official driver. Montague, however, was acutely aware that his rank did not entitle him to a chauffeur, but because Detective Sergeant Wayne Wain always accompanied him during his crime enquiries, Montague had deemed it wise to let him drive. With his smart suits and tall, impressive appearance, Wayne could easily be mistaken for a chauffeur. Indeed, over the months Montague Pluke had come to regard Wayne Wain as his personal driver.

To be driven around by a smart young man gave Montague a distinct feeling of eminence within the police service and indeed within the town. The sight of him being chauffeured to official engagements had certainly impressed the citizens of Crickledale and there were times when he wondered if he should have a flag on the bonnet of his official car. In the light of present financial restraints, though, he felt the Chief Constable might not sanction such expenditure and he didn't feel inclined to spend his hard-earned personal cash upon a flag. Besides, the car bonnet would need modifications to accommodate it, a further costly consideration the Force could not afford. Flag or no flag, he would be driven to the Druids' Circle by Detective Sergeant Wayne Wain.

This arrangement both pleased and relieved the sergeant, because Montague's driving skills were universally recognised as not being of the highest standard. All the police officers of Crickledale, members of the uniformed and plain-clothes branches alike, knew that Montague Pluke crashed his gears, had difficulty coordinating his arm movements and lacked anticipation when using the brakes, a defect which frequently manifested itself at highly critical moments. His driving was guaranteed to put other road users at risk — the term used by some was 'hair-raising' although Montague would have denied that. After all, he had never crashed a car and never had trouble steering or stopping his lawn-mower; furthermore, he had often said that persons of a nervous disposition should not allow themselves to be carried as passengers in motor vehicles. The more vociferous might retaliate by saying that only a raving lunatic would allow himself or herself to be driven by Montague Pluke. Pluke might counter this by saying that his wife, Millicent, never objected. The short answer was that Millicent loved and respected Montague and could see no ill in anything that he did; in fact, so confident was she that she often closed her eyes when he was driving. This was in keeping with one of Montague's favourite quotes — 'love is blind'.

Having received clamorous complaints from experienced police officers who had accompanied him in the passenger seat, particularly those who had passed the Advanced Police Driving Test, Montague had decided he would always allow himself to be the passenger in an official vehicle. It was that momentous decision which had led to the present arrangement.

From a personal point of view, the fact that he was a passenger allowed him time to examine hedgerows, dry-stone walls, ditches and derelict buildings for signs of concealed horse troughs. Indeed, he'd found four in one day while investigating an outbreak of haystack fires, a just reward for his consideration to other road users. And now he was being driven to the Druids' Circle.

'You know where to find the Druids' Circle, Wayne?' He fastened his seat belt.

In spite of the oppressive heat, Pluke wore his ancient greatcoat and heavy suit, while Wayne Wain knew he must not dress casually, even if the sweat was pouring from him.

'Yes, sir. In Druids' Wood, that's on Hunter's Ridge,' replied Wayne Wain.

'It is one of the Nine Sights of Crickledale, Wayne. You knew that, did you?' asked Pluke.

'Yes, I did, sir, as a matter of fact.'

'And can you name the Nine?' challenged Pluke.

'They comprise nine historic places in or near Crickledale, sir, places of interest to sightseers, visitors, tourists and historians. They are — the Keep of Crickledale Castle, the Vaults of the old Priory, the Crypt of St Agnes' Church, the Bells of St Macarius Church, the ancient Nunnery of Trattledale, the Devil's Bridge, the Tower of Turbulent Thomas, the Roman Baths and the Druids' Circle. How's that?'

'Excellent, Wayne. And all are genuine, except the Druids' Circle. That's a folly and consequently not of any great interest,' Pluke proffered.

'I quite like it, sir, and some do say it occupies the site of a genuine temple.'

'It does look impressive, I will agree to that, but it cannot rank alongside the genuine historic sites within the Crickledale district, those to which you have just referred. It was placed there as a folly, nothing more. It has had no religious, ceremonial or historic function.'

'Yes, but with your deep interest in things historic, sir, I thought you'd have researched it …'

'The depth of my knowledge is primarily associated with horse trough history, Wayne, and secondly with other aspects of local history. I concern myself with the *genuine* article, not fakes, and most certainly not fake Druids' Circles. I fail to see the point of studying a fake or regarding it as something historic or even of academic interest, even if it does stand on a site of some possible importance. One has to find the right balance in such matters.'

'But surely it is now a part of our history, sir? History has to start somewhere, it has to begin at some stage of our life-cycle. Besides, the Circle is shown on all the tourist maps, it's one of the Nine Sights.'

'Why is it on the maps, Wayne? Why would tourists wish to visit something which is overtly false? It's like visiting an amusement arcade to look at plastic wall decorations — they're fakes too, made to look like the real things. Like false clay pipes and copies of horse brasses in some pubs. Cheap replicas, Wayne, not for the discerning. I live for the day when the Town Hall horse trough is formally included in the Sights of Crickledale — imagine that as the Tenth Sight!'

'I see no reason why that should not happen, but some people find the Druids' Circle very interesting and I do think it has a certain atmosphere. Mystique, even. Anyway, so far as your horse trough hunting is concerned, there are plenty of moorland tracks nearby, most of them disused nowadays. You might discover a long-lost horse trough or two. The horses of the past would surely need water?'

'I'm sure there would be no troughs, Wayne. Those travellers would use moorland streams, they'd utilise natural water supplies. There are hundreds of springs on the moors and they are still producing endless gallons of purest water, even today. It means there was no need for them to spend days or weeks carving a horse trough from solid rock when there was a ready supply of water nearby. Those moorland springs never dry up, they even flowed during the winter of 1947 and the droughts of 1976 and 1995.'

'Simple logic by simple people, sir?'

'Simple, but not stupid, Wayne. Uncomplicated — and they were very practical. They had to work hard at merely surviving without carving horse troughs which weren't needed. In their day, you didn't find horse troughs for sale in supermarkets. If you wanted one, you made it yourself and if you didn't need one you didn't make one. There were other things to do.'

'Quite, sir,' conceded Wayne Wain, well and truly lectured.

The car moved smoothly away as Wayne drove from the police station yard into the traffic and along the road to the northern extremities of Crickledale. As Wayne drove, Montague Pluke aired his knowledge of the Druids' Circle.

It was quite clear that he *had* researched it in some depth. He said it was built in 1840 by Lord Losky, partially to keep his estate workers employed during a particularly slack time, and partially to impress his friends and neighbours. Roughly oval in shape, its widest portion was about a hundred feet (30 metres or so) in width and its perimeter consisted of two main circles of standing stones, one immediately inside the other with some rising to more than ten feet (three metres or more) in height.

Huge crosspieces straddled them to provide an impression of Stonehenge. Two taller stones, each rising to over twelve feet (about four metres) with a massive crosspiece above, formed the Eastern Gate, which was used as the main entrance. A similar gate of smaller stones created the less prestigious Western Gate. Within the centre was what appeared to be an altar formed from a flat sacrificial stone standing on short stone pillars and this stood near a tall standing stone which was clearly intended to be a phallic symbol.

An additional asset was that it served as the gnomon of a massive sundial, its shadow ticking around the stones like a huge clock. Other standing stones adorned the central portion, and immediately inside the Eastern Gate, on the left as one entered, there was a cavern which extended deep into the hillside. This was thought to be a replica of a tomb, although it had no door.

Further chambers were thought to replicate places of rest for the high priest and accompanying celebrants, while recesses around the complex provided seats for spectators and participants in ceremonial occasions.

It was clear to Wayne that Pluke knew a lot about the folly, even if he denied any special interest. He went on to say that it was surrounded by a mixture of deciduous and coniferous trees, while occupying a large glade in the woodland. There was an unmade track leading to it, but the track terminated at the Circle. Beyond lay only rough moorland without any clearly defined paths or tracks, all part of the local estate.

'Many topographical writers have omitted the likelihood of the Circle occupying a genuine site,' Montague went on. 'If such a claim is true, however, it is just possible that this Circle might not be wholly false. The original stones may have been used. If that is the case, it lends a certain air of authenticity to the Circle and if that were proven, I might take a more discerning interest. But horse troughs are my speciality, Wayne, and today my interest in the Circle is purely professional.'

'I understand perfectly, sir.' Wayne smiled.

'Think about this, Wayne,' Pluke went on. 'The Circle's stones must have come from somewhere. Contemporary records do not tell us where Lord Losky found them. Having examined reports about the site, I do not think they were carved especially for this modern construction. Their shape, size and purpose could have been determined centuries ago. So, Wayne, if the Druids' Circle is not totally false, it might contain forces we do not yet understand.'

'You could be right, sir,' concurred Detective Sergeant Wayne Wain.

'Now, is it open to the public?' asked Montague Pluke, thinking there might even be a horse trough within the complex, a real one, not a fake. It would be very uplifting to discover a trough which had survived since druidical times, or even one made to match a well-executed folly. Were there such things as folly horse troughs, he wondered?

'There is no resident warden, sir,' Wayne Wain told him. 'And no gates to prevent access; anyone can, and does, visit the place without restriction, around the clock too, I might add. There are occasional rumours of all sorts of bizarre goings-on here at night. I believe the estate has placed an honesty box inside a rock near the entrance, in a vain hope of defraying the expense of upkeep.'

'Rumours of orgiastic events do surface from time to time,' acknowledged Pluke. 'Nothing has ever been proven. Now to the purpose of our visit. Who found the deceased?' The car was now gathering speed as the two officers left the confines of the town and made for the hills.

'A man called Winton, sir. Stephen Winton, a photographer. He was sent to photograph the site for a tourist magazine. He called us from his car phone; there is a car-park nearby.'

'I cannot say I know him. Is he from Crickledale?'

'No, sir, from Fossford.'

'And he has been asked to remain there, pending our arrival?'

'He has, sir.'

'Thus he has presented himself as the first, and to date, the only suspect?'

'That is very true, sir.'

'It's always a good start, Wayne. The person who reports finding the corpse must always be a prime suspect, if not *the* prime suspect.'

Montague had remembered that from his days on CID training courses. There were times when killers reported the discovery of their victims in the vain hope it would remove suspicion from them. The truth was it had precisely the opposite effect. Stephen Winton would be closely questioned.

In the meantime, as the officer in charge of the investigation,

Montague Pluke had to make sure that everything necessary for the smooth running of the enquiry had been set in motion. Having never before initiated a murder investigation, he must rely heavily upon the professionalism of Detective Sergeant Wayne Wain. In such cases, delegation was a virtue.

Not to be forgotten, of course, was that there was no confirmation that this *was* a murder investigation. It had not yet been established that the girl had been murdered, even though there appeared to be circumstances of some suspicion. This meant there were questions to ask and answers to seek.

'Has a doctor been called to certify death?'

'Yes, sir, I've done that.'

'And a pathologist to carry out an examination of the body at the scene?'

'Yes, sir.'

'And our own Scenes of Crime teams, photographers, video team, police dogs to search the area, Task Force to do a fingertip search of the site when we are ready?'

'Yes, I've made sure that all our support services have been placed on stand-by, for call-out the moment a crime is confirmed.'

'And suspects? Apart from the finder, has any other suspect vehicle or person been seen in the vicinity? Or leaving the scene of the crime?'

'No, sir, none yet, but it's early days. Everything that needs to be done at this stage has been done.'

'You're a good man, Wayne, and a most capable officer. Very efficient. You appear to have thought of everything. Now, let us embark upon our enquiries.'

At this point, Montague reflected upon the action he had taken and felt he had made a good start. One of the prerequisites of a good supervisor was to have a good deputy upon whom to delegate important tasks. And Wayne Wain was one of the best in the Force, if not *the* best.

Knowing that Pluke depended upon him, Detective Sergeant Wayne Wain pressed the accelerator as they made for the moors. The final half-mile was along a dark lane with a rough, unmade surface upon a stony base. It led into Druids' Wood. This was a plantation created some years ago by the estate and the entrance was via a five-bar gate, standing open. At one side a wooden notice board saying, 'Druids' Circle, 800 yards.'

'Not far now, Wayne,' muttered Montague as the car entered the gloom beneath the overhanging trees and bounced noisily along the uneven lane.

Then a magpie flew from the trees; it fluttered across the lane and when it was directly ahead of the car, Montague hastily opened the car window and spat upon the road.

'You all right, sir?' Wayne wondered if the rough ride had made his passenger sick.

'A single magpie, Wayne. A bad omen. A sign of sorrow. One for sorrow, two for joy, three for a girl, four for a boy ... you must know the verse? Upon seeing a single magpie, you must spit immediately to dispel the bad fortune that it would otherwise bring.'

'I don't believe in that, sir, with all due respect. I think most people ignore such things.'

'No, Wayne. They pretend to ignore such things. They pretend to themselves and others — but how many people think thirteen is unlucky? Did you know that fishermen will never give their boats a name containing thirteen letters? And how many people will begin a new venture or a journey on a Friday? Can you imagine a bride getting married without a horseshoe to bring her luck? And would you ever find a bride getting married in a green dress? Superstition is all around us, Wayne, we're all affected in one way or another. Can I remind you about greenery in the house at Christmas and that we celebrate Easter with eggs as the pagans did — it's all superstition,

Wayne, all of it.'

'Yes but …'

'No buts, Wayne. It's either all or nothing. You can't believe thirteen is unlucky if you ignore magpies and don't take care never to walk under ladders. I don't hide my beliefs, Wayne. Why hide something in which you believe? That is dishonest. I'm an honest man, you see, I'm not devious and secretive. And for people deliberately to avoid a superstition is a superstition in itself.'

'My mother would never cut my fingernails until I was a year old,' Wayne admitted. 'She told me that, then she refused to cut them on a Sunday in case it brought bad luck.'

'Exactly. It happens all the time. Lots of parents, especially mothers, follow superstitious practices and instil them in the minds of their children. They grow up to do things which they never consider superstitious, just because it's the way they've always done it. Yet those same parents might well deny following a superstitious belief. So now you know why I spat when I noticed that magpie.'

As the car moved beneath the canopy of trees, Montague smiled at his sergeant, and then, without warning, shrieked, 'Stop, Wayne, stop! Now!'

'God! What's happened?' Wayne Wain slammed his huge feet to the floorboards and brought the car to a skidding halt on the rough track; even as he did so, Montague was clambering out and hurrying into the trees with coat-tails flying.

'Sir?' Wayne left the engine running and climbed out to stand near his door and shout after his departing boss. 'What is it?'

'Look at this, Wayne!' He was pointing to something in the ditch, something almost hidden by weeds and undergrowth.

Wayne was unable to identify the cause of Montague's excitement, but Montague had seen it, whatever it was.

'The body, sir?' called Wayne as he left the car and hurried towards his boss.

'No, Wayne, a horse trough! See, it was once standing beside this waterway ... the running water would be collected from that gill that comes into this ditch and it would be diverted to fill the trough. The overflow is at the far side ... see? A groove in the lip ... the ditch is dry now, there's been a lot of erosion which might be the reason, but I'll bet the gill can produce more than a trickle in wet weather, even now. To make this trough dry as it is, the course of the water must have been diverted only a little or blocked ... by Jove, Wayne, this is exciting, a real find. I never expected to find a trough in use on these heights. Now, if that trough were moved a short distance to a new site or if the gill were cleaned higher along its route, it might fill with water again. The trough could have a whole new lease of life, it could become a genuine feature of this drive towards the circle ...'

'Sir, with all due respect, we are on our way to a possible murder scene.'

Montague did not hear him as he continued, 'It's on the side of a highway too ... this was probably once a major route across the moors ... now, my camera!'

'Sir, I must remind you that we are going to investigate the report of a suspicious death ...' Sergeant Wain repeated.

'She won't run away, Wayne.'

'But if the support services come and catch us examining a bloody disused horse trough that's been dry for years ...'

'We're not racing to the scene of a major incident in which lives are at risk, Wayne. Two minutes longer will make no difference to the unfortunate victim.' And he pulled his fist-sized camera from his jacket pocket, cleared away as much rubbish as he could with his feet and began to photograph the trough from all angles. Then he took a small personal notepad from another pocket and started to record the date, time and place of his discovery, talking to himself with excitement as he did so. After five minutes' activity and flushed with success, he returned to Wayne.

'I call that a really good day's work, Wayne. Now, if I hadn't spat the moment I saw that magpie I would have missed that trough. As it was, I cancelled out the bad luck which would have been cast by the magpie, you see, and lo! I got lucky and found another trough! Instant good fortune, Wayne. That's a perfect example of what we were discussing only moments ago. Now, onward to the Druids' Circle, eh?'

'Yes, sir,' sighed Wayne Wain, thinking Montague would have spotted the trough with or without the intervention of that long-tailed black-and-white bird that caused people to spit or make the sign of the cross.

But in truth, the whole incident was merely a set of coincidences — wasn't it? Even so, it might just be worth checking the lists of runners. Wasn't there a horse with magpie in its name down to run at Sandown Park soon? And wasn't a horse called Two Joys entered to run at the Ebor meeting? One for sorrow, two for joy ... whatever it was called, it would be worth a bet. And then there were the National Lottery numbers to consider ...

A minute or so later they were easing into the car-park which was a small patch of bare ground made by clearing some of the trees. Rough and dirty, it was not surfaced, although there was a small wooden hand-painted sign announcing 'Car-Park — Do Not Light Fires'. A secondary sign said 'Honesty Box near Gate — recommended charge for park and visit to the Druids' Circle — £1'.

Montague studiously ignored the request for money as he saw a man emerge from a parked car, the only one on the site. In his middle thirties and powerfully built, with a good head of dark, wavy hair and rimless spectacles, he was casually dressed for the sticky heat in trainers, jeans and a T-shirt. Smiling with a hint of nervousness, but striding purposefully forward, he came to meet the newcomers, leaving his car door standing open. Inside, a radio was playing soft music.

'Mr Winton?' asked Wayne. 'Stephen Winton?'

'Yes.' In spite of his size and attempted display of confidence, the man sounded nervous and his face was a pale shade of grey. He seemed to be in a state of shock.

'I'm Detective Sergeant Wain and this is Detective Inspector Pluke. We're both from Crickledale. I believe you have discovered a body?' Wayne Wain had taken the initiative.

'Yes, in there, in the ruins. It's awful ... I ... really ... it is most distressing ...'

'Has anyone else been with the body?' asked Pluke, showing his warrant card to the man. Winton had no idea what he was looking at; it could have been one of the new National Trust membership cards for all the notice he took.

'I don't think so, I came away, here, to my car, to call your office. I have a car phone. I haven't seen anyone else, this is the only way in, although I suppose people could hide in the wood ... I didn't see anyone but I couldn't stay there, not with her, poor creature ... God this is terrible ...'

'We won't detain you any longer than necessary.' Pluke sounded sympathetic and friendly. 'But we must ask you to accompany us to the scene. I want you to tell us exactly what you did and show us where you found her. Then we shall require a written statement; one of us will take that from you in a few minutes, after you have shown us what you found. I'm sorry to ask you to do this, but the sooner we get it done, the sooner we can release you and, of course, the sooner we can determine the course of our official enquiry.'

'Yes, I see, well, all right.'

Winton locked his car but removed his camera and slung it around his shoulders in its large case as he led the two detectives along the final yards of the track. In spite of the shade of the trees the heat was intense, but the unmade surface was slightly damp. The deep shadows of the trees prevented direct sunlight from baking the surface of the ancient track. As they walked, Montague was concentrating upon the ground, seeking tyre marks or footprints. There were no tyre marks, so it seemed no car had been driven to the Eastern Gate, but there were some partial footprints. Many had been obliterated by the light shower of rain which had fallen overnight, but some did remain and Winton's should be among them.

Montague and Wayne were both alert to the prevailing atmosphere as each scrutinised every inch of the way. Each was aware that this road might well have been the point of arrival and departure of the killer, with or without a vehicle. If so, they hoped to find some evidence of his or her presence. But were they destroying evidence by walking upon it?

Montague was asking, 'Did you come this way, Mr Winton?'

'Yes. I parked my car where it is now. I haven't moved it. I took my camera out and came along here, walking exactly where I am now, on this side of the road.'

'And you were alone?'

'Yes.'

'Then I would expect to see evidence of your arrival somewhere upon this track, but it does look to have a very solid surface under that thin natural covering. So tell me about your work, Mr Winton.'

'I'm a photographer, a freelance. I was commissioned to take several colour transparencies of the Circle, it's for a series, "Mystical Tours of Britain".'

'What time did you arrive?'

'Just after eleven o'clock, it would be. I took a few pictures before I found her ... it would take a few minutes, I was still on my first reel. God, it was a shock ... then I ran back to the car to call you ... yes, it would be about ten past eleven I suppose. Quarter past, maybe.'

'Did you take pictures of her? Either on purpose or inadvertently?'

asked Wayne.

'No, neither. I couldn't take any of her … God, that would be disgusting …'

'We will have to develop your film in our studios, Mr Winton, just to see if there are any clues upon it that have disappeared since your arrival.'

'I'm sure I can arrange that, yes, there's only one reel as I said. Then, if I can have my negatives back. My deadline's not until the end of the month, there's a couple of weeks yet, but I do need my pictures of the Circle. The light was just right, you see, I can't repeat them … they are important …'

They had arrived at the main entrance to the fake temple, the Eastern Gate. Before them stood the majestic lichen-covered rocks, rising above their heads with the thick stone crossbeam forming the arch. Inside, they could discern the shape of the giant folly with its circular array of standing stones, its phallic symbol and sacrificial altar, all casting shadows in the hot sunshine. High in the summer sky, the sun had risen above the trees, its brilliance making the ripening berries of the rowans appear like clusters of tiny orange lights; it was bathing the Circle in its glow, the shadows of the stones being sharply defined upon the earth.

Montague entered first, but did not step completely into the Circle. He halted, with the others behind him, scanning the entire vista, memorising details and noting trivia, gaining a lasting impression of the Circle and its environs. There was tourist litter, he noted, several dead fires, empty beer cans and bottles, crisp packets and plastic bags, a couple of wine bottles near the sacrificial altar, a man's hat hanging from a lintel, a man's shoe near the phallic rock, black and befitting a townie, some newspapers, wet and bedraggled, a plastic sandwich box, empty and open, and other miscellaneous discarded items. British tourists were an untidy lot, he decided.

'Our own Official Photographer will take pictures of the interior,

Wayne, with all that rubbish *in situ* and every item listed on a scale plan. Listing it will be a job for the Task Force. Now, Mr Winton, where is the lady you found?'

'To your left, there is a chamber or a cave. It reaches quite a long way into the hillside. Like a tomb. She's in there, in the dark, on a ledge in the darkness, round the corner. It's cool in there, Mr Pluke, so beautifully cool. I saw her in my flash. It's very dark inside, you'll need a light.'

'Wait here, both of you.' Montague took command of the situation. Deputies were all right, but there was a stage when a leader must lead. And that stage had most certainly arrived. As the officer in charge, it was essential that he made the correct start to this investigation. Taking off his panama as a mark of respect for the deceased, he prepared to enter the Circle, leading with his right foot.

*

Amelia Fender had told the Coffee Club all about the vehicle and the comings and goings at the Crowthers' home. And they listened most intently.

'That niece of hers is bringing all sorts of people into the house.' Mrs Fender had leaned forward confidentially and dropped her voice.

Other ears would be flapping in the café and she wanted only the Coffee Club to heed her words.

Although the café was noisy and no one appeared to be listening, one could not be too careful in speaking confidentialities to one's friends.

'I don't know what May would think if she knew they were having parties there, really I don't ...'

'Perhaps she gave the girl permission to bring friends in?' suggested Millicent. 'If it's her niece, that would be quite normal, surely?'

'I very much doubt it!' returned Amelia. 'I mean, you never know who youngsters are likely to attract and besides, the party went on right into the early hours, lights on all the time, cars and taxis coming and going ... I never got a wink of sleep that night, I can tell you. There were men and women ... and a van of some sort full of party stuff. I think May would not want all that sort of thing going on. I heard they'd been to the cricket club as well, partying till all hours, naked too ...'

'That is awful, and in May's house ... and naked you say? What on earth is the world coming to!' Gertrude Nettlewren, one of the other Coffee Club members, was suitably shocked by the allegations of bare people. 'I know I would hate to have strangers in my house when I was on holiday. They treat the place as their own.'

'House-sitter, that's what the girl is,' said Mrs Fender, now wondering what had really happened at the cricket club. 'She is house-sitting while Cyril and May are away. That's what May told me. She said her niece was coming to look after the house, to live in. But that's no excuse for bringing in all and sundry, I ask you ...'

Millicent Pluke looked at her watch. 'Well, I must be getting back,' she said. 'I have a lunch engagement with Mrs Councillor Farrell.'

But dare she broach the subject of the cricket club over lunch, she wondered?

Chapter 5

After only two strides into the Circle, Montague Pluke came to an abrupt halt. He stopped because he experienced the presence of living evil. It was a tangible sensation, almost overwhelming in its intensity, and it was confirmed when a flock of screaming swifts burst from the heavens and cascaded across the sky with a swishing of their sabre wings. Within a split second they were out of sight above the leafy trees, the sound of their shrill voices fading rapidly in the sheer speed of their exodus. Some thought these birds were a gift of the Almighty, but, probably due to the Lincolnshire blood within him, Montague regarded them as the devil's birds. Legend said they were Satan's links with the dead and contained the souls of the lost. As Montague stood in silence during those vital moments he knew beyond all doubt that there was evil nearby. For the second time that morning he spat on the ground.

From his vantage point he could see a well-worn footpath around the inside of the ring of stones. Another path cut across the central grassed area which formed the circular floor of the folly and it led directly to the underground chamber. Taking a deep breath, Montague knew he must continue — he must not be thwarted by the depravity which surrounded him. Everything now depended upon him.

He regarded the cavern in the hillside; its dark opening was a few yards to his left and at its threshold there was a depression of bare, damp and muddied earth. It formed a moist hollow where the feet of visitors had worn away the surface. There were footprints at that point, unidentifiable but numerous.

Because that threshold lay in the shadows of the trees and fractionally within the shelter of the cavern itself, it was always damp; deep inside, the floor was also permanently slightly wet.

Montague observed that the opening was high and narrow, rather like the entrance to a catacomb, as the cavern thrust deep into the side of the mound of earth which formed its roof and walls. The aperture had a pillar at each side; there was no door to enclose it. Anything and anyone could enter without hindrance. No doubt wild creatures sheltered here when the weather was stormy. Each of the pillars which formed the doorway was a standing stone less than six feet tall by ten inches wide and ten inches deep; the lintel was another large stone. That crosspiece, and others within, supported the tons of heaped earth which formed the thick, weatherproof covering above the cavern, earth which was sprouting trees and shrubs. The varieties included deciduous and coniferous trees among them birch, hazel, oak, elm, holly, rowan, spruce and larch.

Montague thought the opening looked like the entrance to a mine. It was similar to those of the ancient iron ore, lead and coal mines which dotted the upper regions of the Yorkshire Dales and, bearing in mind the risks of entering such a place, he wondered if there had ever been a roof fall. But, he told himself, this was not a mine. It was not even genuine; it was the model of a burial chamber, a folly, a rich man's plaything.

So why had that feeling of evil been so tangible?

The lintel was less than six feet above the floor of the chamber and the uneven roof inside seemed no higher, so very tall men would have to duck and remember to keep their heads bowed during their time inside. A nasty crack on the cranium would be the painful penalty for forgetfulness. Montague was not a tall man, especially when carrying his hat. None the less, he approached cautiously, once more leading with his right foot, hat in hand and nose wrinkled at the onslaught of damp earthiness mingled with the smell of stale urine. From a point just outside the entrance he observed that the immediate interior seemed a veritable waste tip, a convenient dumping ground for unwanted garbage, the offal of humanity and the price of tourism. It was evident that the chamber was used variously as a shelter, a toilet, a brothel and a rubbish dump. Paper tissues, used condoms, and old newspapers littered the floor within sight of the entrance; there were empty beer cans too, broken beer and wine bottles and lots of plastic carrier bags. Dark-grey ashes, the remains of fires, along with charred kindling suggested that people had slept there, cooked meals or merely taken refuge from the upland weather, probably when hiking over these heights.

Entering with his customary care, Montague saw that the subdued light of the summer day highlighted that awful miasma, before being extinguished in the windowless space beyond. It was impossible to see what lay in that velvety darkness because after four yards or so the chamber curved sharply to the right. Once inside, Montague experienced the dank coolness of the underground as he trod with precision, wary of the risks of contaminating any material evidence.

As he reached the corner, his heart was pounding with suppressed excitement and he realised he required a light if he was to see any further. One of the objects in his breast pocket was a miniature torch, even if it did look like a fountain pen. He withdrew it and switched it on. The narrow-beamed light, surprisingly powerful, picked out the uneven rock floor and Montague noted it was cleaner than the area near the entrance. The filthy users of this place had not dared venture into these dark bowels of the earth.

Continuing his exploration, he saw that the rock walls a few yards beyond the corner had apparently produced a natural shelf. It looked like one of those lintel stones which formed the crosspieces of the Circle but it was about knee height from the uneven floor. Part of the rock wall on his right, it was wide enough and long enough to accommodate the recumbent form of a human being. And so it did.

It bore the white and naked body of a young woman. She was out of sight from the entrance, while lying on that natural shelf with her head towards the daylight, as if she was asleep. Pale and sombre in the all-embracing gloom of this folly of a tomb, she was alone and, he was sure, quite dead.

He stood for a moment in respect for the dead, his panama dangling in his free hand while his old coat, buttoned tight about his belly, made him appear abnormal in shape, size and even mental capacity. He spoke to her, his voice sounding hollow in this weird place, but there was no response. He listened for breathing — nothing. He tried her pulse — nothing. He opened her eyes — they were dead.

He closed her eyes and knew there was no truth in the rumour that the eyes of a corpse retained the image of the killer. Even now, some killers believed that and ensured the eyes of their victims remained closed after death by placing a coin upon each eyelid, to hold them shut. And, Montague knew, if the corpse's eyes were open, it meant it was looking for a companion to accompany it to the grave … but hers were shut. And she was cold, as cold as the stone which entombed her.

He had examined enough dead bodies to be confident that no life existed in this unfortunate young woman. In addition, there were flies about in spite of the coolness and lack of daylight. They were a further indication of death, seeking somewhere to lay their eggs if they had not already done so. They swarmed in the beam of his torch, buzzing towards the centre of the light source. There was a belief that fleas departed from the body of a dead person, but these were not fleas. They were bluebottles, scavengers, pests and disease carriers and, in the heat of the summer, the coolness of her tomb had probably kept them at bay for a while.

How long had she been here? Not long enough for the body to have decomposed nor to produce the sickly scent of death, but long enough to attract these buzzing insects. Montague waved his torch about to disperse them, without hoping for permanent success, as he said to himself:

'A fly on your nose, you slap and it goes,
If it comes back again, it will bring good rain.'

One did settle on his nose; he waved his hat and it departed.

Knowing better than to interfere with the victim unnecessarily, Montague was aware that a doctor must certify the death, but before that he himself must conduct an initial search of the remainder of the chilly, gloomy chamber. It would take a few moments. A more comprehensive search would be done later by his expert colleagues, but he wished to examine the scene in his own way, before the others disturbed it. One reason was that the darkness might contain another corpse, one overlooked by Winton in the trauma of his moment of discovery.

It was also possible that a living person, a suspect perhaps, or some evidence relating to the girl's death, might be abandoned or concealed here. Her clothes might be here too … she could have undressed to please a man and placed her belongings in a dry place.

His work of detection began as the pencil-slim beam of his pocket light scanned the walls and floor. He noted green moss and dankness, the marks of water seeping through; the uneven floor here devoid of human rubbish; the wall of solid rock at the distant end and the lack of any other entrance or exit, however small. The entire chamber was probably no longer than thirty feet and no wider than six feet and seemed to contain nothing but the body and those items of litter near the entrance.

When they had fashioned this chamber, Lord Losky's workmen had probably not carved it from the earth. To hack a route through solid rock would not have been sensible, particularly to build something as trivial as a folly, so its origins had probably been a natural hollow among large, immovable boulders.

Its present appearance suggested the builders had placed stone beams and lintels over that hollow, the beams then being covered with earth and planted with trees to produce its current near-natural appearance. It was fairly realistic, but Montague reminded himself it had never been intended as a real tomb, even if it possessed some of the attributes. For example, sunshine never invaded its entrance which lay permanently in shadow.

Montague remained acutely aware of the atmosphere of evil in which he worked and at times it was so powerful that he felt he was in a genuine but abandoned mausoleum or family vault. He had to keep reminding himself that this was just a folly, a place of interest and amusement. Now, though, by a quirk of fate, this fun structure was surely serving as a tomb, however temporary it might be. He stood for a few minutes with his torch playing across the body, wafting his hat to frighten the determined and pestilent flies.

She would be in her late twenties, he estimated. A young woman with a beautiful body and a fine, shapely figure. Her legs were laid together; her arms were by her side, almost as if she was lying to attention. Her feet were not tied together, he noted. In some countries and even in parts of Britain, it was thought the spirit left the body via a route between the legs, thus if the feet were tied together, the spirit could not return, nor could the evil spirit of any other creature gain uninvited access to the corpse. Her large breasts appeared to be flat because she was lying on her back and the tuft of hair between her legs seemed darker because her surrounding flesh was so white.

Blonde hair, worn long, was spread about the stone shelf near her head and her face had been one of handsomeness, beauty and some intelligence. And she was totally naked. Apart from the fact that she wore no clothes, she did not even have any jewellery — no rings, no earrings, no watch or bracelet. Nothing. Not even a ribbon or clip in her hair, nor even a flower beside her body. He had never seen

Millicent like this; she'd never allow him to view her nakedness. He sighed a sigh of lost passions.

Holding his hat and the torch in his left hand, he wondered whether she had died here. Peering closer, he noted that the body appeared clean and without wounds. Although he was unable to examine her back without moving her, he saw that all the visible parts of her body were free from cuts and bruises. And she was surprisingly clean; even her feet were clean except for a solitary brown fibre wedged in a slit in her left big toe nail. From a blanket, perhaps? Montague knew better than to turn her over; at this stage of the investigation she must be examined by experts in this place and in this position before anything else was done. Although there was no sign of blood, she might have been stabbed in the back, shot in the head or killed by other means which were not readily visible.

The absence of blood was no firm guide, but in spite of his eagerness to know, he must not move her. The pathologist would determine the cause of death — but the fact that she was unclothed in this dreadful place suggested that her demise was suspicious. That being so, it was time to have the death certified and arrange a full investigation, one of the first tasks being to establish her identity.

Alone in the chamber with the subject of his enquiries, Montague's heart thumped as he felt tremors of excitement and nervousness. So much now depended upon him. To reach a successful conclusion to this mystery would indeed be a challenge — and a great responsibility. It would not be easy; he accepted that. Her killer had made sure that identification would be most difficult. Clothes and jewellery were vital to that process, but every scrap had been discarded. They must be found. The entire surrounds of this place would have to be searched for them and that search would have to be extended over a huge area of moor and woodland.

From what he had seen so far, he favoured the theory, that she had been killed elsewhere and brought here in death in the hope she might never be found. In Montague's mind, whoever had killed her must have known of this remote tomb in the woods. It was not the sort of place you found accidentally, especially during those urgent moments when trying to dispose of a corpse. Having seen all that he wished, Montague emerged from the dank place, pleased to breathe warm but unsullied woodland air once again. Outside, in the shadows of the trees, he halted to replace his panama and approached Wayne Wain and Stephen Winton. They had waited for him at the Eastern Gate.

'She's in there, apparently dead in circumstances of some suspicion,' he told Detective Sergeant Wayne Wain, adding with authority, 'I want the entire Circle sealed and nothing touched or moved until our experts arrive. Wayne, call Control immediately with a situation report and confirm this is to be treated as a murder. Tell Sergeant Cockfield pronounced Cofield to set up the Incident Room.'

'Very good, sir.'

'And, Mr Winton, I need to talk to you at some length.'

'Yes, of course,' muttered the photographer.

'Thank you for reporting your discovery …' began Montague.

'I nearly ran for my life … what a shock … I was exploring the place, looking for atmospheric scenes and backgrounds … I thought she was asleep … I touched her, Inspector, to wake her up … then realised she was so cold, stiff. Dead. I was sure she was dead. I rang your office.'

'Absolutely the correct thing to do.' Montague smiled. To touch a dead person was thought to bring good fortune. He had touched her too. He addressed his sergeant, determined to establish his control over the enquiry.

'Now, Wayne, once you have radioed Crickledale Control Room, you must stand guard at this gateway and keep everyone out of the Circle until the support services arrive. Ask Control to send two uniformed constables to guard the Circle, then await the arrival of the doctor and the specialists. Meanwhile, I'll have a chat with Mr Winton in the car. When our support teams arrive, tell them the body of a young woman is lying in that cavern, on a stone shelf, around to the right, out of sight, out of daylight. She's naked, but there is no apparent injury to the body. It could be murder, but, let's be realistic, she could have died from natural causes. Whatever the cause of death, the usual care and attention to detail is required. Preserve the entire Circle and everything in the cave for examination — rubbish, ashes, the lot.'

'Very good, sir,' said Wayne Wain, realising that Pluke did know a thing or two about the investigation of murder. Montague was clearly in charge and enjoying his role. Wain was suitably impressed. He hoped sincerely that Pluke would solve the crime and confound his critics.

Leaving Wain on guard, Detective Inspector Pluke, with his half-mast trousers flapping around his ankles and his straw hat perched upon his head, led Stephen Winton away from the Circle saying, 'We'll sit in my car, Mr Winton, for our chat.'

Upon arriving at the car, Montague Pluke removed his panama, opened his car door, placed the hat upon the rear seat and invited Winton to be seated in the front passenger seat. The young man consented, easing his bulk into the limited space and placing his camera upon his knee. Montague Pluke turned to face him, noting the young man was pale-faced and very nervous.

'So.' Pluke's voice was now softer, quieter too, although some might say it contained a hint of menace as he addressed the man who was his number one suspect — his only suspect in fact. 'You found her, Mr Winton? Tell me about it, again and in greater detail, please. Take your time, I need to know every step you took, every move you made, even what thoughts were going through your mind.'

'There's not a lot more I can tell you, Mr Pluke, I've said how I found her.'

'You said you had come here to take photographs for a magazine and went into that cave where you discovered her. You ran back to your car, which you had left in the car-park, and called us on your mobile phone?'

'Yes, that's it, that's all. I waited until you got here, like your office said I should do.'

'Good,' acknowledged Pluke. 'You did what every good citizen should do and I compliment you on that. But I fear this *is* a murder-style investigation, Mr Winton, which means I need to know a lot more details about your actions and your purpose in being at this place. Little details, Mr Winton, petty stuff you might think, unimportant stuff you might even say, but most important to us, to me, to the whole investigation.'

At this point Pluke took out his official notebook, found a ballpoint pen among the conglomeration of instruments in his breast pocket and scribbled on the clean page; he was noting the time, the place and the reason for the ensuing entries.

'Your full name, Mr Winton? Age, date of birth, address and occupation please.'

He was Stephen George Winton, twenty-eight years old with a flat on Cragston Moor on the outskirts of Fossford. He said he was a professional freelance photographer and provided his date of birth. He was single and lived alone. He had a girlfriend who lived with her parents in Fossford, but there was no engagement or long-term commitment. Not yet, he emphasised.

'Tell me about the commission that brought you here,' invited Montague.

'It's for a series, "Mystical Tours of Britain", I told you that before.' The man's lower lip quivered as he responded to Pluke, 'A new magazine highlighting places of mystery ...'

'You know the Druids' Circle is a folly, a fake?' Montague put to him. 'It is hardly a place of mystery, hardly the sort of spot to merit any great attention.'

'Yes, I know, but it does attract people, and there is a theory it might occupy the site of an earlier temple and that it is on a ley line, so the editor wants to include it.'

'And your editor, who is he?'

'She, it's a woman. Molly Swift, I have her address and telephone number.'

'I may need those to check your story.' There was a hardness in Pluke's voice because he was in active pursuit of a killer. 'We check everything that we are told, Mr Winton, time and time again until we are completely satisfied.'

Detective Inspector Pluke waited as Winton found a business card in his jacket and handed it to Pluke. It bore Molly Swift's work address, telephone and fax numbers.

'You can keep it, I have her details in my Filofax,' said Winton.

'Tell me more about the commission, Mr Winton,' invited Montague Pluke. 'How you came to receive it, how you were about to execute it this morning.'

'Molly rang me last week, she knows my work. I've undertaken commissions for her before, rural scenes generally. Abbeys, castles, country houses, river bridges, dramatic views, that sort of thing.'

'Published work?'

'Yes, of course. She asked me to produce a set of contact prints of the Druids' Circle, that's all. She wanted to select two good ones for publication. By the end of the month. So I came this morning, the light was ideal. A hint of thunder and dark clouds combined with bright sunshine would produce a marvellous atmosphere.'

'You've been here before?' asked Montague.

'Yes, but not to take pictures. I once came with some friends, hiking, about eight or nine years ago. We had a picnic here, we didn't stay, we were youth hostelling.'

'So this is your first visit for professional reasons?'

'My first visit for years, Mr Pluke.'

'So today. What time did you arrive?'

'It would be around eleven o'clock. I reckoned I could work for an hour or so and allow an hour or so for the drive to York for another appointment.'

'That plan has been thwarted, eh?' Montague's face creased in a sad smile. 'So you drove out here, parked in this car-park and walked into the Circle?'

'Yes. I spent a few minutes calculating the light, to get the right setting, studying angles and views. I wanted to capture the atmosphere, the mystical feel of the place, something to provide the reader with an immediate appraisal of the attractions of the Circle.'

'Did you take your car to the Eastern Gate? I was thinking of you having to carry your equipment.'

'No, I just use a hand-held camera, no portable lighting, tripods or such. Besides, we're not supposed to drive that far, are we?'

'True. So what time did you leave Fossford?'

'Tennish. Maybe a bit before. It's about an hour's drive; a bit less when there's not much traffic about.'

'Did you see anyone you knew as you were leaving? Did you talk to anyone?'

'No, no one. I got into the car and came straight here.'

'Where was your car in relation to your flat?'

'Right outside, parked on the street. I don't have a garage.'

'So there are no witnesses to confirm your departure time? And when you arrived, did you see anyone? Tourists? Hikers? Gamekeepers, estate workers ... anyone?'

'Nobody, Mr Pluke. I had the place to myself. It was eerie even then, I don't mind admitting.'

'I agree, it is a very odd place, Mr Winton. It's redolent of past times. Now, take me through your discovery of the body once again.'

As Pluke and Winton talked, the first of the support services arrived — it was Detective Sergeant Tabler of the Scenes of Crime Department and he was accompanied by three detective constables in their official Transit van. Wayne Wain would brief them well. Then an increasing number of specialist service vehicles began to arrive, along with two uniformed constables to secure the site. All knew their jobs. Wayne would cope and Pluke could continue his interrogation.

He smiled at Winton.

'Like I told you,' Winton was saying, 'I took my camera from the car, which I parked here, and went into the Circle. After selecting certain shots, I took them, all out-of-doors using natural light, but all within the circle of stones. The trees do make it fairly dark in places, but that can be used to advantage. I managed to get the altar in a lovely atmospheric light, then I thought the cave might make a nice pic so I took a few shots of the exterior, the entrance that is, avoiding the litter on the ground inside, and then I went in. I had no torch, so when I got into the dark bit, round the corner, I activated the flash on my camera — it was like walking in lightning during a thunderstorm in the dark: all quick flashes — that's when I found her. God, what a shock, Mr Pluke ... I couldn't believe it ... it was terrible ... at first I thought it was a joke, one of those tailor's dummies, and then I touched her. I knew she was real, but she was so cold, so awfully cold ... and stiff. I knew she was dead. So I ran out and went straight to my car to call the police.'

'You did not touch anything else? Remove anything? Turn her over?'

'No, nothing.'

'And have you seen her before? In life? Do you know her?'

'No. I saw her face ... I'll never forget her face now. No, Mr Pluke, sorry, I can't help you there.'

'How many films did you say you used before you found her, Mr

Winton?'

'Just the one. It has thirty-six exposures. I know you want it, that's no problem. I have others I can use, I have a commission this afternoon, in York, the Minster. I might just get there on time if I can leave now … you can have all those I took — if I can have my shots of the Circle please, before my deadline. I don't suppose I could go back in there now, for a minute or two, to take another reel, now that you are here to supervise me?'

'Sorry, no. It'll be out of bounds to the public for today at least, perhaps longer. We'll develop your film and will make copies of everything we consider useful. I will ensure your negatives are returned to you, probably tomorrow. Now, before you go, I would like you to put all this in writing, in the form of a written statement. If we do it now, I shouldn't have to trouble you later. I might add that a statement from the finder of the body is vital to the investigation. I have the necessary forms in my briefcase.'

And so, as the complement of support services began to gather around Wayne Wain for their first briefing, Montague Pluke wrote down everything said by Stephen Winton, quizzing him once or twice to iron out any queries, and afterwards Winton signed the form. This was merely a witness statement, not a statement from a suspect, and once it was complete, Pluke allowed Winton to leave — after confiscating his film.

'Now, before you leave,' said Pluke, 'my officers will need to examine your car.'

'My car?'

'Yes, and the soles of your shoes. For elimination purposes. We need to be sure you did not convey the body to this place in your car, Mr Winton, and we need to isolate your footprints from those of any other person. We must eliminate you from our enquiries as soon as we can, and this is the ideal time.'

'Am I a suspect or something?' The paleness of Winton's face was turning slightly more grey at this juncture.

'In a murder enquiry, everyone is a suspect until we can officially eliminate them, Mr Winton,' said Pluke. 'Clearly, you are the only person we can talk to at this point. It will take a few minutes of your time, then you will be free to leave. I am sure you wish to be cleared of suspicion? Is it your own car?'

'Yes, of course I do, and yes, it's mine.'

'And how long have you had it?'

'A year. I bought it second-hand.' Detective Inspector Pluke asked the Scenes of Crime officers to examine the tyres for comparison with any tracks they might discover, then they examined the interior of the car, and the boot, to determine whether a dead, naked female body had been carried. If she had been inside Winton's car, she would have left some deposits. Whatever the officers found would be taken away for forensic analysis. While Winton stood and watched the meticulous examination of his vehicle, another detective came to examine his footwear and to take plaster casts of the soles of his trainers.

As these investigations were under way, Detective Inspector Pluke went to check on progress in the cavern. The police doctor had pronounced the girl's life extinct but was not prepared to certify the cause of her death; a local pathologist had conducted a preliminary examination of the body *in situ* but could not provide any suggestion as to the cause of death. He confirmed there were no marks of violence on the body — no stab wounds, bullet holes or other indications of the use of a weapon. He had turned her over for a look at her back, again finding no sign of a weapon having been used, but this examination would have to be followed by a post-mortem in laboratory conditions. He added that, in his opinion, she had been dead for at least twelve hours but the coolness of the chamber had preserved her remains longer than if she had lain outside in the normal heat of the day.

Meanwhile, the Scenes of Crime officers had examined the interior of the cavern and had marked the position of every dot of debris before collecting it all in plastic sample bags. Everything, including the remains of the woman, would be closely examined, both visually and scientifically. Official photographs and a video tape of the body had been completed, and meanwhile the Task Force officers were noting and examining every item found within the Circle, or just beyond the perimeter of outer stones.

Wayne Wain had done a good job as liaison officer and after about an hour Detective Sergeant Tabler located Pluke, took him aside and said, 'We've finished with Winton's car and footwear, sir. We've got all we need for the moment.'

'And?'

'We've got some bits and pieces from it, but on first inspection I don't think he carried her in that car. Prints matching the soles of his shoes are on the track as one would expect; we found them in several places, heading in both directions, and at the entrance to the cavern, in the soft mud. They confirm his account of how he found the body.'

'But they're not inside the cavern, on the floor?'

'No, sir, it's solid rock. We found no footprints there, none at all.'

'So we can let him go?'

'Yes, sir, I think so. I reckon he's clean.'

'All right. Release him, but I think we need to know a little more about him, Sergeant,' cautioned Pluke. 'His eyebrows meet in the middle, you will have noticed. That's never a good sign, Sergeant! It is said that people whose eyebrows meet in the middle are untruthful.'

'Really, sir?' puzzled Sergeant Tabler.

'So that's an action for a good team,' stressed Pluke. 'To examine Winton's life and recent movements in detail.'

After returning to thank Stephen Winton for his public-spiritedness, Detective Inspector Pluke allowed him to leave the scene in his car and returned to locate Wayne Wain.

'If Winton says he didn't kill her, then who did?' he asked as he fell into step at the side of his sergeant.

'We might know the answer to that if we could find out who she is,' said Detective Sergeant Wain.

'And in due course we must have more words with Mr Winton,' said Montague Pluke with determination in his voice. 'For the time being, let him think we have finished with him. I believe he may have more to tell us if we press him. But first, let us complete a tour of the site, Wayne.'

*

Millicent did enjoy her lunch with Mrs Councillor Farrell and six other ladies of position and eminence in the town. The goings-on at May's bungalow, during the absence of May and her husband it was stressed, was a talking point of some interest to the assembled group. All wondered if May had given permission for her niece to hold parties on the premises. It seemed that lots of young people had arrived and although several had left by taxi, some had stayed overnight; there'd been lights too and music. Had that large van been a disco DJ and his equipment?

The big question discussed by the ladies was whether May and Cyril should be told about this upon their return from holiday. No one referred to the incident at the cricket club, however; perhaps such things were not discussed in decent society, so Millicent decided not to mention it to her friends, although, if he would listen, she might tell Montague.

Chapter 6

With Wayne Wain at his side, and taking care to avoid places under close examination by his officers, Detective Inspector Pluke completed a pedestrian tour of the Druids' Circle. It was during this perambulation that Pluke remarked on the presence of some rowan trees, saying, 'Our pagan ancestors planted rowans to ward off evil spirits, Wayne. They were grown near burial grounds to aid the deceased along their path to the heaven of their time. Thus the presence of rowans hereabouts *could* — and I emphasise the word *could* — suggest the location was once a genuine religious site.'

'So even after the passage of centuries, we might expect some rowans, descendants of the parent trees?'

'Yes indeed, Wayne. Very true. Remarkable evidence of continuity down the years.'

While the two detectives had been studying the environment of the giant stones, members of the various support services had been carrying out their detailed and specialised inspections.

'Everyone's finished with the body, sir.' Pluke was eventually approached by Detective Sergeant Tabler of SOCO. Wayne Wain was at Pluke's side.

'Good, then we can move her. Is the shell here?'

'Yes, sir.' Wayne pointed to a parked Transit van.

Pluke strode across to the constable who was standing beside a blue Ford Transit van.

Inside would be the plastic makeshift coffin known as the shell; this was used for the transportation of dead bodies to the mortuary.

'She's all yours now, PC Hughes,' said Pluke, pleased that this part of the enquiry was complete. He did not like dead bodies lying about when there was work to be done, but as it was physically impossible for the large vehicle to enter the confines of the Druids' Circle, its driver reversed it to the Eastern Gate where Hughes recruited the assistance of three detectives to help carry the loaded shell. Pluke walked beside them as they made for the entrance of the chamber where she lay.

'Feet first, gentlemen,' Pluke told the bearers. 'You always carry a corpse out feet first.'

'I've never come across that sort of thing before,' muttered one of the officers. 'It's not in Standing Orders, is it? I can't see that it matters which way a corpse is carried out, upside down, back to front, feet first, head first, sideways and standing on its head ...'

'I insist that things are done properly, gentlemen.' Pluke was not to be deflected from his ideals. 'It is out of respect for the deceased if nothing else.'

He spoke with unaccustomed authority as the team of bearers carried the lightweight coffin into the dark chamber, now illuminated by lights wired to a generator. They lifted the pale corpse into the coffin, working quietly but efficiently, and in a matter of seconds the young woman was lying in the shell, arms upon her body with her hands covering her most personal area as if she were in the bath surrounded by ogling onlookers.

Before the lid was fitted, Pluke looked upon her in the brightness of the temporary lights, hoping he might have seen her in the town, but had to admit he did not recognise her. Pluke was sure she was not a local woman.

'Someone somewhere must know who she is,' he murmured, then asked PC Hughes, 'Has a time been fixed for the PM?'

'Yes, sir, five o'clock this afternoon at Crickledale Hospital.'

The lid was fitted and it covered the mortal remains of the unfortunate young woman. She was then carried out of the chamber feet first in accordance with Montague's instructions and placed in the Transit for conveyance to the hospital mortuary. There, her once-lovely body would be subjected to the horrific carving and brutal internal scrutiny that comprised a post-mortem examination. As the van manoeuvred for departure, Pluke sought the pathologist; he'd noticed him earlier among the busy police officers who had entered the cave for a final check. He was called Simon Meredith, a slightly built individual with half-moon spectacles, thinning fair hair and a matching moustache

'Anything further to report now she's been moved?' asked Pluke. 'Anything beneath the body? Any marks on the body? Anything new that might tell us something, however trivial, Mr Meredith?'

Meredith shook his head. 'Very little to add, Detective Inspector. The condition of the body and a lack of insect infestation suggest she had not been here very long. Although it is a summer day with high external temperatures, the atmosphere in that chamber is very cool and she has been well preserved. I'd say she was placed here overnight; it's almost impossible to estimate her time of arrival, but I'd hazard a guess it happened within the last twenty-four hours, and probably within the last twelve hours. And there is no evidence that she was killed here. No sign of a struggle in that chamber, nothing under the body. I believe she died elsewhere and was brought here, even though we have not found any indication of her means of arrival at this lonely place. Most certainly, she did not walk here naked. Her feet were clean.'

'So you are saying she was killed overnight?' Pluke put to the pathologist.

'I am not saying she was killed, Mr Pluke. I am saying she died because I cannot specify the cause of death. I hope my post-mortem will establish that. Clearly, it is suspicious, but that is all I can say at this stage. Now, I must get back to the hospital. Is five o'clock a suitable time for the PM?'

'Yes, that's quite suitable,' agreed Pluke.

The pathologist left the scene, followed swiftly by the Force Photographer and the SOCO team. Pluke handed Winton's undeveloped film to Sergeant Tabler before he departed, asking that it be developed and copies made for scrutiny by the murder teams. Tabler said he should complete that task by later this afternoon.

Although many experts were leaving, members of the Task Force remained to complete their duties. Eight officers upon hands and knees were conducting meticulous fingerprint searches, gathering anything and everything that had been deposited within the limits of the Circle. Every single item, whether it was a discarded crisp packet, a piece of broken glass or the ejected cartridge of a twelve-bore shotgun, was charted and placed in a plastic bag for later scientific analysis. The detectives knew that such objects could often tell an interesting story even though many would be rejected as being of no evidential value to this investigation. It was amazing what could be deduced from something as innocuous as the lid of a jam jar or an empty beer can.

Pluke had a chat with the inspector in charge of the Task Force, reminding him to search the woodland beyond the extremities of the Circle; the girl's clothing and personal belongings had disappeared and dense woodland was the ideal place to dispose of them. Tyre marks must be sought too — it was highly likely she had been brought here by vehicle, probably after death, and Pluke was assured that this team of highly qualified officers would do everything required of them.

'Ready, Sergeant?' asked Pluke. 'I think we can do no more here.'

And so Detective Inspector Pluke and Detective Sergeant Wayne Wain departed for Crickledale Police Station.

*

At this stage, there were certain formalities to be completed by Detective Inspector Pluke. The Chief Constable had to be notified and so had Detective Superintendent Jack Hart, the officer in charge of the CID. Then the officer in charge of the Control Rooms at both Crickledale and Force Headquarters would have to be briefed so that their officers were aware of the ongoing situation. And Pluke's own divisional commander must be informed. Coping with the demands of internal politics was as vital as solving the murder itself, and upon receiving Pluke's telephone call, the Chief Constable asked, 'Does it look like being a runner, Pluke? From what you've told me, it's hardly a routine domestic, is it?'

'I fear it might take a while to solve, sir,' said Pluke after explaining the prevailing situation.

'I know you are not very experienced at this sort of thing, Pluke, but I want you to remember that we operate on a very tight budget. We can't go spending money like water, even if it is to solve the mysterious death of a pretty young woman. If it is not murder, we can avoid a lot of expenditure, so the sooner we get the job cleared up, the less it will cost the Force. That means we shall have more to spend on important things. In that respect, your duty is very clear — we need a speedy result.'

'I fully understand, sir, and I do have a suspect.' Whereupon Pluke told of Winton's role in the matter.

'It's a beginning, Pluke,' commented the Chief. 'But am I right in thinking this is your first major investigation?'

'I have investigated other sudden deaths, sir, and many crimes, but I must admit this is the first time I have been in command of an enquiry of this kind,' Pluke corrected his Chief.

'Then you will be aware that not everyone who finds a corpse is a murderer, Pluke, and that not every dead body is a murder victim. Don't let old theories blind your judgement, don't get side-tracked into fruitless enquiries and do make sure you don't run away with my year's contingency fund. But equally important, I do not want an unsolved murder messing up my crime statistics.'

'I will do my best, sir,' acknowledged Pluke.

When Montague rang his divisional commander, Superintendent Ronald Casson, Casson said, 'Whatever you do, Mr Pluke, get this one solved as soon as possible. We're talking money, Mr Pluke, serious money, and both the Chief Constable and the County Treasurer have warned us not to overspend during the current financial year. So find that killer, Mr Pluke, and do it without spending a fortune. I don't want you or your detectives thinking there are unlimited overtime payments, those days have gone. For every day your teams remain on the enquiry, it is less money for other things. Think on that, Mr Pluke. And go easy on the forensic exhibits, they cost money, you realise. Big money. Keep costs down, Mr Pluke.'

'Yes, sir,' said Montague Pluke.

After hearing about the investigation, the Chief Constable rang Detective Superintendent Jack Hart and said, 'Jack, is that man Pluke fit to take charge of the enquiry? If my information is correct, he has never been in charge of a murder investigation. He seems to have spent his entire career worrying whether it's unlucky to carry a spade into a house or whether it's the right day of the month to shout "rabbits".'

'He is in charge of the CID of the area in which the body was found, sir,' replied Hart. 'The case is therefore his responsibility. He is quite a good detective, you know, he did solve the Primrose Bank statue damage case and it was he who caught the Hooded Pimper at the Nurse's Home.'

'Well, so long as he gets the job done without spending too much money. And get him to dress in something that looks good on camera — we need a good television image among our senior detectives and at the moment he looks like a bloody refugee from World War One. We need to portray efficiency and professionalism, Jack — and I hope he doesn't concentrate all his attentions on the chap who found the body.'

'If I might say so, sir, those of us who know him well think it wise to let him pursue his own lines of enquiry. This allows the ... er ... more professional detectives to concentrate on the real substance of the investigation.'

'Point taken, Jack. That does make some sense. Nice tactics. And keep an eye on those overtime payments.'

*

Fridays were never a good day to start any new enterprise, so Montague Pluke was pleased that the investigation was beginning on a Thursday. Having notified all those who had to be told, he went down to the Incident Room which was now being established in the parade room. It was a hive of activity with desks and chairs being positioned, telephone lines, faxes and computer links being installed, along with a photocopier, blackboard, stacks of paper and official forms, and tea and coffee-making facilities. People were dashing around and civilian staff were arriving by the carload.

Detective Inspector Horsley was in charge of the arrangements and Wayne Wain was in the thick of it.

Montague made his way through the throng to examine an ante-room, then said to Horsley, 'This will be my office, Mr Horsley.' He took a four-leaved clover from his pocket and laid it on the desk already *in situ*. 'I'll get Mrs Plumpton to find a vase for my clover. It's not often one finds a four-leaved clover in this locality — quite unusual in fact, a sign of impending good fortune and a fortuitous beginning for us. It was growing on the verge just up the road ...'

'So where do I work?' snapped Horsley, a former rugby international who didn't know a clover from a vetch. 'I happen to be the officer in charge of the Incident Room and this is the only office. I would have thought I should have had first choice.'

'And I am the officer in charge of the overall investigation, Mr Horsley,' retorted Pluke. 'Might I suggest you work at a desk among your staff? That way you will be able to keep an eye on things as they happen around you, a very good supervisory tactic. And I do need a secure office; this is ideal which is why I have claimed it.'

Horsley had slipped up. In such cases, it was usually a case of first come, first served and he had been rather slow in staking his claim. And he could not pull rank on Pluke because both were inspectors. He had to admit that luck had been on Pluke's side — surely that had nothing to do with that four-leaved clover, had it?

Having claimed his office, Pluke's next job was to find Mrs Plumpton.

She had been drafted in to supervise the secretarial work and he wanted her to produce the necessary stationery and equipment for his office. He felt it might be beneficial to have his name on the door too and would ask her to bring a name-plate. The next most important job was to convene a conference of detectives. He calculated that all the detectives would have arrived within an hour and decided that, in the meantime, a cup of tea was needed. He found Mrs Plumpton unwrapping brown paper parcels of witness statement forms and asked her to make the tea before she got too involved with other things. And he would have his lunch while enjoying the tea. But then came a telephone call from the Control Room.

'Inspector Pluke.' It was Sergeant Cockfield pronounced Cofield. 'I've received a radio message from the murder scene, it's DC Bray. He has found a gentleman's glove; it is outside the Druids' Circle and appears to have been discarded recently. He wants you to be informed and to make a decision about its examination and disposal.'

Pluke thought for just a moment, then said, 'Tell him I will come immediately. Leave it where it is for the time being.'

Within two minutes, Pluke had located Detective Sergeant Wayne Wain and, forsaking the cup of tea and a chance to have lunch at his desk, was soon being driven back to the Druids' Circle by him. When they arrived, the entire site was encircled with metres of yellow tape and guarded by uniformed constables. After Wain had parked the car, Pluke quickly located DC Bray. 'Ah, Detective Constable Bray.' He beamed. 'You have something to show me?'

'A glove, sir, for a male person, leather, black, right hand, size nine, soft lining, good quality, good condition.' DC Bray had been a former soldier, Pluke recalled.

'And what makes you think it might be relevant?' asked Pluke.

'The glove is damp, sir, but otherwise in very good condition. It has not been here long, sir. One can sense that by its general appearance. It rained gently last night, sir. I have checked the state of the weather at this place. The glove is made of leather, sir, good quality and I deduce it was dropped very recently.'

'Not by a policeman, I trust, DC Bray!' There was a smile on the face of Detective Inspector Pluke. 'But good work and good thinking. Now perhaps you will lead me to it?'

Using a route which had clearly been approved by the detective sergeant in charge of the scene, Pluke and Wain followed DC Bray around the outer stones to a point beneath a beech tree.

The woodland floor was clear of briars and other vegetation at this point, but there was a covering of dead beech leaves, a legacy of last autumn.

'There it is, sir.' And, standing to attention, Bray pointed to the glove.

'You have not moved it?' asked Wayne Wain.

'No, Sergeant, it has not been touched. The facts were acquired without having to move it, sir.' The glove was lying on its back with the label exposed near the wrist.

'Any other clothing nearby?' asked Wayne Wain.

'No, Sergeant,' chanted Bray. 'We have conducted a meticulous examination of the locality but there are no other items of clothing, male or female, within a twenty-metre ring around the Circle. And no footprints either, sir. The covering of dry leaves has prevented anyone leaving footprints. The leaves are damp, sir, under the surface, but dry on top, today's sunshine has dried them on top, sir.'

'Very good work, DC Bray,' Pluke congratulated him. 'Now, have you recorded the precise position of the glove?'

'I have, sir, and had it photographed. Twenty metres due north of stone number nine on our master plan of the site and eighteen centimetres from the base of this beech tree which can be identified by the scroll and heart carved on the trunk, western side. Unmistakable, sir.'

Pluke then asked Bray to mark the position for the record. He did so with a dagger-sized piece of pointed plastic bearing the number 67 and then, lifting the glove carefully, placed it in a plastic exhibits bag.

'DC Bray, this is a very important piece of evidence. I shall have it examined with a view to tracing its origins and its owner. Thank you for your diligence.'

'It is good to be of service, sir.' And Bray stood to attention as Pluke and Wain walked away bearing their trophy.

During their return to the office, Pluke said, 'Wayne, this glove might be a very important piece of evidence. We must not inform the press at this stage — we do not want the owner to dispose of the matching partner. We must determine the name of the manufacturer, the point of sale and, if possible, who bought it.'

'We must be careful, sir, we cannot be certain it was dropped by the killer. We should not spend too much time and money on the glove if it is not known to be relevant. Isn't it odd that someone should wear gloves, thick leather gloves like this, in the height of summer? Very few people wear gloves in summer, especially not men, sir.'

'Criminals wear gloves to conceal their fingerprints, Wayne. Most criminals are not blessed with brains, as we know — so might our villain have been hoping to conceal his prints by wearing this glove? Maybe he used it when driving a car to the scene to dispose of the body? Or when carrying the body!'

'That is possible, sir, yes, I agree.'

'Anything is possible and if this is possible, Wayne, we must consider that possibility. I believe the glove is important. Gloves can be identified by the grains of the leather, rather like fingerprints. This is a very important piece of evidence, Wayne, so it's a good action for our teams — have someone trace the source of that glove and, if possible, identify the owner. Now let us get back to the office. Our tea will be getting cold and I haven't had my lunch.'

*

When Millicent walked into town to do some shopping after lunch, she noticed Gertrude Nettlewren emerging from the hairdressers with a hairstyle that looked like a wasps' nest.

'Your hair looks very nice,' Millicent oozed. 'But you weren't at the lunch?'

'No, Moses wants me to join him at the Magistrates' Association Dinner tonight and the only time I could get an appointment for my hair was over lunch. I was so sorry, I did ring Mrs Councillor Farrell.'

'You missed a treat, Gertrude,' said Millicent. 'There's all that stuff about May's niece having parties at the bungalow ...'

'I saw the van the other day, Millicent, they were taking cameras in. It must have been a very special party, mustn't it, if they were taking cameras and tripods in. I mean big cameras, Millicent, the sort you'd expect for a television programme.'

'Really?' Millicent was intrigued by this. 'Have you time for a cup of tea at Ye Olde Tea Shoppe?'

Chapter 7

Montague Pluke's first news conference did not attract many journalists because non-violent deaths, even those with an element of suspicion, were no longer considered front-page headline news. Even though this was the greatest thing that had happened in Crickledale since the vicar ran off with both the choir mistress and the contents of the parish safe forty-six years ago, the editors in distant towns felt disinclined to commit their staff to the story. It meant a long drive into the remoteness of the moors for something which, on the strength of the advance information, might be little more than the outcome of a domestic tiff or some ribald horseplay.

But those who did arrive found themselves rewarded with a good story and an intriguing detective inspector whose photograph would soon grace their pages. Montague, having had his photograph taken complete with panama, spats and ancient, curiously shaped, buttoned-up overcoat, told the press corps about the discovery of the naked body of a beautiful blonde woman in the burial chamber of the Druids' Circle and added that identification of the deceased was his priority.

The press loved him; they wanted lots of pictures of him at the Druids' Circle complete with magnifying glass in a sort of Sherlock Holmes scenario, but he resisted, saying this was a serious matter and it was a description of the girl they should be publishing. He knew that the story of her death would create useful publicity, even if it was of tabloid standard and content.

There was no doubt the story would be elevated from a routine piece of news about a puzzling death to something salacious laced with mystery and magic in an abstruse setting. The journalists who were present would ensure the story reached the nationals, while those editors who had not bothered to despatch a journalist would now be regretting it. Some were even forecasting that if the investigation did become a long runner, Montague Pluke would become a TV star. On those occasions when there was no further news about the investigation, they would concentrate on the life and work of Montague Pluke. At this stage, of course, they knew nothing of his horse trough expertise. That alone might make a TV series ...

When the journalists asked Montague to specify the cause of death, however, he truthfully said he did not know and that a post-mortem was to be conducted, although he did confirm that it was suspicious. To add words to their stories, he told them that fifty detectives were engaged upon the enquiry, many of whom would be making house-to-house enquiries in Crickledale and the neighbouring villages. As questions were asked about the Druids' Circle, he found himself stressing that witchcraft, a black mass sacrifice and a ritualistic killing were unlikely, although death resulting from sexual activity could not be ruled out. Having said all that, he qualified it by adding, 'We are keeping an open mind.'

Even though Montague emphasised that the Circle was a fake, a couple of photographers persisted in their desire to take pictures of it, some with Montague standing either at or near the phallic symbol or at the entrance to the cavern or near the sacrificial altar, but he declined every invitation.

He had no wish to trivialise the enquiry, but the Force press officer agreed to accompany the photographers to the scene for a picture session without Montague Pluke. Their presence could be tolerated under supervision, even while examination of the scene was under way. In fact, a photograph of police officers searching the scene would make a good picture, while the necessary scientific restrictions would be heeded. In all Montague felt, it was a good and useful news conference and the resultant publicity might produce someone who could identify the deceased. Surely that lovely girl had been missed by her family and friends?

Very soon after the journalists had departed to meet their deadlines, the result of the post-mortem was telephoned to Montague. It produced a dilemma because Mr Meredith could not determine what had caused her death, which meant that further tests would be necessary. Some of her organs would have to be despatched for forensic analysis, or at least a second opinion.

'Are you saying she's been poisoned?' Pluke asked Mr Meredith.

'I'm not saying that because I do not know,' admitted Meredith. 'Drugs, poison, some other cause. You need an expert analysis, Mr Pluke. All I can say is that I can find no evidence of an unnatural death. It seems she died from natural causes, that is what I am saying, but I need a second opinion. Provisionally, I believe she was asthmatic but do not know if that would cause her death. There was no evidence of sexual assault, she was not pregnant and she had never given birth to a child, although she was not a virgin.'

He went on to say that there were no external or internal injuries, she appeared to have been a healthy young woman aged between twenty-five and thirty, around one and a half metres tall (five foot four) and of average build, with long blonde hair and blue eyes. She had kept herself in a spotless condition; every part of her body was remarkably clean and she had good natural teeth. There was no foreign matter beneath her fingernails such as the assailant's skin or hair, nor anything such as earth, dough, food or paint to provide a clue to her occupation or hobbies. Her last meal had been a salad comprising ham, lettuce, tomato and spring onions, and she took a size 5 in shoes.

'I am sorry not to be of more help, Mr Pluke,' apologised Meredith.

'We do have something.' Pluke smiled, admittedly baffled by this outcome. 'We know her death is suspicious — the method of disposal of the body tells us that. But thanks for your efforts. You'll let me have the usual written report?'

'Of course.'

Montague Pluke returned to the Incident Room to ensure these findings were entered in the file and on the computer, and to inform his officers. Even without a known cause of death the investigations would continue and in any case it would soon be time for the first conference of detectives. A check with Mrs Plumpton revealed that all had now arrived in response to their call-out; most had gone to the canteen for something to eat before their evening's duty, but they could be assembled in the Incident Room within a few minutes. Pluke suggested a meeting at six o'clock; it was amazing how the afternoon had flown, and as he glanced at his own watch he realised that Millicent would have his evening meal ready.

He also realised he had not told her of his unexpected commitment, so he decided to hurry home before the conference of detectives.

There was just enough time to do that and he told Wayne Wain of his intention.

*

'Had a nice day, dear?' asked Millicent as he walked into the kitchen to plant his routine kiss upon her cheek, taking care, as always, to stand in front of her in order to achieve this display of purest love. To kiss someone upon the nose, even accidentally, is said to bring trouble between the pair, and to kiss someone while leaning over that person's shoulder was tantamount to stabbing him or her in the back. And Montague had no desire to create trouble between himself and Millicent, nor did he wish to imply he wanted to murder her.

Millicent was a tall lady and rather slim, although the clothes she wore — old-fashioned cover-up-everything pinnies, shapeless skirts and home-made jumpers when in the domestic mood — obliterated any shape of which she might be proud. With grey hair, curled and worn short above the ruddy-red cheeks of a countrywoman, plus rounded, tortoiseshell-framed spectacles which had thick lenses to compensate for her short-sightedness, she was not a very handsome woman. But she loved Montague, even to the extent of tolerating his dress sense.

'Very interesting, dear,' said Montague, having delivered his kiss and hung up his hat. 'I found a new horse trough.'

'How exciting,' she bubbled as she took the casserole from the oven. 'That must be number 350? You'll soon reach your target of 500 at this rate! That is good news, I am so pleased for you … you must tell me about it.'

'I won't have much time,' he apologised. 'I have to go back to work this evening.'

'Oh, dear. Is it important?'

'A young girl has been found dead in very suspicious circumstances and I am in charge of the investigation.'

'A murder? And you are in charge? Oh what a huge responsibility, Montague. And how awful for you, for the town. I hope it doesn't stop the tourists coming. What dreadful things happen these days.' She began to spoon the contents of her dish upon his plate. 'You do work so hard, Montague, you could do without this sort of thing when you are trying to keep crime down.'

'I am not referring to it as a murder, dear, it is merely a suspicious death, but it will be quite interesting, I believe,' he said, sitting at the table and tucking his serviette into his collar. 'But I must admit, it would be nice to catch the killer, Millicent, if in fact that is what emerges. I am sure she met her death unlawfully.'

'Well, you must not work too hard, and remember you promised to lecture to the Local History Society tomorrow night. You cannot let them down, they are looking forward to your visit. Now, you mustn't go working overtime and wearing yourself out, Montague. Do sit down and relax for a while.'

As he chomped at the squares of beef in her stew, his mind was going over the events of recent days, and he asked, 'Millicent, dear. Have you heard any more about the Crowthers? You said they were on holiday?'

'Yes, they are. Two weeks in Majorca. May told me they were going when I saw her at the Embroidery Club. I thought I had mentioned it. Why do you ask?'

'It's just that I hadn't seen either of them around for a while. I was passing the end of their Grove this morning and realised how long it had been …'

Montague had no desire to tell Millicent about the crow and its message, so he smiled his appreciation of the news she had imparted as she continued, 'I should think we should be getting a postcard from them soon. She has a niece, you know, who's looking after the house while they're away. It seems she has friends in Crickledale too, lots of them go round to visit her. She's been having parties there.' And she went on to tell Montague about the observations made by her circle of friends, concluding with, 'Now, dear, do tell me about the horse trough.'

It had long been a rule of Montague's that he did not mix his police work with his domestic life, so he pondered her words for a while, then said, 'Yes, that could be a very interesting discovery and I intend to give it a closer examination before too long. It's near the Druids' Circle, that folly in the woods, close to where the body was found. I was lucky to notice it in the ditch, we've been past before without me seeing it. I find it very interesting that horse troughs were used on that part of the moor …'

A little more than half an hour later, Montague Pluke was back in the Incident Room, suitably refreshed and ready to conduct his first conference of detectives. His hat was sitting on a peg beside his famous overcoat; he was now resplendent in his tight-fitting jacket with its breast pocket full of pens and pencils, his blue bow-tie, his silky waistcoat and half-mast trousers which revealed his spats.

He let it be known to the Incident Room staff that he was pleased to note that brief details of the deceased had been written on a blackboard for all to see, that photographs of her face with front and side elevations were already on display on the notice-board and that a video of the scene showing both the corpse and the surrounds was available. Wayne Wain had been busy.

Also on the notice-board was a photograph and description of the gentleman's glove with a request that officers attempt to find the owner or, more immediately, the left-hand glove which completed the pair. Montague had issued an order that news of the discovery of the glove was not to be given to the press at this stage, since he did not want the killer to dispose of its mate. Having checked the efficiency of his teams, Montague was ready to address them.

When the group of fifty noisy, cheerful and hardened detectives gathered in the muster room for their address by Montague, he felt somewhat nervous. Most of them were very experienced hunters of murderers; most, if not all, were drafted on to every major investigation within the county, but this was the first time he had been in command of so many officers in such an important and difficult case. Montague, however, was determined not to be overawed by the drama of the occasion.

As Wayne Wain moved supportingly to his side, Montague stood on a chair, shouted in his loudest voice and, surprisingly, found that everyone lapsed into a respectful silence. Recalling Swinburne's words that 'Silence is most noble', he began his address. The first part was easy. He told them of Winton's discovery, he told them about Winton and his work, he explained how the body had been positioned in the chamber and gave a detailed description of the deceased with the local pathologist's inconclusive assessment. He added that the body would now be subjected to forensic examination and provided a brief history of the Druids' Circle. He referred to recent police photographs depicting what was there now, including shots of the body and the rubbish in the chamber. He mentioned the glove, showed them photographs of it and said it was the only evidence to hand at this stage — that unintentional joke resulted in a ripple of laughter in the room. It was good-natured laughter — they thought his joke was intentional. He laughed with them — it was a good moment.

Next, he said, was the long, tedious slog of routine enquiries in the town — door-to-door enquiries must be undertaken by teams of detectives, two officers per team. Montague stressed that the officers must interview the people at each house — if there was no response to their knocking, they must return to the house again and again until they got a response. No occupant must be left unvisited or unquestioned. He was thinking about the Crowthers' house — whoever was living there had to be interviewed and seen to be alive.

The enquiries might reveal the identity of the many visitors mentioned by Millicent, but in any case, the crow's presence demanded that close attention be paid to No. 15 Padgett Grove. He also insisted that all the workers on the estate which contained the Druids' Circle be interviewed to determine whether anyone had noticed anything or anyone suspicious at or near the Circle in recent days. Press coverage of the enquiry would produce ghoulish tourists and unwelcome visitors to the Circle; gamekeepers, poachers and trespassers would be traced where possible and quizzed about their movements. Sexual perverts and those with odd sexual tastes such as pimpers, flashers and their ilk would be interviewed — there was a good file on them at Crickledale Police Station. Woods and druids' circles were the known haunts of some very weird people.

'But,' he said as he terminated the conference, 'our main purpose is to identify the girl. Inspector Horsley will allocate appropriate actions to you — we will need to peruse all lists of missing women issued by every police force and to liaise with civilian registries of missing girls and women. Someone, somewhere will know who she is. Our first job is to find a name for the lady in the burial chamber. Inspector Horsley will provide maps of the town, so that a system of house-to-house enquiries can be established. And we need to be told of any found clothing, especially women's items that might have belonged to the deceased. It is vital that we find her clothing and any jewellery she might have worn.'

He went on to state that Stephen Winton's antecedents would be studied, and that any cars seen entering the woodland area must be traced.

Hikers, ramblers, nature students, bird watchers and those with similar pursuits must be tracked down and interviewed. Quite surprisingly, he did motivate the officers and finished by saying that each working day would be from 9 a.m. to 9 p.m. That meant four hours' overtime each day, but due to the Force's dire financial straits, time off would be taken in lieu of payment. Today, the teams would finish duty at 9 p.m., which allowed a little time to make a vital impact on the town. Before the teams left, Pluke said that the video would be constantly available to those unfamiliar with the girl's description or the scene. The teams left the Incident Room full of hope and ambition — each detective aspired to arrest a murderer and hoped this might provide that opportunity.

Each team of two officers was given a specific briefing by Wayne Wain; their action had been entered into a register and allocated a reference number for subsequent cross-reference and checking when the statements began to flow in to the Incident Room files. Every statement would be read and cross-indexed by a team of statement readers who would enter data into HOLMES, the Home Office Large Major Enquiry System's computer. From these efforts, the names of suspects would emerge for future interview.

Having seen his men dash into action, and happy that Inspector Horsley would supervise and administer the Incident Room, Montague decided that, on his way home, he would revisit the Crowthers' house. He must establish whether that niece of May's was at home — he could not ignore the message of the lone crow and continued to ponder its significance in the light of recent developments.

He realised that one of his teams would visit the house during the routine house-to-house enquiries. If they did their job properly, they would establish the holiday whereabouts of the Crowthers and the identity of May's niece. But Montague felt his duty was rather more immediate and as the teams returned from their first, uneventful enquiries in town, he said to Wayne Wain, 'I am going home now, but *en route* I shall be visiting a house of some friends.'

'Sir?'

'They are away on holiday, so I am told on good authority, but as I saw a crow sitting on their roof yesterday, a sign that heralds a death, I felt I ought to call in.'

'As part of this enquiry, you mean, sir?'

'I suppose you could say that, Wayne, although there is no known link between the house and the dead girl. But yes, every enquiry in this town is now part of our murder investigation, surely?'

'Might I ask why you wish to see the house?' Wayne seemed to think that murder enquiry protocol was being breached.

'I want to see whether there has been a death there.'

'You mean the girl might have been killed at that house, sir?'

'It is a possibility that I cannot ignore, Wayne. It has been troubling my mind. I know our teams will be visiting the house in due course, but in this case I have personal connections with the owners. So, do you wish to accompany me or are you going off duty?'

'I'll come with you, sir.' Wayne had no intention of missing this. Pluke could be right, he might know something the others did not. After all, he was a local person with a very extensive local knowledge. As Pluke walked through the town, he received courteous greetings from the townspeople who were out and about, smiling, nodding and raising his hat where appropriate.

'You know a lot of people, sir,' commented Wayne Wain.

'Indeed I do, Wayne, indeed I do. That is part of my job, but also part of the penalty of being a leading citizen in a small town. But in the case of my work, it is an enormous help — local knowledge is of paramount importance, Wayne, and it is one of the factors which has compelled me to return to the Crowthers' house.'

'Return, sir?'

'I did make a quick visit this morning, Wayne, but learned nothing of great interest, except that there were indications of the presence of someone other than the Crowthers. My decision was made in the knowledge that a crow had settled on their roof, Wayne, not because of the girl's death.'

'And there was no sign of a problem, sir?'

'There was one small indication of a possible problem, Wayne, one which I shall retain in my memory should it become relevant.'

'Something you noticed?'

'Something I noticed, Wayne.'

'A piece of superstition?'

'A piece of domestic practice which could be construed as a superstition, Wayne, hence my unwillingness to divulge it at the moment.'

When they arrived, Montague rang the bell. He did not expect a reply but felt he should perform this basic arrival ritual. No one answered and so he said, 'I think a circuit of the bungalow is called for, Wayne. The kitchen door is at the other side and I suggest that a peep through the windows might be helpful.'

After only a few yards he halted and peered through the lounge window into the well-furnished room. He saw that the mirror above the fireplace was still draped with a tea towel.

'See that, Wayne? A covered-up mirror? That was there when I called earlier.'

'Stopping the reflection of car lights in the drive, perhaps, sir?'

'I doubt it, Wayne. It's not the sort of thing the Crowthers would do.'

'The niece, perhaps? Drying the cloth?'

'That is one interpretation,' acknowledged Pluke. 'There may be another. Now, I wonder where the niece is and what she's doing here? Millicent referred to visitors with cameras.'

Although it was almost nine thirty, the evening was light, this being mid-June but none of the house lights was burning. Gingerly, Pluke walked around the path towards the kitchen door, passing the dustbin and opening a wooden gate before entering the back-kitchen garden. The glass-panelled door was now on his left. He knocked and waited. There was no reply.

As he was waiting, Mrs Dunwoody at No. 11a, grey-haired and plump and in her fifties, opened her kitchen door and shouted, 'They're away, Mr Pluke, on holiday.'

'Yes, I know, Mrs Dunwoody. But I am told someone is living in during their absence.'

'That niece of hers, she's house-sitting.'

'Ah, and where is she? Do you know?'

'Well, she was here the other day but not for long, always rushing out somewhere. People coming and going. Vans and cars and things, folks wanting taxis. I said to my George that young lady's never here, she's always gallivanting off somewhere in that little car of hers, but I haven't seen her today so I said to George she might have gone off early or something, you never know with young people ...'

'What does she look like?' asked Pluke with sufficient volume temporarily to stem Mrs Dunwoody's flow of words.

'A bit of a glamour-puss if you ask me, not one for talking to the likes of me and my George. Too old for her, we are, I said to George. Not her kind of people. I said to George that young lady's got ideas above her station, I said, not a bit like her Aunt May ...'

'Appearance, Mrs Dunwoody. What did she look like? That girl?'

'Blonde hair, Mr Pluke. Very clean it was, and long. Pretty face, I suppose, the sort men would go for ... yes, very pretty. Smart with it ...'

Pluke looked at Wayne Wain who said, 'Mrs Dunwoody, if we showed you a girl who is lying in a mortuary, could you tell us whether it is Mrs Crowther's niece?'

'A mortuary? Oh good heavens what a thing to ask ... I'd better have words with George ... he's the one for that sort of thing. I always say when the police come knocking on your door it means trouble ... George, are you there? George? What are you doing? George!'

At her call, there emerged a grey-haired man in slippers who was bearing an egg cup containing the shell of a boiled egg which had been smashed into the cup. He was trying to extract the shell to throw it into the waste bin.

'Good evening, Mr Dunwoody,' greeted Pluke, recognising the fellow. He did countless jobs around the town, including taxi driving and work for the local undertaker. He was always to be seen rushing about Crickledale, running errands, cutting grass in the sports field, doing bits of painting and decorating, and even some bus driving in the summer. A man of all parts.

'What's up?' he growled as he came from the kitchen. 'Oh, it's you, Mr Pluke. I'm in the middle of washing up, a late tea. Damned egg shell's got stuck fast in here ...'

'Sorry to interrupt you during important work, Mr Dunwoody, but have you seen the girl who's staying here?' Wayne Wain put to him.

'Aye, bonny lass. Chatty with it!'

'Mr Dunwoody.' Montague spoke now. 'There is a girl of similar description in the mortuary of the hospital. I need you to look at her and to tell me if it is the girl who was staying here. Will you do that?'

'Aye, right. It'll get me out of the rest of the washing up. Hang on while I get my shoes on.' And he went inside to dispose of his stubborn egg shell.

'We'll check the house when we come back,' said Pluke very quietly to Wayne, as Mrs Dunwoody said, 'I always said no good would come of that lass. Much too flighty. She never dried the pots when she washed up, just left them to drain ... and she never made the bed. And she had people in, it's not as if it's her own house, is it? You could look through the windows and see the sheets all over the place. Not brought up proper, she wasn't. I don't know what May would think to it all, if she ever finds out. Apart from that, my George couldn't take his eyes off her, those shorts it was. I've never seen shorts as short as those shorts, Mr Pluke, then there was her skirt ...'

George reappeared, smiling, and said, 'Right, Mr Pluke. Ready when you are.'

On the way to the hospital, George let it be known that he had done this before, when a friend had been killed in a road accident, and so it was not a new experience.

'Is it that girl found at Druids' Circle?' he asked. 'Word's got around the town, Mr Pluke.'

'She was found there,' confirmed Pluke. 'Yes, that's the girl we are going to examine.'

'Then it'll be a public footpath from now on, eh? Through those woods?'

'Public footpath?' queried Wayne Wain.

'Aye, whenever a corpse is carried across a field or through a wood or anywhere that's private, it becomes a public footpath,' said

Dunwoody with conviction.

'The estate will never allow that,' said Wayne Wain. 'It's private now, although they do allow the public to visit the Circle. But that's with their consent — the public has no right of way.'

'It'll all stop from now on, mark my words,' said Dunwoody. 'Old law it is. Corpse roads become public rights of way, you can't argue with that! So, what happened? Accident with that car of hers, was it? Somebody taking fright and getting rid of her?'

'No, we have reason to believe it is murder,' said Detective Inspector Pluke, ignoring Wayne Wain's puzzled frown at this bold comment.

*

Mrs Peat from No. 14 Padgett Grove, a member of the Flower Rota for the church, rang Millicent. 'Millicent, I shan't be able to replace the flowers this weekend, I'm going to see my sister in Brighton. Now, I wonder if you could stand in for me?'

'Yes of course,' Millicent said. 'Only too pleased.'

'Now, you know Mrs Dunwoody doesn't like red and white flowers together. Something to do with her WVS work at the hospital. Hospitals won't have red and white flowers in the wards and her George is most particular, like blood on bandages he says. Anyway, where was I?'

'You wanted me to help out?'

'Ah, yes. The church. Can you help, Millicent?'

'Yes, of course. And I'll make sure there's no reds and whites together.'

'Good heavens, Millicent,' cried Mrs Peat. 'I'm looking out of my window and there's your husband and another detective, they're at May's place, talking to Ada. What a coincidence I should ring you now. I'll bet it was all to do with that noise that girl and her friends were making … look, I'll pop round to see you about the flowers …'

'There is no need, it is all very clear …' But Mrs Peat had rung off.

Millicent knew that Montague's investigations were very important and highly confidential and that she must resist all Mrs Peat's questioning. Not that Montague told her very much about his work, but with Mrs Peat's potential for gossip, you never knew how far things would go. On this occasion, Millicent decided she would listen rather than talk, because Mrs Peat seemed to know something about the goings-on at No. 15 Padgett Grove.

'Good heavens … your husband is at May's place, talking to that Dunwoody man … I'll bet it's to do with the noise that girl and her friends were making …'

Millicent didn't say that Montague was engaged upon a very important murder investigation.

Chapter 8

On the journey to the mortuary, it became clear to Montague
and Wayne that George Dunwoody loved to identify dead bodies.
In fact, it was almost a hobby with him. He'd seen hundreds, he
told Montague, chiefly due to his part-time work of helping out at
Crumble and Smirch, Undertakers, Embalmers and Funeral Carriage
Masters of Crickledale. During his part-time work he had, from
time to time, been expected to handle corpses, to carry them down
narrow staircases and lift them into coffins; furthermore, he'd often
been asked to help identify those injured in traffic accidents or fires,
and had done a bit of laying-out and measuring for coffins too. But
his proudest moments were as bearer, especially if the funeral was a
big one with a local personality as the dear departed.

During their discussions, it transpired that George was often asked
to identify deceased persons because he had once been a postman.
He had met almost everyone in the town, often at the crack of
dawn, and had thus viewed many Crickledonians in their natural
early-morning state, i.e. women with curlers and without teeth, or
unshaven men suffering from a hangover after a night in the pub. It
meant he could recognise the features of almost any local person,
dead or alive, battered or not battered, in darkness and in light, and
in conditions which would thwart other potential identifiers. People
without their teeth did have a look of corpses, he jested. He added
that if today's corpse was a Crickledonian, he would know her.
George added that he would never shirk from his public duty and
was not afraid of helping Detective Inspector Pluke, even if the lass
in question was a murder victim.

What he did not tell Pluke was that it would be something to boast about in the pub on Friday nights. After all, it wasn't everyone who measured corpses for coffins and got it right first time, even for those with humped backs and big noses — and even if the regulars were rather tired of George's tales of the macabre, his involvement with Crickledale's first murder case would enliven the conversation at the Bay Horse.

When the small official party reached Crickledale Hospital, George was eager to display his knowledge of the network of corridors plus his considerable corpse-handling skills. After Detective Inspector Pluke had satisfied the receptionist that they were not invaders seeking to sit with a sick relative after visiting hours, they were guided by George to the mortuary suite.

'I've been here hundreds of times.' He led them into the bowels of the hospital. 'But I've never done a murder before, Mr Pluke. There's a first time for everything, eh?'

'There is indeed,' responded Montague, remembering this was also his first murder-type investigation and adding, 'We have yet to confirm she was murdered, Mr Dunwoody. At the moment, it is officially nothing more than a suspicious death; I shall be pleased if you will treat the possibility of it being a murder with the confidentiality it deserves. All we need from you is a name for the deceased if, of course, you recognise her.'

'Aye, well, I know that. I shan't go blabbing in the pubs about this, you know. I know when to keep a secret. Us folks in the public eye must behave right, eh?'

'That is very reassuring.' Inspector Pluke beamed, unconvinced.

When they reached the mortuary suite, the attendant, a cadaverous character called Clarence, bade them wait near the empty operating plinth as he went to Drawer number 14 and hauled it open. It was like a giant filing cabinet in which each drawer could be filled with a corpse instead of masses of paper, and each was refrigerated. As the huge drawer eased out of the bank of cabinets, it filled the room with the distinctive sweet-sickly smell of death and disinfectant. Montague saw that it contained the body of the girl found at the Druids' Circle. She was the only resident this evening, the other drawers being empty if the blank labels were any guide.

Pluke saw that the subject of their visit lay feet first in the cabinet, her head at the handle end of the drawer with her blonde hair spilling around her. Below the neck, her nakedness was concealed beneath a white shroud which reached down to her feet. Only her face was visible. Montague Pluke was pleased about that, pleased that her modesty had been respected.

'That's the one,' muttered Wayne Wain at his side.

'Mr Dunwoody.' Montague spoke with authority, his voice echoing in the sepulchral space of the mortuary as he carefully avoided the use of George's Christian name. 'Can you examine the body of that young woman in drawer number 14 and tell me if it is the woman you recognise as the niece of Mrs Cyril Crowther?'

'Aye, right.' And George moved manfully towards the head of the drawer, cap in hand, and peered at the dead face. His decision took a fraction of a second.

'Aye, Mr Pluke, that's her. Mrs Crowther's niece, I'd swear to it.'

'And do you know her name?'

'No, sorry, Mr Pluke. No idea.'

'But you've seen her at the Crowthers' house?'

'I have.'

'When was the most recent occasion, Mr Dunwoody?'

'Well now, that's a good question. Today's Thursday, eh? Which means yesterday was Wednesday and the day before that was Tuesday, haircutting day. I'd say Tuesday, Mr Pluke. Tuesday morning. When she left in her little car.'

'Left where, Mr Dunwoody?'

'Cyril and May's house, Mr Pluke. She was house-sitting, so I understood, they're away on holiday and I definitely saw this lass go off in her mini on Tuesday.'

'Where to? Any idea?' asked Wain.

'Turned right she did, outside the bungalow, but I have no idea where she went from there.'

'What time was that, Mr Dunwoody? When she left the house?'

'After breakfast. Coffee time. Half-ten, summat like that.'

'And did she come back?'

'She must have done because the lights were on, later, that was. I never noticed her, though. Mind, folks can come and go from that house, by the front door that is, without us knowing.'

'And her car? Did you see it parked outside upon her return?'

'No, but she did use the garage. Cyril drove his car to the airport, you see, so the garage was empty for that lass to use.'

'What colour was her car, then? And registration number?'

'Red, a dull red. Nearly plum-coloured, I'd say. But, well, Mr Pluke, I have no idea of its number, I mean you don't, do you, take car numbers, unless you are a car number spotter. There was no cause, was there? She was just a lass having a break herself, looking after the house for her aunt ...'

'What was she wearing? When you last saw her? Can you remember that?'

'Now you're asking hard questions, Mr Pluke. She allus dressed well, in mighty short skirts or shorts ... thin blouses ... white I think. I nobbut noticed the top in the car, driving seat. A white T-shirt, that's all I can say.'

'Any idea where she lived, Mr Dunwoody? Her home address? I need to know who she is and where she lived or her parents' name and address. Or next of kin.'

'Now that's summat I do not know. She's definitely not from Crickledale, that's for sure. But before May left for Majorca, she told us her niece was coming to live in, to house-sit. She never gave us a name or said where the lass was coming from.'

'She was definitely May's niece, then? Not Cyril's?'

'Aye, her sister's lass, she said. May's youngest sister is called June — her elder one's called April, daft, eh? April, May and June … Anyroad, before May went off, she said we shouldn't have to worry about putting lights on and taking in parcels and things because June's lass was coming to live in. She had some work to do in these parts, so May said, a summer job.'

'So if the girl hadn't come, you would normally have looked after the house?'

'Aye, me and Ada allus do that, Mr Pluke, look after each other's houses, water the plants, take parcels in, that sort of thing, put lights on, draw curtains at night … We've a set of keys for the bungalow, for when they're away.'

'But surely she must have mentioned a name for the girl? A Christian name?'

'Nay, Mr Pluke, she never did, not to me or our Ada.'

'When she left the house in her mini on Tuesday, was she alone?' pressed Pluke.

'I think other folks came and went while she was here, there was a lot of partying and things, cars and vans coming and going at night, but personally speaking, I never noticed anybody else with her on Tuesday.' He thought hard. 'Nope, Mr Pluke, I reckon she was alone. Chugging off somewhere alone that Tuesday, she was. I said to Ada afterwards that I thought her car needed its plugs cleaning, it was chucking out a fair bit of smoke and one plug was misfiring, you know, making plopping noises … I told Ada I would offer to put it right for the lass, but Ada said it was nowt to do with me and I had to mind my own business.'

'You've been a great help, Mr Dunwoody.' Montague thanked him and nodded to the mortuary attendant who began to close the drawer and conceal the body until it was next required. 'At least we know she had links with the Crowthers.'

'Sorry about the name. I can ask our Ada …'

'I will ask her when we return,' countered Pluke.

Wayne Wain wondered what time he was going to finish duty tonight. Once Pluke found himself hot on the trail, he would work all night. Wain had memories of the great stolen gnome case some two years ago. Pluke had worked all one night but, to give him due credit, he had traced the culprit and had found him in a garden shed full of stolen gnomes.

But on their return to No. 11a, Pluke, while standing at the door, questioned Ada without receiving any further help. George was at her side as Ada said she had seen the lovely blonde girl coming and going, dashing off in her mini and returning with plastic bags full of supermarket groceries and drinks. Sometimes the girl had waved at Ada as she'd peered through the kitchen window, but they had never spoken. The Dunwoodys' overall impression was that May's niece lived respectably even though she had had lots of young people in from time to time. A party of some kind, Ada thought. The Dunwoodys said they had no complaints about loud music or noise.

'Not yet, anyroad, touch wood!' George grinned, reaching for the frame of his doorway. 'They've not caused us any bother!'

Pluke established that Cyril and May had left in the early hours to drive to the airport in their own car and the girl had arrived the same day, which was last Saturday. Ada confirmed the timing. The girl had arrived in the middle of the afternoon and had unloaded her belongings while clad in a red T-shirt with wide sleeves and a neckline down to her knees.

Her white shorts had left nothing to George's imagination. His lawn-mowing that afternoon had taken three times longer than normal and he had commented about the gummed-up plugs of her car, even offering to sandblast them for her. She had declined with a smile that compelled George to offer to test his dip stick in her sump but she said the man at the garage had done that this morning.

'Which garage?' asked Pluke.

'She never said, Mr Pluke. She never said where she had come from and I never asked,' admitted George, thinking that if he had been forty years younger he would have had her name, address and telephone number within moments of his first meeting.

'She said not a word about where she'd come from and May didn't either, Mr Pluke,' confirmed Mrs Dunwoody. 'And I never asked. I'm not nosy, you see, I don't poke my nose into other folks' business. Not like some I could name — like her at No. 14, the Peat woman. Right nosy, she is. You should hear some of the things she comes out with at the Coffee Club; you ask your Millicent, Mr Pluke.'

'The girl's home can't be very far away if she arrived in, say, half a day. If she'd called at a garage to have her oil checked and tank filled, then driven here to arrive by mid-afternoon, she can't have come all that far,' observed Pluke. 'I'd guess she's come from the north, somewhere between the Humber and the Tweed, maybe.'

'Come to think of it, I think she did have a Durham twang when she spoke,' recalled George. 'Not quite Geordie, nicer than the Middlesbrough sound. County Durham, I'd say, judging by the way she said stuffed.'

'Then we must make sure all the papers, radio stations and television news bulletins provide a description. Now, I fear we must examine the house,' announced Pluke. 'I have reason to believe she met her untimely death in No. 15.'

'Oh, my God,' murmured Mrs Dunwoody. 'Not on May's best carpet — she just had it cleaned a fortnight ago ... such a nice young man came with his chemicals and wafted scent all over afterwards.'

'You'd think we'd have heard something, Mr Pluke,' said George. 'Or seen him taking her out ... I mean, you can't shift dead bodies without somebody seeing something. I should know all about that,

I've shifted plenty.'

'Precisely, Mr Dunwoody.' Pluke beamed. 'Somebody, somewhere, must have seen something or heard something or know something. There are other neighbours we must talk to for it is our job to find that person. Now, I believe you have a key to the bungalow?'

'I'll get it, it's for the kitchen door, but shouldn't we ask the Crowthers first?' asked George.

'Don't be silly, George!' snapped his wife. 'They're in Majorca!'

'They might not be, they might be dead too, in this very house.' Pluke decided to shock them into silence and submission. 'I have reason to believe that a suspicious death has occurred within this house and must therefore examine the property to ascertain whether or not that is the case. We are permitted, by law, to enter the premises in such circumstances, Mrs Dunwoody. Rest assured we shall leave the house as we find it.'

When George produced the mortice key on a plastic keyring depicting Mickey Mouse, Montague asked the Dunwoody pair to remain in their own premises, saying that if murder had been done inside, there would be masses of evidence which had to be preserved from the feet of neighbours and incomers. Only he and Detective Sergeant Wain would enter.

At this stage, the summer night was growing darker and it was necessary to switch on the house lights as they entered the kitchen door. The two detectives stood side by side in the kitchen, their trained observational powers absorbing every detail down to the unwashed mugs and plates in the sink, the half-consumed pan of spaghetti bolognaise on the cold oven ring, the opened cans of Coke on the table, things Pluke had not been able to see from the outside during his earlier visit.

'She's obviously had company, Wayne, one or two persons.' Pluke pointed to three empty plates on the draining board, each bearing the remains of a meal of spaghetti bolognaise. 'Three plates, three forks. Someone who doesn't like washing up. So, other than those party-goers, who has been here with her, I ask myself?'

'We might discover more, sir. The neighbours said she'd had visitors.'

'We will need to preserve those Coke cans, dishes and other items for fingerprinting.'

Without touching anything in the kitchen, they passed through and entered the passage which ran towards the front door, turning left and left again into the lounge, switching on the light. This room overlooked the street and the garden, and it was here that Pluke had earlier noticed the covered mirror.

'I think somebody hung that tea towel up to dry, sir.' Wayne Wain smiled. 'A strange place to put it, if you ask me.'

'Very strange and very interesting indeed,' commented Montague Pluke.

The mirror was hanging above the mantelpiece which in turn was above the gas fire and it seemed, at first glance, that someone had indeed suspended the tea towel over the mirror so that it would gain from the waves of heat rising from the gas fire. Portions of the mirror that could be seen revealed a sturdy wood-framed looking glass of oval shape suspended on chains from a hook in the wall. It was positioned lengthways and the wooden oak frame was dark with age, its vintage probably being pre-World War Two. The tea towel, depicting scenes from the North York Moors, was draped between the two points where the chain was attached to each end of the mirror and almost covered the entire glass face.

After Pluke had scrutinised the towel without removing it, he said, 'I need that towel to be photographed *in situ*, Wayne. I regard it as very important.'

'Yes, sir,' agreed Wayne Wain. 'Nothing will be moved, that is the normal situation with an enquiry of this kind. Move nothing, photograph everything.'

'Precisely.'

Their inspection of the lounge, achieved by standing at each doorway without touching anything, revealed nothing else of a suspicious nature in that room, so they adjourned to the bedroom. And there, in the master bedroom, the mirror on the dressing-table was covered with a white sheet, although the littered dressing-table was not.

It contained the usual complement of perfumes and make-up, but Pluke noticed the inhaler beside some lipstick.

'An inhaler, Wayne. Note that. It confirms what our pathologist thought. He mentioned asthma. Have that photographed in due course. Neither of the Crowthers used one.'

'Very good, sir.'

The bed was tidy and fully covered, although it did appear to have been used since the Crowthers' departure. The covers were crumpled and one of the bedside mats was crooked; May always made sure everything was smooth and symmetrical. In the second bedroom, the mirror of the small dressing-table was covered with a pink bath towel but the single bed was unmade. The sheets and pillows were rumpled, while the duvet was lying partially on the floor and partially on the foot of the bed; the single wardrobe door was standing open and, from their vantage point, Pluke and Wain noticed it contained the clothing of a young woman. The deceased's clothing, surely? All of it? That kind of clothing did not belong to May Crowther.

'If and when we trace her relatives, Wayne, we must find out which items of her clothing are missing. Did the killer strip her here and are her clothes therefore in this wardrobe?'

'I'll check as soon as I am able, sir,' said Wayne Wain.

The bathroom contained some make-up, toiletries and recently washed underwear comprising two black bras and two pairs of black knickers, all hanging from a line suspended over the bath.

The bath was empty although Pluke did discern the faintest of tide marks around the inside at high water level. Somebody who had bathed here had not cleaned out the bath afterwards, just as they had not washed the pots used for their meal. But here, in the bathroom, the mirror was also covered, this time with a smaller towel which had been tucked behind the glass to hold it in place as the length of it draped across the glass.

'So, Wayne,' said Detective Inspector Montague Pluke. 'What do you deduce from all this?'

'There is little doubt,' the sergeant said, after a moment's thought, 'that the young woman lying dead in the mortuary is the same person who has been living in this house. It appears she was here with the permission of the householders. That has yet to be confirmed by them, however. It seems she has not been alone either. She has had visitors or a visitor. That other person or persons must be our prime suspect, probably being the last person or persons to see her alive. It seems that all or most of her clothes are here too. It suggests she was killed, or died, in this house, and that her body was removed to the Druids' Circle for concealment.'

'My conclusion precisely, Wayne. A good deduction. So we need to have the entire place meticulously examined by our forensic experts and Scenes of Crime officers, do we not? Fingerprints must be taken for comparison with those of our growing list of suspects as and when they are brought to our notice. And if this bungalow is the scene of her death, it needs to be photographed and examined in meticulous detail. Bedding checked, sample fibres retained for forensic. Attics, dustbins, garden and every nook and cranny must be searched for evidence. We need to take the place apart, Wayne, we need to identify the owners of any fingerprints we find, not just those of any suspects.'

'Had we better inform Mr and Mrs Crowther, sir?' asked Wayne.

'I fear we must, Wayne. That time has come — besides, they need to be eliminated from our enquiries, but we must break the sad news of the death of their niece, plus the awful fact she might have met her death in this bungalow. And we must obtain details of the girl's name, address and next of kin from the Crowthers, so that is an action for this evening, Wayne. Trace, interview and eliminate the Crowthers, identify the deceased. The Crowthers must also rank as suspects until we can prove they were out of the country at the time of the girl's death. Might I suggest we start with the travel agent?'

'I'll set things in motion, sir.'

'*We* will set things in motion, Wayne. I shall accompany you to the home address of Mr Holliday of Holliday Holidays. I know where he lives. He will trace the Crowthers for us and we must ask them to put a name to that girl, Wayne. Then we have the awful job of asking her parents to come to Crickledale formally to identify her.'

'Yes, sir, but shall we emphasise to the Crowthers that there is no urgency for their return? I am thinking of our work in their house, sir, it'll be far easier in their absence.'

'A good idea, Wayne. They will not be able to use their home for a few days anyway, not while our men are searching it for evidence. We must be careful to break the sad news gently, Wayne, a dreadful matter for someone enjoying a Holliday holiday in the sunshine.'

After studying the interior, the garage and the exterior in silence for a few minutes, Pluke decided it was time to leave. He told the Dunwoody couple that he was impounding their key to No. 15 Padgett Grove, that the house was sealed and that he was now going to contact the Crowthers in Majorca. Meanwhile, a policeman would be ordered to guard the property until the teams of forensic scientists and Scenes of Crime officers arrived. Pluke radioed for an officer and determined to await his arrival. Having briefed him, Pluke decided to leave.

'Good-night, Mr and Mrs Dunwoody,' said Montague Pluke. He raised his panama in farewell to Mrs Dunwoody, 'And thank you very much for your valued assistance. I shall be in touch when I have some further news.'

On their way to the Holliday abode in Wayne Wain's car, Pluke asked his sergeant, 'Do you regard George Dunwoody as a suspect, Wayne?'

'Well, sir, he has to be eliminated, like anyone else.'

'Yes of course, but what I mean is, Wayne, is he in the frame, as we say? A positive suspect, one worthy of closer examination?'

'You clearly do not think so, sir, you took him into your confidence, telling him it was a murder when we haven't had the official confirmation.'

'I wanted to test his reaction if he thought we were treating it as murder.'

'And?'

'I am still judging his response, Wayne, I asked him to respect the confidentiality of that information. Officially we have not yet confirmed it is a murder enquiry. I want to see how things develop.'

'So you do suspect him?'

'He is one of many suspects, Wayne, do you not think?'

'I didn't feel that, sir. I got no gut feeling that he might have done it. I felt he was merely a neighbour keeping an eye on the bungalow.'

'Consider it anew then, Wayne. Here we have a neighbour who, by his own admission, is accustomed to handling dead bodies in difficult places. Naked dead bodies. Lifting them about, moving them from place to place ... it's something he's quite proud of. And he had a key to the bungalow. And he took a shine to that girl, according to Mrs Dunwoody.'

'There was no indication he might be guilty, sir, was there?' Wayne interrupted.

'Let us suppose that he went into the house to attempt a seduction of the girl and things went wrong. He could say he saw her leave the premises when in fact she would be lying dead until he had the time and opportunity to move the body in secret. And he is a taxi driver, Wayne, working for a firm in town, out and about at all times with access to vehicles and no questions asked. And, note, he did not mention operating a taxi from that party at No. 15, although cars and taxis were seen there. Was he afraid for us to know he was somehow involved?'

'I can't see that such negative things are important, sir. Besides, there was no sign of a struggle. I'll agree the bed looked crumpled but not as a battlefield might.'

'And her clothes were in the wardrobe, not thrown away as we first thought. She might have been nude while in the house, Wayne.'

'Nude, sir? When she was killed? Doesn't that imply she consented to something?'

'Not if she was in the bath, Wayne. And remember that body in the Druids' Circle was very clean, was it not? And there was a tide mark around the bath, indicating it had been used since the Crowthers left — May would never leave the bath in that state.'

'Am I right in thinking we need to know more about George Dunwoody, sir?'

'I am sure that is a wise decision, Wayne. That is a task for our teams tomorrow. Now, let us talk to Mr Holliday of Holliday Holidays.'

*

Millicent's visitor had arrived while Montague was working late. Millicent, ever the welcoming host, offered Mrs Peat coffee even though she said she had merely come to discuss the altar flowers.

'I am sure I saw a nude man in May's house,' she later whispered to Millicent when she realised that Millicent was not going to talk about Montague's work. 'Not that I was watching, of course, but, well, one of them opened the door to go outside to get something from the van, and the bare man darted across the hall ... starkers, he was. Young, dark-haired. Quite big, too. And there were lots of people in the house, Millicent. Now, with all that stuff on the news and with Mr Pluke being there earlier, I did wonder if May's house was involved because that would be awful …'

'Mr Pluke never discusses his work with me,' said Millicent proudly, but she became determined to learn more from Mrs Peat and then to ask Montague what was going on at No. 15 Padgett Grove. After all, he had asked her about May and Cyril, hadn't he? He'd never said why he was asking, the devious man!

Chapter 9

Ephraim Holliday was the chairman, managing director and proprietor of Holliday Holidays. This was a modest empire which comprised a chain of Yorkshire travel agents with its headquarters in Crickledale. Ephraim, a self-made man, lived quietly in an end-of-terrace house of gigantic proportions. In a desirable and peaceful part of the town, an area once favoured by Victorian businessmen, it boasted spearheaded iron railings which had avoided confiscation for the World War Two effort, and it was endowed with a garden full of rhododendrons and a summer house. The family home for several generations, it had seven bedrooms, lots of reception rooms, an attic, a cellar and Adam-style fireplaces. It dated from 1802 and was in Heft Road, No. 47, complete with a conservatory and highly polished brass doorbell. There was also a thing for scraping mud off shoes, positioned at the top of a wide flight of stone steps which climbed to the front door.

Leaving Wayne Wain in the car, Montague Pluke climbed the steps and rang the bell which produced a prompt response. Ephraim, a tall, heavily built man of some half-century in age and with iron-grey hair, appeared in carpet slippers and an old cardigan. He was smoking a large curved pipe and looked like Sherlock Holmes.

'Why, hello, Mr Pluke! To what do I owe this honour at this time of night?' He puffed a cloud of smoke into the mild night air.

Montague explained that it was not a social call, nor a matter relating to one of the town's voluntary organisations, nor indeed an official visit to ask whether anyone had seen a burglar or armed robber legging it through the streets.

He went on to say that his arrival was part of an investigation into a suspicious death which had occurred in or near Crickledale. Montague managed to create an immediate air of mystery by saying he wished to trace two of Ephraim's customers, Cyril and May Crowther, who were thought to be holidaying in foreign parts. Suitably horrified and shocked, Ephraim admitted Pluke to his hallway with its ornate umbrella stand, Victorian mirror and tiled floor, then after hearing that the Crowthers might be able to assist Pluke with his enquiries, he offered to escort the detectives to his business premises in town from where he could trace the wanted man-and-wife team.

Five minutes later, with Ephraim's slippers exchanged for sensible town shoes and his capacious pipe tucked into the pocket of his cardigan, Pluke and Wain followed Holliday's grey Volvo into the town centre until it drew to a halt outside Holliday Holidays in Market Street. The travel agent's window was brightly illuminated and filled with a selection of model aircraft flying over Alpine views and blue Adriatic seas with a backcloth of colourful brochures and glamorous posters. He led them to his desk at which there was a computer VDU and keyboard. It was the work of but a moment or two to access the Crowthers' file.

'Cyril and May have always been very good customers,' proffered Mr Holliday. 'I've never had trouble with them before. I always thought they were nice people. They have always paid cash for their holidays, Mr Pluke. They habitually take an overseas break at this time of year ... now, here we are. Yes, they departed at 11 a.m. on the 17th — Saturday — by air from Manchester Airport. For two weeks.'

'Where did they go, Mr Holliday?' checked Pluke.

'Majorca, it was part of a package tour and I booked them into the Hotel Palacio on the Costa Blanco.'

'Good, I need to speak to one or other of them.' Pluke was

relieved that their departure date provided both with a good alibi; if it could be proved they had actually departed on that day, neither could have caused the death of their niece. She had been seen alive after they had gone, Montague realised.

'Shall I obtain the telephone number of the hotel?' suggested Holliday. 'What time is it in Majorca now, you might well ask ... not too late to make a call to their room or to reception ... unless you wish to ring Interpol to arrange an arrest?'

'I am not thinking of arresting the Crowthers, Mr Holliday, certainly not upon the information currently in my possession, and in addition I am not fully conversant with the extradition procedures involving British holiday-makers in Majorca. I merely wish to have a conversation with them about the deceased. Now, can we be sure they took the flight?' asked Pluke.

Inspector Pluke wished to eliminate the Crowthers positively from his investigation, at the same time as notifying them of the decease of their niece. Ephraim, now sensing Holliday Holidays was not going to be the focal point of a sensational headline-hitting hunt for killers across continental Europe, approached his sophisticated computerised holiday booking system. This enabled him to access the flight records and to confirm that a Mr and Mrs Crowther had taken their seats on the 11 a.m flight last Saturday to Majorca. Or, to be precise, someone bearing their names and in possession of their passports, had taken the flight.

They were booked in the hotel for two weeks i.e., to return a week on Sunday, leaving Majorca at 2 a.m. Thus it was almost certain they had been out of the country at the time of the supposed death of the blonde in the Druids' Circle. That pleased Montague — the idea that Cyril and May might have been involved in a suspicious death was dreadful to contemplate; their guilt would have had a drastic effect upon the town's social activities. You couldn't really have a murderess or even a suspected one running Crickledale Flower Club or hosting a coffee morning.

'You can ring from here,' invited Ephraim, showing them the telephone.

Even if the Crowthers were not going to be escorted back to England with an armed guard, Ephraim was anxious that his part in an international police enquiry should be seen to be as great as possible. Apart from confirming his role as a worthy citizen, it would be good for publicity, especially if men from Interpol used his agency to book a flight to Majorca to arrest and bring home any guilty parties. Ephraim reckoned to understand secret police jargon and was sure that the phrase 'we need them to help with our enquiries' was tantamount to saying they were suspected and would have to be interviewed, with an arrest in due course. So what on earth had Cyril and May got themselves involved in? puzzled Ephraim. A drug-smuggling racket, arms dealing, forgery cartel, white slave traffic?

While Ephraim pondered possible publicity, Montague fretted about the offer of a free telephone call. He had to consider whether or not this was an attempted bribe, but felt it wasn't. It was, he believed, a genuine desire by a leading Crickledonian to help the police, although Montague did realise he would be imparting terrible news of a devastatingly personal nature to the Crowthers, news that would be overheard by a third party. Yet, on reflection, there would be nothing that would not appear in tomorrow's papers or become public knowledge in the town. It didn't matter, he decided, that Ephraim would overhear the conversation — in fact, it might be of advantage to the enquiry if he did so, because, with his knowledge of the comings and goings of many Crickledonians, he might be able to provide useful information at some future stage. Perhaps the killer had fled overseas? The house-to-house enquiries would include his abode in due course and so Pluke decided to avail himself of the telephone call. He considered his decision to be very politically sound.

'That is very noble of you, Mr Holliday,' he acknowledged.

'I will dial the hotel for you,' offered the travel agent, eager to please and determined not to disappear into a back office where he could not overhear conversations. In an amazingly short time, Pluke was speaking to the receptionist of the Hotel Palacio.

'Good-evening,' began Pluke in his best speaking-to-foreigners English accent. 'I am an English detective. My name is Detective Inspector Pluke of Crickledale Criminal Investigation Department Yorkshire England yes — Pluke. That is correct. P-L-U-K-E.'

The person at the other end was clearly attempting to write this on a message pad because Pluke was obliged to pause before continuing, 'I wish to speak with Mister or Madame Crowther English holiday-makers who are residents at your hotel.'

'Putting you through to their room, sir, room 316,' said the voice in remarkably good English and with remarkable speed.

'Hello,' said a masculine Yorkshire voice.

'Is that Mr Cyril Crowther? The Mr Cyril Crowther of No. 15 Padgett Grove, Crickledale, Yorkshire, England?' asked Pluke.

'Aye, that's me. Who's that?'

'This is Detective Inspector Montague Pluke of Crickledale CID.'

'Oh, now then, Mr Pluke, 'ow's things? Are you in t'same hotel or summat? Wanting us to 'ave a drink with you in t'bar? Now that's a good idea, eh? Or mebbe you're ringing from 'ome. We 'aven't been burgled, 'ave we?'

'Er, no, it's not that ...'

'Thank God! 'As somebody rung to say our May's forgotten to turn up at one of her meetings?'

'I am ringing from England, Mr Crowther ...'

'Aye, I guessed that. You can call me Cyril, you know ...'

'I am ringing from England with some very bad news for Mrs Crowther.' Montague realised that Mr Crowther sounded rather jolly and wondered if he had been having champagne in the bath or drinking foreign brandy from pint glasses.

'She's in t'bath, Mr Pluke. Now there's a sight for you, eh? I'll bet you've never seen owt quite like that. Any 'ow, 'ow can I 'elp? She didn't come away and leave t'oven on, did she?'

'No, it is a very serious matter, Mr Crowther.' He thought of ringing back, but decided it was not fair to use Mr Holliday's telephone a second time. 'I have some very bad news for your wife. It concerns her niece.'

'Niece? She 'asn't got a niece, Mr Pluke,' returned Crowther.

'Has she not?' This revelation caused Pluke seriously to reconsider his strategy and he paused for a long moment before continuing. 'But there was a young lady living at your bungalow, a blonde-haired lady in her late twenties ...'

'Oh, 'er. That's Sharon. Nay, Mr Pluke, she's not a niece. She's an 'ouse-sitter, she said she 'ad to be in town for work and 'ad nowhere to stay, so we said she could use our 'ouse, us being away. She's the daughter of a friend of a friend of May's ...'

'Ah, I see. Well, that's rather remote from your own family, isn't it? The daughter of a friend of a friend. It certainly eases things a little from my standpoint, Mr Crowther, because I have some awful news concerning her. I need to trace her family very urgently. She has been found dead, you see, in the Druids' Circle. You know the stone circle in the forest? We have reason to believe she met her death in suspicious circumstances ...'

'Oh, bloody 'ell!' There was a long silence. 'What a thing to 'appen! Not murdered, you mean? Bloody 'ell ... what shall I do now? Shall we come 'ome as soon as our May gets out of t'bath?'

'I don't think that is necessary, Mr Crowther, particularly as you are not her next of kin. But I do have to have her identified and that ought to be done by relatives; besides, they do need to be told — by us, I might add. I must know the name and address of her next of kin.'

'Old Dunwoody next door to us is pretty good at identifying bodies, Mr Pluke.'

'Yes, but we do need a relative at this stage, Mr Crowther, for a positive identification. Perhaps you can tell me whom to contact?'

'She's from West 'Artlepool, Mr Pluke. Sharon Pellow. 'Er mother's a friend of a friend of our May's. They, Sharon's folks that is, live at Apedale Gardens. I can't remember t'number off — ' and, but 'er dad works for British Rail, summat to do with cleaning carriages on t'East Coast expresses. 'E sings in pubs, they reckon 'e does a smashing Elvis.'

'Thank you very much. That is most helpful. Now, I can confirm she is definitely not a relation of yours. You see, Mrs Dunwoody next door to you led me to believe the girl was Mrs Crowther's niece.'

'Did she, by gum! So that's why you rang me?'

'Mr Dunwoody explained that the blonde girl was the daughter of Mrs Crowther's sister, June. I understand someone had told him so.'

'Mrs Peat at No. 14 it would be, Mr Pluke. She's a nosy old cow and Ada Dunwoody's not much better. May told Mrs Peat about that lass being 'er niece to stop her quizzing us about why we'd let a woman who wasn't a family member live in our 'ouse. We knew she'd gossip about it, pass the word around. It made things easier at the time, saying she was family, as I am sure you will understand, knowing the Mrs Peats and Mrs Dunwoodys of this world. Poor lass, though. Suspicious death, eh? What a bloody awful thing to 'appen.'

'It is indeed very tragic, Mr Crowther. So, if you don't mind me asking, how did you come to offer your house to her? To someone you did not know in person?'

'It was through a friend of May's, Mr Pluke. One of those women she meets at 'er clubs and societies and things. Sharon is that woman's friend's lass, and she said Sharon was looking for somewhere to live for a couple of weeks in Crickledale, summat to do with a job she was doing, and what with one thing and another, our May offered that lass our bungalow while we were away. It seemed a good idea, 'aving somebody living in and looking after things. I thought it would keep burglars away — I never reckoned we'd get a murdered lass instead. It was murder, you said, Mr Pluke? I'm not 'earing things, am I?'

Montague explained how and where the body of the girl had been found, adding that she had been nude when found in somewhat suspicious circumstances. He did add that murder had not yet been confirmed, but admitted it was a murder-style investigation. Pluke added that he would now contact the girl's parents and invite them to examine the body with a view to identification. He added that there was no need for the Crowthers to come back to England before the conclusion of their holiday — he also explained that their house would be examined by the police and forensic experts because it was where the girl had been living. It might, he said, contain vital evidence of her friends, contacts and even her killer.

Cyril said he understood. 'I reckon we'd better come back, though,' he said eventually. 'I mean, Mr Pluke, if our 'ouse is involved, we should be there, shouldn't we?'

'It is not absolutely necessary, I assure you,' affirmed Pluke. 'But clearly, I am not in a position to prevent you coming home. There is absolutely no reason to return ahead of your normal scheduled flight, and it would give us time to examine your house whilst it is unoccupied. That would make it easier for all of us.' Montague Pluke was thinking of the time it would take to strip-search their house and personal belongings.

'Does that mean you'll poke and pry into our private belongings, Mr Pluke?'

'My officers will have to conduct a very thorough search, Mr

Crowther.'

'I think I'd rather 'ave burglars, Mr Pluke. Our May will worry about 'er mucky washing and dust on the mantelshelves. Ah, 'ere she is now, looking like an 'alf-drowned 'en after a thunderstorm. Have you ever seen a naked old 'en wearing a shower cap, Mr Pluke? Well, there's one 'ere. 'Ang on while I tell 'er.'

As Crowther imparted the awful news to his freshly bathed wife, Montague put his hand over the mouthpiece of the telephone and said to Ephraim Holliday, 'Sorry it's taking so long; he's telling his wife now.'

'Think nothing of it, Mr Pluke. I'm glad to be of assistance. How awful, how terrible that this should happen in Crickledale of all places ... you never think things like that will happen here, do you?'

'Did you, by any chance, come across the young lady in question in the course of your work or private life?' asked Pluke, keen to take advantage of the lull.

'Not to my knowledge, Mr Pluke. My dealings with the Crowthers ended when they collected their flight tickets, and they never mentioned that their house would be occupied. But they wouldn't need to tell me, would they? Not being a neighbour.'

'Of course not. Ah, he's back. Yes, hello, Mr Crowther.'

'May says to tell your men not to look in t'bottom drawer in t'main bedroom because it contains her mucky washing. She's a mite fussy who sees her knickers and my underpants, especially clarty ones. And she says to ignore that pair of socks with 'oles in t'toes ... She 'adn't time to do t'washing before we set off, you see, undies and things.'

'Tell her I will pass the message on and that our officers will behave with the utmost confidentiality.' Pluke tried to sound reassuring.

'And tell Mrs Pluke that our May forgot to remind 'er about making tea tomorrow night, for t'Local History Society meeting. It was 'er turn, our May's that is, and she forgot to find a replacement.'

'I will tell Mrs Pluke and am sure she will find a replacement.'

'And we'll come 'ome as soon as we can. We won't be 'appy out here now, will we? May says she wrote a postcard to that lass, Mr Pluke ... 'ow sad, eh?'

'You might care to contact me upon your return?' suggested Pluke. 'To acquaint yourselves with any developments in the case?'

'Aye, right,' said Crowther. 'Is that it, then?'

'Yes, it is. I'm sorry to have to call you like this, to ruin your holiday.'

'Think nowt about it, I was worrying about my taties, carrots and beetroot anyway, wondering if that lass 'ad thought to water 'em now and then.' And the phone went dead.

Montague looked blankly at the handset, then slowly replaced it and thanked Mr Holliday.

'We shall need to take a statement from you,' Wayne Wain informed Holliday. 'About what has transpired this evening. For our files.'

'I understand,' said Ephraim who had now produced his vast pipe and ignited the contents which spewed clouds of dense smoke into the atmosphere. It was like being in a railway station of bygone times.

'Thank you for your courtesy, and for helping us trace the Crowthers,' said Montague Pluke. 'You have been of great assistance. Now, we will leave you; we have work to do.' And the two detectives departed, leaving Ephraim to lock up and to ponder the means by which his agency might gain useful publicity from these events.

'You said we had work to do?' asked Wayne Wain as he settled behind the wheel of their car. 'I thought we could knock off now, sir, having made such good progress. It is getting late.'

'It is precisely the wrong time to knock off, Wayne,' said Pluke. 'Is there not a saying "strike while the iron is hot"? It is very hot right now, and we must reach the parents of the deceased before her killer does likewise.'

'Is that likely, sir?'

'Who can tell, Wayne? And we must also talk to the lady at No. 14.'

'No. 14, sir?'

'No. 14 Padgett Grove. Mrs Peat. The gossip mentioned by George Dunwoody and Cyril Crowther. Gossips are such lovely persons to interview, Wayne. They poke their noses into the affairs of everyone else and love to impart juicy titbits, even to the police and especially during a major investigation. Perhaps we will talk to her tomorrow though?'

'So tonight we are going to West Hartlepool?' anticipated Wayne Wain.

'Yes, Wayne, we are. Immediately in fact,' said Pluke, placing his panama on the rear seat as Wain accelerated into the night.

*

During the forty-mile drive, Pluke asked Wayne Wain whether he considered Mr Holliday to be a prime suspect and Wayne replied in the negative. There seemed nothing to link the travel agent with the girl's death and, having aired the possibility, Pluke said he was inclined to agree. A suspect — yes, like everyone in the town — but not a prime suspect, not one to be placed in the frame, as the detectives would say. None the less, Holliday's movements and background would be scrutinised by one of Pluke's team.

After calling at Hartlepool's Divisional Police Headquarters in Raby Road to acquaint the local police with their presence, Pluke asked if he could examine the electoral register to ascertain the address of the Pellow family.

He knew it was in Apedale Gardens but did not have the number. Having discovered the Pellows occupied No. 79, Pluke next asked the way and was told it was a tower block in West Hartlepool. Under Pluke's directions, Wayne found his way there without any difficulty, parked on a rubbish-laden patch of concrete and both climbed the urine-saturated staircase to No. 79. Pluke, being the leader, knocked on the flaking blue paint of the door on the seventh floor and it was opened by a huge, untidy woman wearing a red track suit.

'Yes?' she asked, not inviting them inside, but puzzled by the man in the panama hat and funny old overcoat.

'Mrs Pellow?'

'Who wants to know?'

'Police,' said Pluke, showing his warrant card with a flourish.

'Our Darren's done nowt this time, mister, you lot are allus picking on him and his mates ...' And she prepared to slam the door in their faces. Acting with incredible foresight, Wayne Wain placed a large foot in exactly the right place to hold it open while Pluke thought that this woman was hardly the sort to be a friend of a friend of a friend of Millicent's or even a friend of a friend of the Crowthers.

'No, Mrs Pellow, it's about your Sharon. We have some bad news ... You see, a body was found ...'

'Her on the news tonight? In that Druids' Circle?' The woman's eyes widened in genuine alarm.

'Yes, well, I am dreadfully sorry to have to impart this terrible news to you, but we have reason to believe it might be your daughter, Sharon.'

'Don't be daft, mister policeman. She's in her room is our Sharon. Thursday's her night for washing her hair and doing her nails, so she's here. Hey, our Sharon, come here ...'

'You what?' bellowed a voice from within.

'Here, now!' screamed the mother. 'There's the old bill ...'

After a lapse of a few moments, a beautiful blonde girl with a massive bust and deep-blue eyes appeared at the doorway, clutching a dressing-gown about her ample body. It was moments like this that made Wayne Wain forget any regrets about having to work late.

'Yeh?' she asked.

'Are you Sharon Pellow?'

'What if I am?'

Montague Pluke had to think with uncharacteristic speed at this stage. This girl was supposed to be dead. 'I understand you were to make use of a bungalow in Crickledale, Sharon, for a few days while the owners were away, so that you could do some work there ...'

'Yeh, but it fell through. Tracy went instead.'

'Tracy?'

'A lass I met at the studio. She said she'd do it, so I said about the house and off she went.'

'So who is Tracy?'

'Dunno.' She shrugged her shoulders and her breasts wobbled under the dressing-gown. Pluke tried not to notice; Wayne couldn't help but notice. 'Just Tracy.' There followed a few moments' silence as Wayne attempted to drag his eyes from the intriguing bodily movements and Pluke tried to decide what to ask next.

'Sharon, we have reason to believe that the girl who occupied the bungalow — the girl we thought was you — has died in suspicious circumstances. I am sorry to bring this news.'

'Murdered, you mean?' she screamed. 'Tracy?'

'We want to know whether the dead girl is Tracy. We thought it was you, you see, which is why we are here ...'

'Oh my God ... the bastards ...' she screamed.

'Sharon, will you come with us now, to Crickledale, to look at the girl who has died? To tell us if it is your friend — and if so, we will need to find her next of kin. Maybe you know where we can find her family? Her address?'

'You'll have to go, our Sharon ... thank God it's not you ... I saw it on the news,' said Mrs Pellow, now speaking more quietly. 'You never think it's as near home as that, do you ... so you go with the er, gentlemen, Sharon ...'

'Yes, and I'll be happy to drive you back home,' breathed Wayne.

'Give me five minutes to get summat on, then.' And Sharon smiled at Wayne as she engineered a final wobble of her chesty bits.

Her dazzling smile would have melted the heart of the most severe of men — it certainly gave Wayne the biggest thrill of his day so far and even made Pluke think she was beautiful. The snag was she'd be like her mother in a few years' time; you couldn't make silk out of sows' ears ...

'I'll come with you,' said Sharon's mother, to the dismay of Wayne Wain.

'No, we'll be fine ...' said Sharon, smiling again at Wayne.

'You never know who's about,' said Mrs Pellow. 'Come on, our Sharon, hurry up and get summat on.'

'We'll wait in the car,' said Pluke as Wayne Wain withdrew his foot from the doorway while Sharon vanished inside, with yet another smile in his direction.

They waited, with Wayne thinking romantic thoughts about the physical attributes of the gorgeous Sharon and deciding to display for her benefit his prowess as a highly trained police driver, while Pluke wondered what on earth was happening in Crickledale.

*

Millicent settled down to watch the regional news which followed *News at Ten*. There was a brief item about the body which had been found at the Druids' Circle and a picture of Montague outside the police station. He looked at the camera and described his victim, then asked for possible names for her, but there was no suggestion she was May Crowther's niece.

Millicent felt very proud of Montague at that stage and wondered what time he would be home for his cocoa.

Chapter 10

During the hour's drive from West Hartlepool to Crickledale, Detective Inspector Pluke established from Sharon that she and Tracy were models. When he asked what they modelled, meaning did they work for fashion houses, catalogues, department stores or mail order companies, Sharon said it wasn't that sort of modelling.

'It's not the posh sort, Mr Pluke,' she tried to explain. 'Me and Tracy don't go jettin' off to sunny places to have our pictures taken in smart clothes or even wearing bikinis or less. We work here, in the north-east.'

'Yes, I gather that.' Pluke was half-twisted round in his passenger seat so that he could observe them in the rear as Wayne Wain, using all his considerable driving skills, guided the fast-moving car across the expansive moors. 'But I am still not absolutely sure of the kind of modelling you undertake.'

'Page Three work, Mr Pluke,' butted in Wayne Wain.

'Page Three? Page Three of what publication, might I ask?'

'Where have you been, Mr Pluke?' Sharon laughed. 'I mean, everybody knows what Page Three means, although it's page five in some papers and other pages in other papers.'

'Topless modelling, sir ...' Wayne Wain added his comments.

'They was always hoping for better things, Mr Pluke,' interrupted Mrs Pellow. 'You've got to start somewhere, you know, it's a tough life, you can only do it while you've got the looks, it's a very short life at the top ...'

'So, you met Tracy at a studio while modelling?' Pluke pressed on.

'Yes, in Middlesbrough. There's this agency, run by a bloke

called Ron. He finds girls and does deals with magazines and video companies, films and things.'

'Modelling deals?' asked Pluke.

'Photographic modelling deals, sir,' put in Wayne.

'Oh, I see. So you have your photographs taken for specialist magazines and get paid for that work? By this man Ron?'

'Yeh, that's about it, except Ron doesn't actually take the pictures. He gets somebody else in for that. Ron trained us up, you know, showed us how to stand or sit or lie, to show our best bits off, if you understand. Bits of tape help a lot ...'

'Bits of tape?' puzzled Pluke.

'For the boobs, to keep 'em where you want 'em when pictures are being taken,' advised Mrs Pellow.

'They're nude models, sir,' clarified Wayne Wain.

'Nude? Really, for artists?'

'Not the sort of artists you think, sir.' Wain smiled. 'These people are not your Rembrandts and Renoirs.'

'They are artistic models, Mr Pluke.' Mrs Pellow grinned from the rear seat. 'Nudes, doing poses, artistic poses, doing other things an' all if the money's right. Our Sharon's in films.'

'You mean porn films?' suggested Wayne Wain.

'We don't call them that, er, Wayne,' breathed Sharon. 'We call them artistic productions.'

'I'm not sure I like the sound of this,' muttered Pluke, beginning to understand what had really been happening in Crickledale and having a suspicion, just the tiniest of suspicions but real none the less, that the Crowthers might somehow be involved. Maybe his officers should research their backgrounds as they would for a murder suspect? It seemed they could not, at this stage, be eliminated from his enquiries and so he made a mental note to investigate Cyril and May before continuing, 'Are you saying that you and Tracy were involved in pornographic modelling for films and video tapes?'

'I'm saying me and Tracy were involved in artistic work for still cameras, videos and films, Mr Pluke. Very versatile we are, according to Ron. I didn't say it was porn. Our stuff's not for dirty old men, Mr Pluke, it's for men of distinction, men with money. You've got to earn a living and well, me and Tracy are not bad looking, big, busty and blonde, as Ron says, and that's all we need — and it was work, Mr Pluke. There was none of the other business, you understand.'

'Other business?' asked Pluke.

'You know,' said Sharon. 'None of that.'

'Drugs you mean?' Pluke suggested.

'No, none of that neither. We was never mixed up in drugs, Mr Pluke,' stressed Sharon. 'We kept ourselves clear of that. We never broke the law. Ron made sure of that, he never wanted none of his lasses getting in bother with the law.'

'Tell me about this Ron,' asked Pluke.

'Nowt much to say really,' responded Sharon. 'He has this place, studio, off Dunthorpe Road. Up that alley opposite Kitto's Kaff, No. 4.'

'For taking photographs? So he is a photographer, is he?'

'Not really, no, like I said, he doesn't actually take the pictures. He fixes things. Does deals. If a magazine wants summat, they'll ring Ron and Ron'll find a girl or two, and a bloke or two if they've got to perform, and then a photographer or cameraman or somebody with all the gear, lights and that. Then they fix up a day to start shooting …'

'Always in the studio?' asked Wayne.

'Oh, no, we go out. Woods, moors, lakes, quiet places. Houses, flats and things.'

'But some pictures are taken in the studio?'

'Yeh, it's amazing. He can make it look like a desert island with palm trees or a mountain top or a lake side or, well, owt he wants.

He uses drapes and things, props. He once did a street scene in the middle of Paris, without going out of the studio, for that one we did about the Frenchman with big onions. Amazing, is Ron, a real Mister Fixer.'

'So who is he, this Ron?' asked Wayne.

'Dunno, just Ron. Everybody calls him Ron.'

'So if we wanted a word with him, about Tracy, if it is Tracy we're going to see, how would we do it?'

'Go to the studio. I don't know where he lives or owt else about him.'

'Been good to our Sharon, has Ron,' said Mrs Pellow. 'Not often she's out of work, he really sees to her, he really does. Don't know what she'd do without Ron. Pays cash an' all, no cheques or tax worries with Ron.'

'So your friend, Tracy ...' Pluke decided to quiz the women about Tracy. 'Tell me about her links with Crickledale.'

'You don't really think it's her, do you, Mr Pluke? Dead, I mean? It should have been me, you see, on that job. I could be dead, couldn't I? It makes you think, it really does ...' Sharon's voice was subdued now. 'There was this job to do, in the woods out there.'

'Job?' queried Pluke.

'Filming job, an artistic film in the woods, nymphs and shepherds.'

'A job that Ron had fixed?' suggested Wayne Wain.

'Yeh, Ron had set it up.'

'And you couldn't do it?' pressed Wayne.

'No, I wasn't fit that time, so I asked Tracy if she'd take it on. Ron said it was all right because she's big, busty and blonde, just like a nymph, he said, so it was all right.'

'So if Tracy replaced you, how did she come to be living at Mr and Mrs Crowthers' house?' asked Pluke. 'We have reason to believe she was living for a while in the house, as a house-sitter, while Mr and Mrs Crowther were on holiday.'

'It should have been me in that house. My mum heard about it, through some friends …'

'Yes, I did,' chipped in Mrs Pellow. 'A friend of a friend of a friend of a friend of mine, Elsie she's called, well, she'd heard May Crowther was going off on holiday and was thinking of having somebody in to look after the place while they was away. So when our Sharon got this offer, we asked if she could use the house and the Crowthers said yes, delighted. So they left a key under a brick in the drive, for that Saturday when they went. If Sharon had gone and done that job, she would have used the house.'

'Just to live in?' Pluke asked Sharon.

Sharon did not answer for a moment or two, then said, 'Well, no, not exactly, Mr Pluke. We might have done a bit of filming there, you know, in a real house in a real bed, not a lot, but we always tidy up afterwards.'

'You mean you use other people's houses for making porn films?' cried Wayne Wain.

'It saves the expense of renting places,' she replied. 'Very expensive is renting houses for filming, Ron says, so we use the places we house-sit in … I mean, we never leave a mess or owt like that. You'd never know we'd been.'

'But the owners do not realise this?'

'Oh, no, we never tell them, they'd want money, wouldn't they? And we are doing them a good turn by sitting in the houses for them, stopping burglars and things. Watering plants an' that. I mean, when television hires houses for filming they pay a fortune, but Ron hasn't that sort of cash, Mr Pluke. Not yet, anyroad, but he will, when he gets into the big time, when he makes his million or summat.'

'So when they gave permission for their bungalow to be used by you, Mr and Mrs Crowther had no idea it would be used for filming — pornographic filming in fact, Sharon?' Pluke was shocked.

'Not porn, Mr Pluke, artistic films. No, they wouldn't know, but why should they have to know? I mean, if I house-sit for them, look after the place and keep it dusted, what's it matter to them what I do with my time? I ask you! They wouldn't want to know if I listened to Beethoven or had friends in for a pizza or what, would they? Or if I practised my violin or studied French. So why shouldn't I let a mate take a photo of me in bed with a bloke, doing what folks do in bed? There's no harm in that, is there? I allus washes the sheets afterwards.'

'And when you home-sit and then use a house for filming, you never tell the owners?'

'No, not ever.'

'So it is quite feasible that somebody who knows Mr and Mrs Crowther and who has been to their house could recognise it if they saw the film?'

'Well, yeh, I suppose so, but that would be real nice, wouldn't it, to think your house was in a film. You'd be famous. We all want to be famous, Mr Pluke.'

'Neither Millicent nor I would desire our house to star in such a film,' stressed Pluke as he attempted to understand Sharon's logic. 'So you are saying that when you decided not to take part in the filming Tracy took your place?'

'Ron said it was all right, Mr Pluke, I mean, he had no objection, she's very good, you know, very professional.'

'But Mr and Mrs Crowther did not know that Tracy was going to occupy their house instead of you?'

'No, there was no need to tell them, was there? I mean, one house-sitter's as good as another, especially lasses like me. No, Tracy was told where the house was and where to find the key, and off she went.'

'How did she travel, Sharon?'

'She's got a car, a mini, an old one.'

'Colour?'

'Reddish, dark red.'

'You wouldn't know its number, or where she lived, do you?'

'No, no idea. I seen the car sometimes when we've been out in the country, but can't say much about it. And I don't know her place, she never invited me back there, never talked about her folks or her home or owt like that.'

'Ron would know, you think?' asked Wayne.

'I expect so, he seems to know everybody in Middlesbrough. Votes Labour, he's well in with the Council.'

By now, Pluke's official car was speeding into Crickledale dale and the lights of the town could be seen in the distance.

'Crickledale, here we come.' Wayne's fast and daring driving brought them off the high moors and down into the outskirts of the town.

It was approaching midnight and the place appeared to be silent and at rest; rows of amber street lights illuminated the rows of sleeping houses, but many would be extinguished at midnight.

'Police station or hospital, sir?' Wayne put to Pluke.

'Hospital, Wayne, I know it's late, and the mortuary attendant will have gone home but we can have access. I know the routine.'

At the hospital, Wayne eased the car into a parking space near the main entrance and Pluke led the ladies into the building, followed by the faithful sergeant. After explaining his purpose, Pluke was led by a porter down to the mortuary complex, but halted outside.

'Sharon,' he said with due solemnity. 'This will not be easy for you. The girl we wish to identify is dead, she is lying in a refrigerated cabinet and everything but her face is covered discreetly. All I want you to do is to look at her face and tell me if this is the girl you know as Tracy. If it is, then we shall have to talk to Ron.'

'All right, luv?' hissed Sharon's mum.

'Yeh, fine. I'm all right, honest. Let's just get it over with, shall we?'

Wayne Wain took the precaution of standing close to Sharon in case she fainted and Pluke gave the nod to the porter. As the drawer emerged on well-oiled rollers, Wayne took Sharon's arm and led her forward.

'Take your time, Sharon.' Wayne spoke softly. 'Take a good look.'

Sharon did, and burst into tears.

'Yeh, that's her, Mr Pluke. That's Tracy … Oh, God … she looks dead, doesn't she … poor kid …'

'And can you categorically state that you know nothing further about her — surname, home address, names of next of kin, anything?'

'Sorry, no.' She sniffed. 'I just wish I did, I really do … doesn't she look peaceful, though, I mean, that work in the woods has done her good, look at that tan she's got, better than I would have got, working in the studio …'

'Don't distress yourself, our Sharon,' said Mrs Pellow. 'Think yourself lucky you didn't take that job on, else it might have been you lying there.'

'I'll have to take a short written statement from you,' said Wayne Wain. 'But we can do that in the police station, it's not far away.'

'I could do with some fish and chips,' said Mrs Pellow.

'I think they'll all be shut now,' said Wayne. 'But I reckon we can produce a cup of tea or coffee down at the nick. Come along, and thanks, Sharon. You were great …'

'I once had to act a scene like that.' She was wiping her eyes. 'Dead awful it was, dead moving an' all, right weepy. But this is real …'

And she burst into tears again.

'While you are taking a statement from Sharon, I shall go into the Incident Room, Wayne, to note the actions we need to set in motion tomorrow morning. We have lots of enquiries to make, Wayne, lots, and don't forget we need to eliminate the Dunwoodys, Mr Holliday and the Crowthers. I feel we have made a very good start to this investigation.'

'Shall I drive Sharon and Mrs Pellow home, sir?' asked Wayne.

'Yes, if you wouldn't mind. I don't think I shall join you on this occasion. I shall walk home to ponder the night's events.'

Wayne was exceedingly pleased to learn of that decision by Pluke. It meant he would have time to acquaint himself with the luscious Sharon, perhaps to comfort and console her.

*

After completing his tasks, it was around 1.15 on Friday morning as Detective Inspector Pluke walked alone from the police station, returning via his familiar route, albeit without the presence of the people he normally encountered. Although some traffic was moving, including Dunwoody's taxi, the town was pleasantly quiet; people were in their homes and most were in their beds, even though a few lounge lights were blazing. He knew that whatever time of night an event occurred, someone, somewhere would be out of bed to witness it, and that his progress through the streets would not go unobserved. Vigilant Crickledonians would be aware that something of major importance had occurred because Mr Pluke was returning from work at such a late hour.

Montague Pluke realised that the ill fortune which would result from starting a venture on a Friday had been overcome because the investigation had started yesterday, a Thursday. And as he walked, he noticed that the full moon was rising above the roofs of the town; it had been full for a few days, he realised.

He began to count. Full moon had been on Monday — he felt sure that the girl had died on Wednesday, i.e. the third day of the full moon. There was an old superstition which said that criminals should beware of committing their crimes on the third day of a full moon, because if they did, their actions on that day almost guaranteed discovery and capture.

As he turned into his garden with the lights still blazing at his home, he was satisfied that the omens were all very good indeed. He felt very confident that he would succeed in solving the case and trusted that Millicent would have his cocoa ready.

*

'Had a busy day, dear?' called Millicent from the kitchen as she boiled his milk.

'Exceedingly.' He dropped into an easy chair to remove his shoes and replace them with his slippers.

'I saw you on the television,' she shouted. 'You were very good, Montague.'

'Did they broadcast my appeal for witnesses?' he asked.

'Oh, yes, and that poor girl. Someone said they had seen you at May's and Cyril's bungalow, Montague.'

'You know I never discuss police business at home, Millicent.' She came through with his cocoa. 'And thank you for waiting up.'

'I was rather worried, you know, but knew you were very busy.'

'I may be busy other nights too,' he said, sipping from the mug. 'I am confident I shall bring the enquiry to a satisfactory conclusion.'

'I am sure you will,' she said, heading for the stairs.

'That girl was not May's niece, you know,' he called after her. 'The Crowthers really should be more careful about their choice of house-sitter.'

'I am sure you are right, Montague.' And now she wondered if Montague knew about the nude man at No. 15 Padgett Grove.

Chapter 11

Detective Inspector Montague Pluke had looked under the bed before settling down to sleep. It was a nightly ritual. He did it because his mother and grandmother had always looked under the bed before going to sleep, and they had encouraged him to do likewise. As a child, he had never questioned the procedure, but had come to assume it was something to do with monsters lurking in the dust. It was perfectly true that he had never discovered one there, but as his wisdom matured, he realised that sensible monsters would not hide there anyway, not when the place was inspected on a daily basis. Now, looking under the bed before settling down to sleep had become a habit, a superstitious habit. After all, one never knew what might be lurking there and if there was nothing, then one could sleep more soundly.

Having performed that modest ceremonial Montague Pluke had slept very well indeed. He had rested safe in the knowledge that the enquiry had been blessed with an excellent start and, in spite of his late finish, he awoke next morning at seven, his usual time. He checked his watch, took several deep breaths and climbed from his bed, making sure he left it, as always, on the correct side.

One should never climb out of bed on the left — that was the famous 'wrong side of the bed'. If people got out of bed on the wrong side, they were agitated, antagonistic, bad-tempered or simply plain awkward for the rest of the day. The reason for this, Montague knew, was that the devil had been seated at the left-hand side of God before being banished from heaven. Since that time, the left had been associated with bad things and ill fortune; for that reason,

Montague never voted for Labour. He climbed out of the right-hand side of the bed, therefore, put on his right sock first and then his right slipper. That was essential if a good day was to follow. Then he followed with his left sock and left slipper. Millicent was still snoozing in her own bed as he went about his routine ablutions, but once he was out of the bathroom and dressed, she would climb out of the right side of her bed. Montague insisted that she never got out of the wrong side.

In the bathroom, he followed the same routine as he did each morning — toilet, shave, teeth and shower, with hair washes every other day. He was blessed with a good head of hair, thick but now greying, and was very aware of the ancient belief that hairy people were lucky — and men without hair on their chests were destined to be thieves. Montague had a considerable amount of hair on his chest, he was pleased to note.

It was amazing how many thieves had hairless chests, he had often contemplated, while thinking that that logic might be applied to female shoplifters. Not that he would ever be allowed to inspect the chest regions of a female shoplifter, or any other female criminal. That morning, thinking of women's chests (probably due, in part, to the experiences of last night) he recalled one of his first arrests. It was a woman he caught late one night, stealing lead from one of the church windows. She had explained she had sore breasts and that she was seeking a cure, something that not every police officer would have believed. She had then gone on to say that one old remedy was to steal lead from a church window and shape it into a heart which had to be worn on a chain around her neck. She had told the court it was a very good cure for sore breasts and was given two years' probation.

Making a huge effort to turn his mind away from the female anatomy, especially at this time of the morning, he dressed in a clean shirt, put out last night for him by Millicent, donned his famous blue bow-tie, drew his belt tight about his waist and went down to collect the mail and have his breakfast. Montague ate sensible breakfasts with fruit and black coffee, after which, clad as always in his panama, old coat and spats, he left the house precisely on time, having bidden farewell to Millicent.

And so it was that, in the midst of a town rife with rumours and worries about murders and rapists, Detective Inspector Pluke was *en route* to the police station to begin another day. And today was a Friday. Hangman's Day. In bygone times, criminals were always hanged on Fridays and since then, criminals have believed that burglaries committed on Fridays are rarely successful. Montague had to admit that the burglary figures for Crickledale were generally lower on a Friday, although that could have something to do with the fact the pubs were open all day, this being market day. Petty criminals spent the day getting too drunk to burgle, he thought, although by tomorrow they would be penniless and breaking into shops and houses to get cash for more drinking, preferably away from Crickledale.

It was during his morning walk through the market square that Montague slipped into Samuel Purslane's, newsagents. He wished to acquire a copy of all the morning papers to examine them for renditions of events at the Druids' Circle. As he waited to pay and to request a receipt so that he could recover the cost in his expenses claim, he noticed the array of colourful girlie magazines on the top shelf of the news rack and was tempted to buy copies of those too, to see whether he recognised any of the artistes or interiors of houses. But he felt his actions might be misconstrued. He settled for a copy of each of the national dailies and the local weeklies. But as he was paying Samuel he noticed a black beetle crawling across Samuel's shoe. 'You have a visitor, Mr Purslane.' He pointed to the shoe as the shopkeeper was totting up the amount on the till.

'They come from the storeroom, Mr Pluke,' said Purslane, using

Montague's copy of the *Guardian* to flick away the beetle. It fell to the floor and made for the open doorway, Purslane allowing it to have its freedom because the totting up of Mr Pluke's large order was of more immediate interest. But the incident worried Pluke — it presented such a riddle.

He managed to reconcile matters as he continued towards the police station with a look of determination beneath his panama. Montague Pluke knew that, in observing him that morning, the residents would realise they had a champion in their midst. Mr Pluke would catch the killer, they knew; Mr Pluke could not let them down.

'Nasty business up at the Circle, Mr Pluke,' was the oft-repeated phrase as he progressed through the town.

'Indeed, yes, a very nasty business,' was his unsmiling response.

'You'll soon be announcing an arrest, I expect,' was the second most oft-repeated comment.

'We are making very positive progress,' was his solemn response, the sort of reply he would give to the newspapers at this morning's press conference. After much panama-lifting, smiling and wishing of good-mornings to everyone from Moses Nettlewren to Whistling Jasper, plus a few asides about the thundery feeling which persisted in the air, Montague arrived at the police station. He was a few minutes later than normal and perspiring slightly, partly due to his diversion into the paper shop and partly because he'd been hailed so many times by so many people. He had been spoken to by more than the usual number of Crickledonians and he regarded that as a sign of his increased stature within the community. Now he was beginning to understand how members of the royal family felt while attempting to do ordinary things like buy clothes or park their cars.

'You're a bit late this morning, Mr Pluke,' noticed Mrs Gossip, the cleaner who was finishing off her polishing of the public enquiry and reception area. He stepped over her mop, leading with his right foot, throwing caution to the wind. There was probably some ancient advice about not stepping over mops, because if that had been a broom which had fallen, you should never step over it. That is a sure way of bringing bad fortune, just as unmarried girls should never step over a brush. It means they will become pregnant before marriage.

'I have been putting at rest the minds of the citizens about recent events,' he told the inquisitive woman. 'I have been giving reassurance to the townspeople, putting the corporate mind of Crickledale at ease. My conversations this morning show that Crickledonians are very concerned about what goes on in their home town and, more important, it shows they have great faith in me and my officers. Such a rapport between police and public is most reassuring.'

'I do hope you catch the bloke what did it, Mr Pluke; there again, I'm sure you will.' Mrs Gossip stood erect, clutching the mop to her shoulder like a guardsman on parade; she seemed to be preparing for a long conversation. 'I said to my best friend, Alice, I said ...'

'I must get on, Mrs Gossip. As you rightly said, I am rather late and have a lot to do this morning.' He managed to create a useful distance between himself and the aptly named earwigging lady.

Before Mrs Gossip had an opportunity to respond, he poked his head around the Control Room door to ask, 'Anything dramatic to report, Sergeant?'

'All quiet overnight, sir. I think news of our intense activity has kept the criminals at bay. You can't beat a session of house-to-house enquiries for putting the wind up the villains,' responded Sergeant Cockfield pronounced Cofield.

'Good. Is Detective Sergeant Wayne Wain in?'

'Yes, sir, he said to tell you he's in the Incident Room if you want him; he was in very early, sir.'

'A good man, is Detective Sergeant Wain, very dedicated.' Pluke smiled.

'I don't think he's been to bed, sir, he was with a woman all night,' retorted the sergeant.

'I hope his endeavours were fruitful and he was conducting meaningful enquiries, Sergeant,' replied Pluke, closing the door and heading for his own CID office. He would check his in-tray before heading into the Incident Room, knowing that once he got involved with the drama of this investigation he would have no time for routine duties. Placing the newspapers on his desk for Mrs Plumpton to scan and take the necessary cuttings, it took a mere half-hour to straighten his desk after Mrs Gossip's dusting and cleaning, to deal with his mail and to dictate replies to Mrs Plumpton in yet another of her flowing, chest-concealing dresses.

Only then did he enter the Incident Room, exhorting Mrs Plumpton to follow as soon as possible. He advised her to bring her routine work to the Incident Room, she could complete it there. When he entered shortly after 9.30 a.m., it was full of detectives. The morning CID conference was due to start at 10 a.m., followed by a news conference for journalists at 10.45 a.m. Detective Inspector Horsley would have prepared the Action Book and divided the detectives into teams of two, some comprising a detective sergeant and a detective constable, others being made up of two detective constables.

In any murder enquiry, there was a lot of administration, lists of detectives to compile particularly so that overtime payments could be made, duty rotas to be completed and tea money collected. There would also be a sweepstake to see how many guessed the name of the arrested suspect — the frame, a mock-up of a bookie's frame at a race meeting, was already hanging from a hook on the wall.

The finder of the body, Stephen Winton, was being quoted at evens — most felt he'd be arrested eventually as the culprit. In fact, no other name was in the frame — but Montague felt there would be one or two additions before the day was over. What would be the odds, he wondered, on Dunwoody, Holliday or the Crowthers? Even before Detective Inspector Pluke was able to settle in his chair, Detective Sergeant Wayne Wain appeared in the doorway. He looked unshaven, haggard and tired, his skin having faded to a dull shade of grey and his eyes looking like tea holes in the snow.

'Have been working all night?' commented Pluke, indicating a chair.

'Yes, sir, you could say that.' Wayne sank on to the chair with a loud sigh. 'I thought I should speak to you before you addressed the assembled detectives.'

'A productive night's work, then?' Inspector Pluke smiled.

'Beyond all doubt, sir.' Wayne sounded exhausted.

'Perhaps, after our conference, you should go home for a few hours' rest?' Pluke was concerned about the welfare of his officers and it was folly to expect a man to work all day and all night without refreshments and relaxation. Wayne looked awful; he was in dire need of sleep.

'I'll see how I get on, sir,' he said, not wishing to admit that Sharon had greeted the morning as fresh as the proverbial daisy. Insatiable, she'd been. 'I might survive the day ...'

'So, Wayne, what did you learn last night?'

It was a loaded question which could produce lots of fascinating answers but Wayne realised that his boss was referring to the investigation.

'On the way to West Hartlepool last night, sir, Sharon Pellow took me to the studio, Ron's place. And Ron was there. We did not admit that I was a police officer, sir. Filming was going on, on a set that looked like a Greek temple. Many of the cast have full-time jobs, so they work on the films late in the evenings. I was able to speak to several of the cast.'

'Well done. A wonderful piece of luck. Highly commendable. So what did you learn, Wayne?'

Detective Sergeant Wayne Wain had discovered that Ron was really called Marcel Boussicourt, but for his work in England he had adopted the pseudonym of Ron Brown. He produced what he described as artistic cinematograph films and videos which were for sale to clubs and societies, chiefly by mail order. Members could opt to receive them through the post in plain brown envelopes. He also arranged still photographs of naked women for a range of magazines both in the UK and overseas.

'Pornographic material, you mean, Wayne?'

'They describe it as having artistic merit, sir, films with finesse, aesthetic artwork, lots of stagecraft with virtuoso performances.'

'I still say it is pornographic material, Wayne,' said Montague. 'And Sharon was one of the girls used for filming? And Tracy?'

'Yes, sir, and through Ron I managed to obtain a full name and address for Tracy. She was also used in the filming, stills as well. Artistic poses.'

'Well done. Good, so your overtime work was worthwhile?'

Wayne explained that Tracy was Tracy Bretton with an address in Stockton-on-Tees; she was thirty-one years old and had been married but divorced two years ago. Wayne had traced Tracy's father to break the awful news and had asked him to visit the mortuary at 12 noon today, Friday, formally to identify his daughter. He had also given a description of Tracy's red mini, complete with its registration number.

'Good man,' said Pluke. 'This is remarkable progress, Wayne. Early identification of the victim is vital in such enquiries. Now we need to trace all her movements and contacts in recent weeks.'

'She had come to work in Crickledale, sir, to make a film. She was replacing Sharon Pellow as we had been told. She was using 15 Padgett Grove, sir. For the filming. This is what the girls do, sir, Sharon was right. Through a network of contacts, they offer to house-sit for people who are going on holiday, then use the houses for making pornographic films. It seems there is a whole group of houses, some used regularly throughout the year, and the owners know nothing of the filming. They know a house-sitter is in residence, sir, but not that they are inviting film crews and photographers in to make pornographic films.'

'That supports our views on 15 Padgett Grove, then, Wayne? Are the forensic and SOCO teams doing their examination of the house today?'

'Yes, sir, they'll be reporting here very soon.'

'Good. Now this man Ron Brown, otherwise known as Marcel Boussicourt. Do we need to put a team on to him and his operations?'

'Yes. We do need to know which of his many film crews — freelances they are, sir — was due to shoot tapes of Tracy at No. 15. Remember our last visit? There were unwashed-up pots and pans in the sink, with prints on. And that inhaler. It was Tracy's, I believe. Her father said she suffered with asthma and wouldn't go anywhere without one. When SOCO have done their stuff, we can check all Ron's freelance crews against the prints we find — for elimination. And we might take the opportunity to see which houses they have been using recently. If only in our town, sir. Crickledale might well turn out to be a den of iniquity, sir.'

'Not when it is within my purview, Wayne. This is a decent town and it must remain so. Even if there is no criminal offence in taking pornographic pictures in private houses, the matter should be halted, Wayne. On moral grounds.'

'You'd have to be very careful how you did that, sir!'

'I am sure the decent citizens of the town would rally round in support, Wayne. But we have more immediate matters to concern us. Now, it is time to prepare for the CID conference.'

At 10 a.m. precisely, Detective Inspector Pluke addressed the fifty or so detectives who had assembled. After repeating his account of the bizarre circumstances of the discovery of the body, he outlined everything that had happened since, placing due emphasis upon the possibility that empty houses were being used as sets for filming, probably without the knowledge of the property owners. That information was not for the press at this stage, but the possibility must be borne in mind during the enquiries. Any information about an influx of cameras and equipment at the homes of absent owners should be noted. The names of those involved were vital — one of them could be the killer of Tracy Bretton. Tracy's movements in the town had to be traced too, along with her car. Where had that gone? Now that its registration number was known, it should not be difficult to locate. Once the girl had been formally identified by her father, details of her car and of her own personal description would be given to the press in the hope that members of the public had noticed her during her brief stay in Crickledale.

Detective Inspector Horsley followed up by displaying a magnified map of Crickledale divided into sections comprising housing estates and manageable areas embracing streets and roads. Teams of detectives would saturate each of those well-defined areas and ask about Tracy and her car, or other evidence of film-making in private houses or other premises. He allocated all the teams to specific tasks.

Briefing of the detectives lasted until 10.45 a.m. when it was time for the morning press conference. As the detectives were despatched about their enquiries, a band of reporters and photographers were arriving for their news conference. This was held in the lecture room at the police station and when Pluke arrived, it was full of journalists — the death of a nude woman in a fake druids' circle had stimulated their interest — and that was of benefit to the enquiry because the story would be read by thousands of potential witnesses and informants. Montague Pluke stressed that the cause of death was not yet known and that, at the moment, he could not confirm it was a murder enquiry. He did confirm, however, that the death was suspicious, that a forensic examination of the body had been arranged and that the investigation was based on a murder-type enquiry. Without giving the suspected name of the dead girl, Pluke went on to say that it was believed the deceased was a model from the Teesside area, aged about thirty, with long blonde hair and a well-developed figure. He did not refer to Ron Brown and his studio — he guessed the press would ferret out such a connection anyway — they'd know of all the local studios which produced such films and would make their own enquiries.

Pluke did say, however, that the investigation was concentrated in Crickledale where house-to-house enquiries were under way. He added that the deceased girl was thought to have had a red mini, qualifying that by saying neighbours had seen such a car in Crickledale, while not making any reference at this stage to No. 15 Padgett Grove. He did not give a full description or registration number because the girl had not yet been formally identified; her family had to know of her death before details appeared in the news bulletins. If any readers, listeners or viewers had noticed a red mini used or abandoned hereabouts, they were asked to ring the Incident Room at Crickledale Police Station while being told not to touch the vehicle.

In the question time which followed, Pluke was asked a range of leading questions about sexual scandals in semi-detached Crickledale, orgies in ordinary suburbia, debauchery in druids' circles and fornication with frolics in far-flung forests. He parried all the questions with aplomb, knowing that some elements of the tabloid press would produce their own brand of so-called news. Even if such innuendo did not help the enquiry, it might provoke some kind of tourist influx to Crickledale. Busloads of ghouls and gawpers would come hunting nymphs in forest glades with pensioners' outings wondering why life hadn't been like that in their youth.

When the press had departed to telephone their stories for their evening editions or more immediate news bulletins, Pluke returned to his office, whereupon he was met by Detective Sergeant Tabler. He had a fist full of developed colour prints.

'Winton's film, sir,' he said, handing the package to Pluke. 'He's not taken any photos of the corpse, they're all innocuous shots of the Druids' Circle. Three dozen in all, one film fully used.'

'Is there anything of evidential value, do you think?' Pluke asked the sergeant as he speedily scanned the collection, his heavy brow wrinkling at some of the scenes.

'I've examined every picture, sir, by blowing up each one to eight times its normal size on screen. I could even count the flowers in the grass, but I found nothing further which I felt was connected to our investigation. Some bits of litter show up quite well, but we've got those logged. I was looking for something else in the background, but found nothing. I don't think they are of any value to us.'

'But you have retained a copy of each of these, duly endorsed? For the file?'

'I have, sir.'

'Good, well, the negatives and one set of prints can be returned to Mr Winton as soon as possible with our compliments. He requires them for his work.'

'I will send one of my men to Fossford with them, sir.'

'No, I would like to take them, Sergeant. I wish to see where this man Winton lives, I wish to have another chat with him on his home ground and to discuss these pictures with him. I think it would be a very useful exercise.'

Leaving the teams of detectives to undertake their local investigations, Detective Inspector Montague Pluke with Detective Sergeant Wayne Wain at the wheel, set off for Fossford just before noon that Friday.

During the journey, Pluke examined the photographs more closely, studying the dramatic effect of light and shadow at the Druids'

Circle. They were good photographs of a highly professional standard, but his initial inspection had suggested that Winton was a liar — this closer examination had confirmed it, but he kept that opinion to himself for the time being.

'It's rather odd, sir, the officer in charge of an investigation performing a chore of this kind? Couldn't a patrol car have done it for us?'

'There are questions I wish to ask Mr Winton, Wayne. Please be patient.'

During the drive, Pluke observed that Wayne Wain was looking even more shattered than he had earlier this morning. His eyes had vanished into a pair of panda-like black rings, but he insisted he was fit to drive and had no wish to miss anything remotely connected with the investigation. He wondered what Pluke had discovered — he realised his boss had not telephoned Winton to announce his proposed arrival either, so he must hope to produce an element of surprise. No doubt he regarded that as beneficial in the circumstances and he was somewhat relieved when he noticed Winton's vehicle parked outside the flat.

'Our man is at home, so come with me, Wayne,' ordered Pluke.

The flats were in a converted and spacious pre-war terraced house. The front door was standing open and was held in position by a large metal knight on a white horse. The floor was tiled and polished and at the distant end was a staircase to the upper floors. There was a range of doorbells on the wall outside, one marked 'Flat 2' with the name Winton. Pluke pressed the bell and waited. They heard it ring inside, apparently in an upstairs room, but got no response.

'He won't be in bed, will he?' yawned Wayne, thinking that's precisely where he would like to be — and alone for an hour or two. He looked up at the first-floor window; the curtains were open.

'It's nearly lunch-time, Wayne,' snapped Pluke. 'All good freelances work a solid day, they don't lie-a-bed hoping to earn money without working … try again.'

For the second time, the bell echoed in the big house and this time it produced a response. A middle-aged woman wearing an apron and hair curlers materialised from behind a curtain on the ground floor; the curtain shielded a corridor which led past the staircase and into her flat. She padded towards them in her bedroom slippers and greeted them on the threshold.

'Is it Mr Winton you want?' She peered at them short-sightedly, rubbing a plate with a grubby tea towel as she addressed them. She saw a tall, smart young man and a shorter fellow in yellowish checked clothes, a blue dicky bow and a hat that looked too small. She wondered if they were salesmen.

'Yes, we do. Would you know if he's in?' asked Pluke in his most policeman-like voice.

'Well he was in last night because I saw him, eight or nine o'clock it would be, because he was getting something out of his car, a camera I think. I haven't heard him go out this morning if that's what you mean,' she responded. 'He usually gets his breakfast with Radio 2 blaring away, but not this morning. Is his car still there?' She peered down the street towards the parking place.

'Yes, it's outside, parked just down there. Mrs … er …'

'Pallister, Emily Pallister. This is my house, you know, I rent it out as flats, that's since my husband died, I need the money, you see, and — you're not bailiffs, are you? He doesn't owe money, does he? He's always good with his rent, I must say that for him …'

'If his car is there, Mrs Pallister, does it mean he's likely to be nearby?'

'He never goes anywhere without his car, mister, not even down to the chippy or the shops. Young folks never walk these days, do they? Not like in my day when you had to walk a mile to get a loaf of bread and then carry it back …'

'We're not bailiffs, Mrs Pallister, but we would like to speak to him. I have some things I wish to return to him, you see, important things, to be received by him in person.'

'Some of his pictures, eh? Well, I should come in and hammer on his door, if I were you, just in case his bell isn't working. Upstairs, first landing. There's a number two on the door.'

As she vanished through her curtain they climbed the carpeted stairs and turned sharp left at the top. There was a first-floor flat with bathroom at the top of the stairs, and two further rooms on the same landing. One door had 'No. 2' upon it, a plastic figure from a DIY shop by the look of it. Wayne Wain, having the biggest fist, volunteered to hammer on the door. He did, with resounding and thunderous noises, but it produced no response. He then resorted to shouting 'Mr Winton', but this produced no response either.

'We've missed him,' said Wayne Wain. 'We should have rung.'

'Or he might be inside, injured,' said Detective Inspector Pluke, looking steadily into the dark, bloodshot eyes of his battle-weary colleague. 'I think we should check, Wayne.'

'Have we any authority to do that, sir? Go in, I mean, without the consent of the occupier?'

'I am sure we have the authority, under Common Law, to break and enter any premises if we suspect that the life of someone inside those premises is at risk, Wayne. Besides, the Police and Criminal Evidence Act of 1984, section 17, empowers us to enter premises for various reasons — the purpose of saving life or limb being among them. It is quite reasonable that I believe I am going in to save a life, Wayne — and I can use force if necessary.'

But the door was not locked. It was fitted with a mortice, rather than a Yale, lock and when Pluke turned the handle the door opened into a kitchen. There was no key on the inside of the door either. The curtains were open, and as Pluke entered, he saw the table had been used for a meal, probably last night, because on it were a dirty plate and a mug, with an empty container that had held a pre-

prepared dish from Marks and Spencer. Shepherds' Pie. A meal for one. Used.

'Mr Winton?' Pluke was calling the fellow's name as he ventured deeper into the flat.

'The bedroom's to the left, sir,' said Wayne, noticing the door leading from the kitchen.

'Mr Winton?' Pluke was calling his name as he inched forwards, and then, as he peered into the bedroom, he halted. 'He's here, Wayne, on the bed. And I fear he has been murdered.'

*

Millicent was looking forward to the Friday Society this morning. She could explain to her friends how Montague had appeared on television about the girl in the Druids' Circle, and then there was all that unresolved business at May's and Cyril's bungalow. Mrs Peat had seen Montague there, she'd said, but Montague would say nothing about it ... but surely there was no connection, was there? Between May and Cyril, and that dead girl in the Circle? She wasn't May's niece after all, even though May had said she was, so it was all very curious. Or had someone got the girls mixed up? Maybe the ladies of the Friday Society would know something?

Chapter 12

Montague Pluke and Wayne Wain stood in shocked and surprised silence as they looked upon the body of the man they knew as Stephen Winton. He was dressed only in green boxer shorts, the rest of his body being completely naked. Even his feet were bare. He lay on his back, spreadeagled across the covers with some dried blood showing near the left side of his head. It had stained the duvet, the dark red showing against the tan-coloured fabric. Pluke, with the file of Winton's photographs in his hand and taking great care not to touch anything, stooped to examine the source of the blood and gently touched the flesh of the chest. It was cold and stiff, the feel of a corpse. That he was dead was a certainty.

'It's a bullet wound, Wayne, in the temple. Small-calibre weapon, I should say. Point two-two by the look of it.'

'He is dead, is he, sir? Definitely, I mean?'

'Yes, Wayne, he is quite dead. What a blessing I managed to get a statement from him before this happened That means we must call the local police as we are outside our divisional boundaries, but before we do so, I need to examine this room. After all, we do have an interest in this man's death.'

'This will not be our case, sir,' pointed out Wayne Wain. 'Perhaps we should leave things alone?'

'Normally I would, but surely the motive for this man's death is linked to his discovery of our corpse? I am sure the two deaths need to be considered together, so for the moment I am going to ignore the inter-force courtesies and politics. Now, let us carefully examine this flat. I want a few moments before the local police arrive but first we must search the premises in case the suspect is hiding.'

That was important in every such case — the police searched the premises to see if the killer was still hiding there — in the attic, the wardrobe or anywhere else. But they drew a blank. Satisfied that there was no immediate urgency to this case, Montague Pluke took his personal camera from his pocket, checked that the flash batteries were charged and that there was a film in place. He next positioned himself beside the bed, not moving an inch, as he committed to memory the appearance of the scene of Stephen's death. It was murder this time; of that there was no doubt because there was no firearm near the body, on the floor or beneath the bed. Suicide could be ruled out; Winton had not shot himself.

'See, Wayne, the mirror on his dresser?'

It was draped with one of Winton's sweaters.

'Hung out to air, sir?'

'Like those mirrors at No. 15 Padgett Grove? Another link, surely?'

'Who'd do that, sir? I'd say the sweater was airing, there's nothing more sinister than that. You can't think it's anything to do with an MO, can you? Surely the victims hung those things over the mirrors, not the killer. All we have to do is prove that the tea towels or sweaters or whatever else was used belonged to the victim, logic would then say the items were placed there by them. I cannot see how those actions can convince anyone that the same person killed both the girl and this photographer.'

'What alternative is there, Wayne? It might be difficult to regard those signs as hard evidence or even an MO — it might be said that Winton himself hung the sweater there to air as you have suggested, but I would suspect something more interesting. However, that is a question for the local police and I shall pursue my enquiries on the grounds that the same person is responsible for both deaths.'

'It means Winton did not kill the girl, surely, sir? He was innocent.'

'Not entirely, Wayne. Not entirely. I feel he must have been involved.'

'His involvement was finding the body, but why kill him for that?'

'I do not think he "merely" found Tracy's body, Wayne. I think he was involved in her death, although to what extent I am not sure at this stage. I think he knew why she died and how she died and I think he helped remove the body to the Druids' Circle once she was dead.'

'I saw no clues that would lead us to that conclusion, with all due respect, sir.'

'There are two things to consider, Wayne. When Winton found the corpse, it was not his first visit to the Druids' Circle. It is my suspicion that it was at least his third visit, not his second as he tried to make me believe. He admitted calling there as a young man, youth hostelling, he told us, and you can be sure he explored the place at that time and discovered the underground chamber. It's there for everyone to see. I'd guarantee that every visitor pokes his or her head into that chamber before leaving the Circle. That was his first visit, the one to which he referred. He told us he had never returned until yesterday, but I fear he was lying. He did call there again, at some stage before he found Tracy.'

'That is not mentioned in his statement, sir. He clearly stated it was his first visit since his youth hostelling days and that he had been sent there on a photographic commission. How can you assume he visited the site before finding the body?'

'I can accept the story of the commission, Wayne, although the precise arrangements for that will have to be checked. But it is clear from his photographs.' And Pluke slipped his own camera back into his pocket for a moment, then opened the file in his hands. 'Examine these, Wayne. Winton took these pictures yesterday morning; he told us that he took them just before he "found" the body. They are shots of the Druids' Circle, taken around 11 a.m. — a useful alibi perhaps. He said he arrived around 11 a.m., took some pictures and then found the corpse. I have no reason to disbelieve him so far as that timing is concerned.'

'Yes, I remember him telling us that.'

'But when I examined the prints that we developed from his film, the prints I have with me now, it is very evident they were taken on different occasions or at a different time. The first ones on the roll were taken during the mid-afternoon, I would suggest, or later, perhaps around tea-time. I re-examined these on the way here in the car and confirmed my original belief.'

'He can't have taken them yesterday afternoon, sir, that was impossible! We had that film in our custody at that time. There is only the one film, isn't there?'

'Yes, one roll of film with thirty-six exposures. That means he had been to the Druids' Circle on a previous occasion, during an afternoon, with his camera — I would suggest the day before he found the body.'

'But how do you know that, sir?'

'Look at the shadows cast by the sun, Wayne. See, these are the more recent photographs, taken around 11 a.m. yesterday.' And Pluke showed a selection to his sergeant. 'The sun would be almost due south, casting shadows of that altar and phallic symbol; the shadows show to the right of the objects in question as we enter the Circle from the Eastern Gate. He took the pictures from that vantage point. That means the shadows point towards the north, away from the sun. Also, there are shadows on the left of the pictures, they're from the overhanging trees — those shadows point to the right, that's to the north of the Circle too. So those pictures were taken yesterday, shortly before our arrival.'

'I understand, sir.'

'And these prints are from one reel of film, Wayne. He was unable to separate the earlier pictures from the more recent, although I would suggest he had no idea of the messages they would provide.'

'Go on, sir.'

'But some of those other pictures, Wayne, show the same locations — the altar and phallic symbol — with shadows pointing towards the Eastern Gate. That suggests the sun was in the west when the pictures were taken, Wayne, and we know it doesn't reach that point of the sky until late afternoon at this time of year.'

'So it means Winton was at the Circle, taking photos late one afternoon. You're right, sir.'

'Precisely, Wayne. It might even be possible to calculate precisely what time he was taking those pictures — that phallic symbol acts very like the gnomon of a sundial which means we might be able to calculate the exact time he was there. But more important — it also means he lied to me when I questioned him. That is why I wanted to talk to him again. In any murder investigation, liars become suspects. We cannot say with any certainty which day or at what time he was there on that earlier occasion, but if the pictures are on the same reel of film, one may assume that they were taken very soon before the others on the same film. Professional photographers go through reels of film as if they are worthless. Another point, Wayne, is that if he was taking photographs for a magazine feature, he would surely have rediscovered the cavern he'd first known about as a youth — the cavern is not concealed in any way. He would have rediscovered it during that afternoon visit, whatever day it was.'

'And he would recall it when the question of disposal of the body arose?'

'Exactly, Wayne. Imagine that he was present when the girl died — irrespective of whether someone else killed her — and I think he was present when disposal of the remains became necessary. He remembered the burial chamber at the Circle. So she was taken there and left naked on that shelf of rock ...'

'How, sir? How was she taken there? We examined Winton's car and it bore no traces of her presence.'

'How about her own car, Wayne? Where is it? Where has it gone? Suppose someone placed the body in her own car, covered on the back seat as if she was resting, or even asleep, and then drove her to the Circle for disposal? After that, the perpetrator or perpetrators could get rid of her mini. It is quite common for cars to be disposed of in these forests, burnt out by thieves for example. I hope our press appeal leads us to it, but I suggest the Task Force might rake the forests for signs of burnt-out cars.'

'We found no tyre marks on the track, sir, nothing to say her car had been here.'

'It had rained overnight, Wayne, gentle but persistent rain will soon obliterate tyre marks from earthen tracks. It suggests she was driven there before the rain came.'

'So you believe that Stephen Winton was present when Tracy was killed — with a possibility that he might have killed her — and that he therefore knew too much? And you are also saying he disposed of, or helped to dispose of, her remains, then later called the police to say he had discovered her body, hoping that would remove suspicion from him.'

'Yes, I think that is a fairly accurate assessment, Wayne, but once we established our enquiries, we began to uncover something more sinister than we realised and Winton had to be silenced. And so he was. That is my view.'

'Sinister, sir? Like what?'

'It could be associated with the use of those houses by supposed house-sitters for making pornographic films. That kind of filming is big business, Wayne, with rich profits. We might have uncovered the proverbial nest of vipers.'

'Are you saying this photographer was involved in that kind of film-making, sir?'

'It is quite likely. A search of his car and flat might reveal something along those lines, Wayne, but I am now convinced he was present at the death of Tracy Bretton whether by accident or on purpose. And he has paid with his life. Clearly, someone thought he knew too much or would talk too much.'

Replacing the photographs in the file, Pluke retrieved his pocket camera and began to take a selection of pictures of the interior of the flat, showing the body, the state of the bedroom, the contents of the dressing-table, the sweater draped over the mirror and other general scenes. He then photographed the kitchen with the remains of its meal, along with more general views, and he achieved all this without touching anything. He valued the need for an uncontaminated scene of crime and would allow the incoming officers that privilege.

When he had finished, he said, 'Now, Wayne, it is time to call the local police. I shall not disturb the flat. But I would like some pictures of his car too. I can take those while awaiting their arrival. In the meantime, could you telephone the Fossford CID? Don't use the instrument in this flat — it will be necessary to trace the last calls made from Winton's phone. Perhaps the landlady downstairs will oblige?'

'I'll do it right away, sir.'

'Good. And while you are talking to her, you might question her about visitors to this flat and find out what she knows about the lifestyle of Stephen Winton.'

*

Temporarily alone with the body of Stephen Winton, Montague Pluke visually explored the flat, not touching anything and walking only along a route he would describe to the incoming detectives. He took his time too, working slowly around the interior of the flat.

The double bed was in a corner of the room and Winton's body lay crosswise. His head was to the left of the pillow and his legs slightly apart, pointing towards the right of the foot of the bed. His right foot dangled over the side, not quite touching the floor.

The shot was in his right temple, blood staining the duvet where it covered the pillow. There was no weapon either; again, he searched the floor and beneath the bed without moving anything and found no firearm. That ruled out suicide.

Bearing in mind the remains of the meal in the kitchen, and the state of undress of the body, plus the fact that a bedside table bore a wrist-watch showing the present time and a handkerchief, Pluke deduced Winton had been shot at bedtime. He had probably died while preparing for bed. The fact that he lay on top of the duvet suggested he had not actually got into bed before his visitor had shot him, nor had he climbed out to greet the intruder. The absence of any sign of a break-in suggested he had opened the door to his killer, but would he do that in a state of near undress? Pluke noticed some day clothes on a chair in a corner of the bedroom — a light-grey T-shirt and pair of jeans, with trainer shoes under the chair. The curtains were open, but the windows were covered with lace — so either Winton went to bed with his curtains open, or the killer had opened them before leaving.

Some intruders did that when they invaded houses at night — it prevented nosy people wondering why the curtains were closed in daylight and often gave a criminal a few more hours of grace before his deeds were discovered. The bedroom was fairly tidy, Pluke decided, although far from the meticulous standard demanded by Millicent, and the intruder did not appear to have searched it, or any other part of the flat, for any reason. All the drawers in the dressing-table were closed and Winton's jeans, hanging over the back of the chair, did not appear to have been searched for money or credit cards. There was no sign of a fight either, no ruffled rugs, disturbed furnishings or indications of defence by Winton. Burglary, Pluke decided, could be ruled out, as could a battle with a burglar.

Whoever had come to this flat, Pluke decided, had come for no purpose other than to shoot Winton. And Winton had admitted

him. Thus they knew one another. Apart from the remains of
the meal on the table, there was little of interest to Montague in
the kitchen, other than Winton's camera which stood on a shelf
above the eating area. There were films too, unused, and the other
accoutrements of a professional photographer, all together so
that they could be gathered quickly if an urgent mission arose. He
would not inspect the camera to see what was contained on any film
that might lie within — that job would be done by the incoming
detectives.

The bathroom told a little — a solitary toothbrush lay near the
taps of the washbasin with a squiggle of paste upon it. It seemed
that Winton had been disturbed moments before cleaning his teeth
as he prepared for bed.

Montague took photographs of the bathroom and kitchen, then
became aware of heavy footsteps on the stairs. He went back into
the kitchen and waited. Two large men in dark suits materialised in
the doorway.

'Who are you?' demanded the tallest, a six-foot-six-inches (two-
metre) giant with shoulders like an ox. He had dark hair shorn close
to his head and dark, staring eyes.

'I might ask the same question,' replied Pluke.

*

The big tall man looked at the panama-hatted figure in the untidy
overcoat and spats and grimaced towards his smaller companion as
he said, 'We've a right one here, George.'

He redirected his attention towards Pluke. 'I ask the questions.
I am Detective Inspector Boddy of Fossford CID and this is
Detective Sergeant Sole from the same department.' And both
showed their warrant cards. 'And if you are thinking what I think
you are thinking, it's all been said before. We've heard the lot, we've
heard all the jokes. Now, having established that, sir, who the hell
are you and what are you doing with what I am told is a body in this

flat?'

'I am Detective Inspector Montague Pluke from Crickledale CID.' Montague drew himself to his full height, an action which caused his trousers to rise like a flag on a flag-pole and his overcoat to tighten around his belly. 'And my companion downstairs, the one who rang for you, is Detective Sergeant Wayne Wain.' And Montague produced his own warrant card which the officers studied briefly.

'So what the hell are you doing on my patch without my knowledge and with a dead body?' demanded Boddy. 'Control Room said nothing about any CID from anywhere being at the scene!'

Montague provided a succinct account of his purpose, at the same time expressing his belief that Tracy Bretton's death was linked with this one, then led them into the bedroom to show them the body of Stephen Winton.

'What have you touched?' asked Boddy.

Montague explained precisely what he had done, whereupon Boddy said, 'I shall need a very detailed statement from you, Mr Pluke. Being the person who found the body, you have made yourself a suspect and will need to be eliminated. Now, what's in that packet you are carrying around as if it contains the Crown Jewels?'

Montague explained and showed the photographs to Boddy and Sole, at which Boddy said, 'I will need those.'

'Most certainly you cannot have them,' snapped Montague. 'These are material to my investigation — I will arrange for copies to be sent to you.'

'So you are trying to say this guy was involved in the death of your victim?' Boddy said.

'Yes, that is my belief. I came here simply to hand him these photographs and to ask him to explain whether or not he had lied to me on a previous occasion.'

'Paul?' Boddy spoke to his silent companion. 'Take Mr Pluke into the car outside and get a statement from him. I'll seal this room and call in the troops. It is a murder enquiry, Paul — contact Control and set things in motion.'

'Yes, sir.'

'And Mr Pluke — you and I will have to confer over this one.'

'That will be my pleasure, Mr Boddy.' Montague smiled as they left the flat and the corpse. 'Ah, here's Detective Sergeant Wain now.'

As they emerged on to the landing, Wayne Wain was climbing the stairs, having been given an earwigging by the voluble landlady below. If he looked shattered before, he was even more drained now. Non-stop woman's talk had that effect upon him.

'Gentlemen, this is Detective Sergeant Wain, my colleague. Wayne, this is Detective Inspector Boddy and Detective Sergeant Sole of Fossford CID.'

'Boddy and Sole?' Wayne Wain smiled.

'What's he been doing?' demanded Boddy, cutting short any further opportunity for a joke about their name.

'I went to call your office. I couldn't use the phone in here, could I? It took a while to get back. Traffic, you know,' replied Wain, deciding not to say he had been interviewing the deceased's landlady.

He let them think he had made the call from a distant call-box. These two urban heavies might not like a rustic detective carrying out work on their patch.

'You were there with your inspector when the body was found?' asked Boddy.

'Yes, I was.'

'Right, we want a statement from you as well. In the car, both of you. And next time you rustic plods come on to my patch, I want to know.'

*

Pluke and Wain drove away about an hour later. In that time, Pluke had been mercilessly grilled by Boddy, feeling that he was a suspect rather than the person who had found the body. But now that ordeal was over and the death of Stephen Winton had been officially handed over to Boddy and his officers, Pluke and Wain were returning to Crickledale — and they had managed to retain the photographs.

'I did not get an opportunity to examine Winton's car, Wayne,' said Pluke as they drove away. 'Those detectives arrived more speedily than I thought. I would dearly have liked to take a second look at his vehicle and a more detailed look at the contents of the flat.'

'His car was given a thorough going-over by our lads yesterday, sir.'

'Yes, it was. I suppose that would have found anything relevant, although I might have to ask Fossford police if I can examine it again if the need arises. Now, Wayne, what did you learn about Winton?'

'He was a good tenant,' began Wain. 'He's been in that flat about three years and has always paid his rent on time. Mrs Pallister's had no trouble with him about noise or bad behaviour. Sometimes, she said, when she went out of her own flat, she could hear his radio of a morning, but not this morning. She thought nothing of it — she knew he sometimes went out early to catch the morning light and darkness, or the empty streets — but then she saw the car outside and wondered if he was all right. In fact, she went up and tapped on his door — that would be about eight forty-five this morning — but got no reply. She didn't try the door.'

'He'd be lying dead at that stage,' said Pluke. 'So, visitors, Wayne. Did she see any visitors? Does he have many visitors?'

'He seemed to have quite a lot of friends,' Wayne said. 'Both sexes too. There were quite a lot of callers, people of his own age as a rule, and sometimes he held small parties with a dozen or so there. They were seldom a nuisance to her, but she does not know who the visitors were. He never introduced any of his friends to her.'

'And last night?'

'Someone called late, sir, by car. Half-twelve or thereabouts.

They left the engine running, she heard it ticking over outside. The visitor ran up the stairs but didn't stay long, then hurried away. She thought little about it because he often had callers like that, friends or sometimes people delivering photos to him. Whoever it was had heavy footsteps so she thought it was a man. She was in her kitchen at the time, making herself a drink before going to bed, and was in her night clothes. So she didn't look out or shout good-night. She has no idea who it was.'

'So she did not see the car in question?'

'No, sir. She did say that Winton sometimes took deliveries of printed pictures late in the evening, cars and vans often called, she said, so its arrival wasn't all that unusual. I suppose we can check out the people who develop his prints?'

'Yes, we can, or Boddy and Sole can. It's their case, after all! So what about the sound of a shot?'

'She didn't hear a shot being fired but .22s don't make a lot of noise, do they?'

'OK, Wayne, well done. We'll have to await the results of the post-mortem and forensic tests on this new death, which means I shall have to bother that unpleasant Boddy man for his findings,' announced Pluke. 'And I think we should make greater efforts to find the killer of the young girl — the same person, I sincerely believe. It would be nice to make an arrest before our Inspector Boddy does so, don't you think, Wayne?'

'It would indeed, sir.' Wayne Wain smiled.

'I wonder if there have been any developments in our own Incident Room?'

*

Gossip at the Friday Society centred upon Padgett Grove, hitherto regarded as such a nice area. But if the bungalow at No. 15 and its owners had been involved in murders and nude men and things like that, then it called into question the eligibility of May Crowther for membership of the various eminent societies and clubs in Crickledale. Letting her home be used for undesirable purposes was not the sort of conduct one should tolerate. It lowered standards to those of seedy nightclubs and brothels. In a true society, standards had to be maintained. And the Friday Society was a modern example of high standards in a world which was slipping into sensuous oblivion — only the finest of ladies were permitted as members. Someone had to save the country.

It was Mrs Councillor Farrell who asked, 'Millicent, I really do think you ought to find out from your husband just what May and Cyril have been doing. You are in the finest possible position to help us. After all, May is so closely involved with so many organisations that any hint of scandal could be devastating to us all. We'd all be tainted. Do try and find out, will you?'

Chapter 13

Montague Pluke's Incident Room — already nicknamed The Plukedom — had been busy that morning. As a result of tasks already allocated to the teams, there had been much productive activity while Pluke and Wain were in Fossford. They, on the other hand, had broken their return journey to enjoy a late lunch of sandwiches and coffee in a bistro. As a notice said the eating of one's own food brought on to the premises was forbidden, Pluke kept his packed lunch in his pocket for a future occasion. It was while eating his open prawn sandwich that Pluke had accidentally knocked a fork from the table; as he'd retrieved it, he'd said, 'Knife falls, gentleman calls; fork falls, lady calls; spoon falls, baby squalls!'

'I suspect we might be receiving a visit from a lady, Wayne,' he commented seriously. 'Perhaps a witness in our enquiries?'

'I hope she produces something worthwhile, sir.' Wayne Wain smiled, hoping that his response did not sound too dismissive.

From time to time Wayne Wain wondered whether Montague's entire life was structured around his superstitious beliefs, but conversely whether any of tomorrow's race meetings sported a horse with a name like Fork Leaf, Lady Caller or Tumbled Fork or something similar. He'd check before having a modest bet.

Upon their return to Crickledale, Pluke and Wain discovered that the teams of detectives had already produced a wealth of information which was presently being analysed. An additional factor was that the early news coverage had also resulted in an encouraging response from the public.

Much of it would be unrelated to the investigation but the

detectives knew that, among the masses of messages, there could be one single gem, one snippet, which would provide the breakthrough and lead them to the killer.

'Before we examine the new information in detail,' Pluke told the now-motivated Inspector Horsley, 'I must tell you that Stephen Winton is dead. We found him at his flat in Fossford, shot in the head. It was not a self-inflicted wound, the weapon was not with the body. We called the local CID, that's 'F' Division. Boddy and Sole from Fossford are dealing with the enquiry. I am sure his murder is linked with the death of Tracy Bretton, so we will have to establish a system of liaison with them.'

'I'll make sure everyone's told. This'll beef up the investigation, Montague — the murder of a witness. Not that he was particularly vital, of course ...'

'Wait!' said Pluke. 'I believe that Winton was more vital than we realised and his demise might frustrate things somewhat. I was hoping to glean more information from that man; I am convinced he did not tell me the truth. Indeed, Mr Horsley, I would classify him as a prime suspect.'

Montague adopted a solemn tone as he informed Horsley of his opinions relating to the photographs and to Winton's earlier visit to the Druids' Circle. In providing this account he asked Horsley, while assessing the incoming data, to bear in mind the scenario that Winton could have been involved with the death of Tracy Bretton and that he might have helped to dispose of her body.

In Pluke's opinion, there was a distinct possibility the body had somehow been conveyed from No. 15 Padgett Grove to the Druids' Circle, possibly in the girl's own car with the assistance of Winton. Any sightings of incidents which might have been relevant to that removal were sought — he asked Horsley to ensure that all detectives bore that in mind during their enquiries.

'So what have you got for me?' Having imparted his news,

Montague settled in the chair in his dingy office and addressed Horsley. Wayne Wain, yawning broadly, had brought in another chair and Horsley occupied a third in front of the desk, his arms full of files. Murder enquiries did generate a mass of paper.

'First, your man, Stephen Winton. Stephen Winton deceased, I should now qualify that,' said Horsley. 'Our findings might well fit your theory, Montague. We did a standard check at the Criminal Record Office and discovered he has form. He left college, couldn't find a white-collar job and eventually got work as a coal heaver; but then he was sent down for two years for attempted rape. In his defence, he said his uncrushable urges were brought on by sniffing coal dust. No one really believed that. He studied photography in prison and found himself excelling at it; he could compose very artistic pictures, especially rural scenes, and began working as a freelance on release. He did well. However, there've been several cases of rape and attempted rape which are unsolved, both in this region and elsewhere; he was working in the vicinity at the time of more than a dozen of those attacks, and was questioned. There was never enough evidence to charge him, but it was felt that the freedom to roam which he enjoyed in his job, enabled him to find his victims and escape without detection.'

'He sounds just the sort of man to be involved in Tracy's death,' commented Montague. 'Anything else?'

'Yes, we've had words with the editor who commissioned him. Molly Swift by name. He has done work for her in the past, she reckons he is — was — competent and efficient. She knew he'd been in prison but did not know for what offence. The fact he had a record did not worry her — all she required was photographs worthy of publication, which he supplied on time. On this occasion she did commission him to take a series of colour photographs, including some of the Druids' Circle, but had no idea of his movements. Her deadline was at the end of this month, as he told us, but he didn't inform her when he would be heading out to the moors to take his pictures.'

'I asked Mrs Pallister, his landlady in Fossford, about his movements on the day Tracy's body was found,' interrupted Wayne Wain. 'She did see him leave his flat that morning, around 10 a.m. as he said to us, and he told her he was heading this way, but added that he had to return in good time for a picture session in York Minster.'

'That tallies with the story he told me. Do we know precisely what job he was doing in the Minster?' asked Pluke.

'No,' admitted Horsley. 'That's another action for my teams.'

'We need to know whom he met there and at what time,' Pluke said. 'He'd be late for that engagement because he was assisting us with our enquiries at the Circle. And we need to know how long he stayed and whether anyone returned to his flat with him.'

'Leave it to me,' said Horsley.

'In short,' added Montague, 'we need to trace anyone who has made contact with him since we interviewed him.'

'Next,' said Horsley. 'Your gossip who lives at No. 14 Padgett Grove. Josephine Peat. We've interviewed her.'

'Good.' Montague Pluke actually smiled, knowing that some of the best crime-fighting information in the world came from women who glanced through net curtains and couldn't prevent themselves talking about what they had seen. 'So what did she see?'

'Almost everything!' Horsley beamed. 'She saw the Crowthers depart for their holiday — they'd asked Mrs Peat to keep an eye on the house and who better? She'd been told that a niece of May Crowther was to live in, and last Sunday noticed the arrival of a dark-red mini with the beautiful blonde at the wheel. All as expected.'

Montague smiled at the deviousness of the staid Crowthers in making the nosy neighbours think May had a niece.

Horsley went on, 'Mrs Peat lived up to expectations. I don't think a fly, or even Father Christmas, could have entered that house, at any time of day or night, without her noticing. She noticed the arrival of some friends of the girl; they came for a party one night, she thinks it was the Monday after the girl arrived. Last Monday in fact. They came in a small personnel carrier, one of those twelve-seaters, and carried a lot of stuff from it into the house. She couldn't say what it was with any certainty, but she guessed it was crates of drink and boxes of food. She cannot swear to that, of course. She merely saw boxes and crates and other objects which she could not identify. A taxi brought a man too, a bit later than the others, but she couldn't describe either the man or the taxi as it was getting dark.'

'I think the objects she noticed might have been the equipment they needed for filming,' commented Pluke.

'You're probably right. Now, she didn't get the registration number of the personnel carrier, but thinks it had the letters N and R in the number, and the figure 3 or 8. That's all she can say — she's most upset at not obtaining that kind of detail!'

'We can run a Police National Computer check on carriers with those numbers in that combination of registration figures, although it'll take some time to make that kind of search,' said Pluke. 'And we can question all local taxi firms and their drivers. So, that was Monday night. What time did the party conclude?'

'In the early hours. Half past one or two o'clock, she thinks. She was in bed and heard the chatter of the guests as they left, and car doors banging.'

'Have we any descriptions of these people?' followed Pluke.

'No, except she didn't recognise any of them, she thinks none was local. Very vaguely, she thinks they were all in their late twenties or thirties, casually dressed, some men with long hair, girls in short skirts, fun people in other words. She wasn't sure how many there were, with all the comings and goings. Five or six, she guessed. But it might be significant that she saw a naked man darting across the hall;

the front door had opened to let some of the revellers out just as this character was running somewhere, probably the bathroom.

'She described him as a large man, youngish, in his late twenties or early thirties, and he had dark hair. She could not tell us anything else about him.'

'Was it Winton, do you think? So what about any other visitors? Such as tall young men looking like Stephen Winton?' was Pluke's next question. 'Did she notice Winton, or anyone like him, at any other time?'

'Yes, as a matter of fact she did.' Horsley smiled. 'There were no other groups arrivals but the girl in her red mini did leave the bungalow most days to drive off somewhere, usually mid-morning, and returned around seven each evening. A man did return with her on Wednesday night, noticed Mrs Peat. About seven o'clock or thereabouts.'

'Wednesday? Well done, Mrs Peat! Description?'

'Rather vague, but close enough to Winton's appearance to have been him. She said he was very tall, dark-haired, good-looking and casually dressed — she mentioned jeans and a T-shirt, light coloured. She can't swear that it was the man she saw naked, but agrees it could have been. He was in the passenger seat of her mini when the blonde girl — Tracy we are sure — parked it outside the house. They got out and she unlocked the front door; he followed her in. They seemed friendly, I might add, chatting like old pals. Mrs Peat didn't think the girl was being pressed into something she did not want. There was no suggestion he was forcing his attentions upon her. In fact, the pair of them stopped on the drive to chat to George Dunwoody who was washing his taxi in the drive of his bungalow.'

'So her visitor appears to have been welcome. If it was Winton, he lied again. He told us he did not know the dead girl and had never seen her. And afterwards? Did she see the man leave, or notice any other activity?'

'No, none, Montague. The house was quiet on Thursday morning, she did not see anyone around, no sign of the occupants. The red mini was not there either, that's the following morning, Thursday. Yesterday. Mrs Peat assumed it had been put in the Crowthers' garage, which was where the girl kept it. The Crowthers used their own car to travel to the airport, so we know the garage was available.'

'All very sound information, Mr Horsley,' said Pluke. 'I know we cannot make unproven assumptions, but it does seem possible that Winton left his own car somewhere on Wednesday evening, was taken to No. 15 Padgett Grove by Tracy in her car and then spent at least part of the evening alone with her. Had he spent the whole day with her, perhaps on a photographic session before returning to the bungalow? And if he did return with her, did he kill her and remove her body in her own car, dump her at the Circle and then collect his to return to Fossford? He was in Fossford on Thursday morning — his landlady saw him leave his flat and her sighting tallies with his statement to us, including the time of his arrival at the Druids' Circle and his subsequent call to us about "finding" the body.'

'We can only guess at that scenario, Montague, unless our enquiries reveal some formal connection between the girl and Winton, photographic work, I mean, commissioned work. We cannot be sure the man with her at the bungalow was Winton. We must be careful not to make too many assumptions.'

'I agree entirely. Now, we are looking into her recent movements, are we?'

'I have three teams doing that, Montague, covering Crickledale and her contacts on Teesside. While you were away, her father came to the morgue to make a formal identification. It is definitely Tracy Bretton. She was a model, aged thirty-one, home address — Stockton-on-Tees. Full details are in the file. Her dad had no idea about her porn work; he thought she modelled for fashion stores and catalogues — which she did, so she didn't lie to her parents. It's just that she didn't tell the whole truth. The fact is she did porn — male order poses, I suppose you could call them! Extra activities for cash. Poor kid, what an awful life. And she was asthmatic, the inhaler found in the bungalow was hers. It proves she was there too. Her body has been taken to Leeds for a forensic pathologist to ascertain the cause of death. He's going to operate this afternoon. I hope to have a result before we knock off tonight.'

'Let's hope we get a positive result,' said Pluke. 'Now, did you know that a diet of boiled carrots eaten for two weeks is said to be an effective cure for asthma? Next, it's vital that we find her car, even if it is a burnt-out wreck in the forest.'

'We've got its registration number from her father; a PNC check on the number has thrown up the engine and chassis numbers too. Even if it has been destroyed, we should be able to identify it. I have passed a message to motor patrols and C10, but we really need the Task Force to search the forests.'

'We can get them to do that when they've finished at the Circle. I have asked the press to publicise it, the evening paper should carry the story. An article in the newspapers will help immensely,' said Montague. 'Holiday-makers, forestry workers and local people can do the work of hundreds of police officers. When it's found, we must make sure it's examined for fingerprints. If it contains the fingerprints of Winton — and we'll have those on file if he has form — it'll help to establish he either travelled in the car or drove it.'

'Sir,' butted in Wayne Wain, stifling another huge yawn. 'Even if Winton did visit the house, even if he did spend time with Tracy and even if he did drive her car away, it doesn't mean he killed her. I am sorry to harp on about this, but it would be dreadful if we labelled him a killer when he wasn't. And he's hardly in a position to defend himself, is he?'

'Point taken, Sergeant,' said Inspector Horsley. 'Now, if we can prove Winton was the killer, we can terminate this investigation. The file can be closed because he can't be prosecuted. But if he was not the killer, it means the killer is still out there. Winton's killer may be Tracy's killer — and I regard that as a strong option. That alternative means we can't wrap up this enquiry, gentlemen. We must press on. Now, the SOCO teams are at No. 15 Padgett Grove this morning, checking it over with a fine-tooth comb before the Crowthers return. They're seeking fingerprints — Tracy's, Winton's, those of the Crowthers of course, and hopefully any others that might appear, even some of the Dunwoodys next door and other visitors. We need to eliminate a lot of people from suspicious associations with that bungalow. If any of those visitors to Tracy have form, we'll track them down. And I have teams working on the Dunwoodys, Holliday, Ron Brown alias Marcel Boussicourt and the Crowthers. We shall be probing every part of their lives.'

'I am afraid we shall create consternation in Crickledale,' commented Montague. 'But so long as we emerge with the truth, that is what we seek. Now, I understand the Crowthers are planning to return very soon. They may tell us if any blankets are missing. I am sure we shall find them most helpful in tracing the people who have had legitimate access to their house. What else do I need to ask, Mr Horsley? Has anything been ascertained about that glove?'

'Nothing, not yet anyway. There's no manufacturer's name inside and so far, we've drawn a blank from enquiries in shops around town. It's the sort of glove any man could buy in a department store, mass produced, not special in any way. Size nine. There's a label inside which says "Made in England" and the size, nothing else. But we are on the trail of one or two likely manufacturers. There might be some means of tracing its journey from the factory.'

Well briefed by Horsley, Montague and Wayne spent the next couple of hours or so studying the file of processed statements.

Many came from householders in the town, people who had been
visited by teams of detectives, and most contained nothing of value.
After being typed and duplicated, every statement was read by a
team of statement readers; their job was to note anything which
might be relevant to the enquiry, highlight it and make a reference
to it in the HOLMES computer. One such relevant item was the
missing red car. All detectives had been told to ask for sightings of
the car during their enquiries, but none had emerged at this early
stage.

One team had been especially commissioned to visit every garage
and filling station in and around Crickledale to make specific
enquiries about Tracy's car, the registration details of which were
now available. Some garages noted such numbers in their petrol sales
records, even when cash was paid. But no sightings, other than those
of the neighbours in Padgett Grove, had been recorded.

When the press arrived for their late-afternoon news conference,
Montague could confirm the identity of the deceased. He knew
the papers would highlight her private life, but this might produce
sightings of her and perhaps identify people with a knowledge of
her and her work. It could produce personal contacts, all of whom
would have to be eliminated from the enquiry. The identity of the
victim was today's big item for the media, although it was too late for
the early editions of the evening papers. It would make TV, though,
and the Force Press Officer had procured a photograph of Tracy in
one of her more modest modelling poses. This would be used by
TV and the newspapers, hopefully to good effect.

The next major development occurred that afternoon when a lady
arrived at the enquiry counter of Crickledale Police Station shortly
before 5 p.m. She asked for the officer in charge of the murder
enquiry and the constable on duty referred her to the Incident Room
where she encountered Montague Pluke. In Pluke's opinion, she was
not entirely unexpected — the falling fork had given him adequate

warning.

'Yes, madam.' He beamed when she said she had something to tell him. He noted she wore sensible walking shoes and a long, loose dress of many colours — a lady in her mid-forties with dyed blonde hair. He asked, 'What can I do for you?'

'It's about this enquiry of yours, Mr Pluke. Well, I had two of your detectives round earlier,' she said. 'Asking about that girl at the Circle.'

'Tracy Bretton.' Montague provided the girl's name.

'Yes, well, they asked about red minis, her car, they said. She had a red mini, they mentioned, and said you were looking for it. Well, I think I know where it is.'

'You do? This is wonderful. And you are Mrs Braithwaite, aren't you? I believe we met at one of my wife's events, in the Church Hall? Millicent Pluke. A plant sale last year?'

'My word, Mr Pluke, what a memory. It'll be your training, of course. Yes, I am Mrs Braithwaite. Ruth Braithwaite,' she identified herself. 'Tavern Lane. No. 22. I took my dog for a walk this afternoon, you see, three o'clock we set off. I take the car to the moors and we walk up there whenever we can. Me and Patch.'

'Up where?' Montague smiled.

'On the tops above Russetdale, that old railway track. It's flat up there, I puff a bit when I have to climb hills, you see, and, well, anyway, I let Patch off his lead — he's a Jack Russell terrier — and he ran about like he does. Anyway, I saw this car, in a dip on the moors. Burnt out, well most of it burnt out. It had been red, I could see some colour left on it. Anyway, Mr Pluke, I went for a look — it wasn't burning then of course — but there was nobody with it. So, well, hearing about that poor girl and her red car, I thought you ought to know about this one.'

'So you think it had been driven along the old railway track and then deep into the moors?'

'Yes, I'm sure that's what happened,' she said. 'I mean, people do take their cars along that old track, it's very firm and made of cinders, but this was well into the heather, quite a long way off the track. I was lucky to notice it, Mr Pluke, it was in a dip in the moors. It was just a fluke that I saw it.'

'If I get a map, could you show me where it is?'

'Yes, of course.'

Minutes later, Pluke knew where to find the car; he summoned two detectives to take a statement from Mrs Braithwaite for entry into the filing system and HOLMES, and called Wayne Wain. His face now looked a weird shade of grey with deep lines about the dark-skinned eye sockets, and eyes like pick holes in the snow. He was yawning with increasing regularity.

'You should be in bed, Wayne!' snapped Montague Pluke.

'I'll knock off soon, sir.' His voice was hoarse now.

'I think we have found the missing car, Wayne, I was going out to look at it.'

'Then I wish to come, sir.'

A quick call to the Fire Brigade and to Crickledale police Control Room showed that no car fires had been reported in recent days, although one report of a small moor fire at that location had been received at 11 a.m. on Thursday morning. Such fires were fairly routine during the summer months and often burnt themselves out very quickly.

In this case, a search had failed to find the source because the smoke had ceased by the time the Fire Service arrived; a lack of smoke meant they did not conduct a localised search and so they had not discovered the car. Whoever had burnt that car had found a very secluded place. It suggested someone with a very good knowledge of the local moorland. After briefing a two-men team from SOCO to follow their vehicle, Wayne Wain led the procession high on to the moors above Russetdale and actually drove along the old railway track. There was no doubt it could easily accommodate a motor car or vehicle of similar size. It took a few minutes to locate the car. It was a burnt-out shell, all rust-coloured with blackened portions which had once been the interior furnishings. The heather and bracken around it were scorched and blackened, while the tyres had completely vanished in the blaze. Very little of the vehicle remained, although some red paint had survived on the sills and under the wings.

The registration plates were missing too, probably having been removed in the hope it would frustrate identification of the car, but the engine compartment was intact and the engine number *in situ*.

Beyond all doubt, this had once been Tracy Bretton's car.

*

The Crickledale Tea Circle that afternoon enjoyed cucumber sandwiches and homemade cakes. It was Mrs Peat who held court. Having been interviewed by detectives, she explained to the shocked ladies that No. 15 Padgett Grove was indeed the focus of a murder investigation and the victim had been the young woman assumed by the neighbours to have been the niece of May and Cyril Crowther. But the young woman was a fashion model, she said, and there was talk of sex parties with orgies of naked men and women being filmed at the house.

There was even a hint that the woman was not really May's niece so what had May and Cyril been up to? That's what Mrs Peat wanted to know. She enlivened the Tea Circle with a graphic description of a dark-haired young man she'd seen with no clothes on and was positive that other people had been gallivanting about the house stark naked …

'I shouldn't say this but I will.' She spoke in confidence to her open-mouthed audience. 'But did May and Cyril *know*? I mean, did they agree to those goings-on …?'

'You *are* going to ask your husband about it, aren't you, Millicent?'

persisted Mrs Councillor Farrell. 'And I will ask my husband to bring it up in Council. We don't want that kind of behaviour in Crickledale, do we? Not in such a nice area ...'

Millicent blushed. How could she possibly ask Montague again about his confidential work and especially about matters relating to overt sexual activity?

Chapter 14

Montague Pluke was locked in a moment of silence as he examined the scorched moorland which surrounded the charred, twisted remains of the little red car. In pondering the start of the blaze, he was aware of an old belief — one that went back to the pagans — that a fire could never be ignited when beams of sunshine were shining directly upon it. That was not true, of course, but there was another very strong belief, prevalent even today, that if a fire ignited very quickly without any artificial aid, then the household in question would receive unexpected visitors very shortly afterwards. Judging by its almost totally consumed condition, this vehicle appeared to have caught fire without any difficulty, so perhaps the person who had set it on fire would soon receive some unexpected visitors — police officers, in all probability. But had Winton done this? It was a question that must be answered. But how?

Detective Constable Sykes, one of the SOCO team, approached Montague. 'Sir,' he said. 'I've searched for bodies; there's none in the shell of the car and none lying on the neighbouring moor. Shall we get to work on it now?'

'Yes, yes of course, DC Sykes. What do you think? Any chances of prints or other evidence?'

'I doubt it, sir, it's burnt to cinders — those places which would have borne prints have gone — internal mirror, steering wheel, dashboard, door handles … but we'll give it a thorough going-over. Is there anything we should be looking for especially?'

'The owner's prints, obviously, or anything belonging to her — jewellery, that sort of thing. Some of her belongings may have been disposed of — they might have been placed in the car for burning. Perhaps a blanket that covered her nakedness. And anything belonging to whoever drove it here. Man or woman. I need to know who brought this car here, DC Sykes — he or she might have left something behind, something which has survived the blaze. And remember whoever did bring it here had to get home afterwards. There might be some indication how that was achieved — two people, maybe, the man who fired the car and an accomplice — and I'll get a team working in this area to see if anyone noticed the flames or smoke. Not all moor fires, or suspected moor fires, are reported. And there may be footsteps in the earth, tyre marks, discarded cigarette ends, anything.'

'I'll make sure we give the entire scene a thorough going-over, sir,' promised Sykes, returning to his own vehicle for his equipment.

'Let me know if you find anything of interest,' requested Pluke, adding, 'I do not believe in interfering with experts while they're doing their duty.'

As this was formerly railway territory, Pluke realised it was scarcely good horse trough country and decided to return to base immediately. He went to his car, but Wayne was in the driving seat, fast asleep. Montague Pluke smiled as he went to arouse him, poking him in the ribs and saying, 'If you are going to stay asleep, Sergeant, I shall be compelled to drive us home.'

'God! Anything but that sir! I am awake, I was just resting my eyelids …' And he jerked himself into wakefulness and set about driving his boss back to the office.

Montague, wary of Wayne's excessively tired state, offered to drive, but Wayne would hear nothing of it. Even in his exhausted condition, Wayne considered he was a safer driver than Montague. During the journey, Montague kept Wayne awake by discussing the logistics of this case.

'What I want you to calculate, Wayne, is whether it is feasible that

Stephen Winton could have killed Tracy Bretton on Wednesday, probably at No. 15 Padgett Grove and probably during the evening. Consider whether he put her naked body in her own car, suitably covered, and drove out to the Druids' Circle for disposal of her corpse. Remember the watchfulness of Mrs Peat too. Did she see Winton at the house? And if so, was he there in suspicious circumstances? And remember that Winton said he did not know the girl — he told me that, he said he had never seen her before. We know he lied about visits to the Druids' Circle, so was he lying about this too? It would appear so. Certainly, Mrs Peat saw someone who looked like Winton and that same person also talked to Dunwoody in the presence of the girl. See what Dunwoody can tell us about that. He did recognise the girl, by the way, in the morgue. And having checked all that, find out if Winton could have driven her car on to these moors to set fire to it, and then returned to Fossford so that his movements or his absences were not unduly different from his normal routine. How feasible is it that he might have done all that alone, without help? If he did not set fire to her car, who did? And why?'

'I'll check his movements minutely, sir,' said Wayne, making a great effort to remain alert. 'I don't think he is guilty of murder, I'd like to see him cleared.'

'I know, Wayne, but if he had an accomplice throughout all this, who was it? We need to know that, and to know it quickly. The accomplice might be the killer, don't forget. And don't forget, too, that somebody has killed Winton. Was that done because Winton knew too much, got himself into this far too deeply perhaps? If Winton was killed for that reason, then he might not be the last of the killer's victims. This makes me wonder who else is involved and what, precisely, they are involved in. Has Winton's criminal record any bearing on this? And we need to find out what's behind the use of empty houses for making porn films. Perhaps the whole range of factors are intertwined, Wayne?'

'I'll do my best,' said Wayne, yawning long and loud.

In the police station yard, Wayne Wain parked carefully and locked the car, as Montague Pluke returned to the Incident Room.

'Go home and get some sleep, Wayne,' was his parting order. And so he did.

It was now four o'clock and some of the officers had broken off to have a cup of tea and a sandwich; those engaged on house-to-house duties had come in to the office to file their latest reports, while those working beyond easy access to the station would make their own arrangements for a tea-break. There was a lull in the activity but not in the conversation, for the officers on the case persisted in chatting about it even during their break periods.

When Pluke entered the Plukedom, he apprised those present about the car on the moors, stressing that it had belonged to the dead girl, but that the person who had torched it remained a mystery.

He asked them to bear the car in mind when making their enquiries. Details would be formally circulated in due course but what was desperately needed was a witness to describe anyone seen driving or being carried in the little red car in and around Crickledale since Saturday, with special emphasis on sightings since Wednesday.

One of the positive results of the house-to-house enquiries was that the detectives discovered another occasion where a private house had been used for making videos while the owners had been in America. It was an old-fashioned detached cottage at the west end of the town; the owners had returned unexpectedly to find their house-sitters — a man and a woman — engaged in film-making, using the house as a studio. That was about eighteen months ago, the detectives were told. As nothing illegal appeared to have happened, the house-sitters were told to leave, along with the film crew, and nothing more had been thought about it until the current investigation. It was not known whether the film had been pornographic or whether the completed film had been distributed. In view of the current enquiry, Montague's detective now questioned the house-owners, a Mr Tim and Mrs Catherine Moore, and they confirmed that the house-sitters had been found through a mutual friend.

They had not been hired through a known agency. Apart from their use of the house as a film set, the Moores did not have any other complaint — the sitters had tended the garden, cut the lawn, watered the flowers and fed the cat. On top of that they had left the house in a clean and tidy condition.

The Moores had not seen the film in either its complete or incomplete stages, but were now very concerned that their nice home could have been used for purposes which were abhorrent. Efforts would be made by the detectives to trace the couple concerned.

It was during these discussions over tea that the telephone rang and a voice called to Montague, 'It's for you, sir.'

'Who is it?' he asked.

'Doctor Taylor, sir, about the PM result.'

'I'll take it in my office,' said Pluke. There were times when the precise cause of death had to be kept from the staff, just in case they inadvertently let the press know, when the police wished to keep that knowledge to themselves. Accordingly, Detective Inspector Pluke adjourned to his tiny office and the call was put through.

'Good afternoon, Doctor Taylor,' greeted Pluke.

'Detective Inspector Pluke, nice to talk. You sent me a real puzzler here, you know.'

'Did I?' cried Pluke. 'In what way?'

'She was a young woman whose only medical problems were due to asthma. She was otherwise fit and healthy. An examination of her organs has not produced any indications of any toxins of any kind. She was not poisoned. She was not choked or asphyxiated in any way and I have found no internal injuries of any kind either. There was no drugs dependency, no needle marks on her body, she's not had injections and she was not an epileptic. There is no sign of embolism, no water in the lungs although there are slight signs of soap or shampoo beneath her nails ... very clean she was. That she died in the bath is a distinct possibility, Mr Pluke, as I believe you have already suggested. Just like your Mr Meredith, I cannot find any suspicious cause of death, Mr Pluke. There was no rape, no pregnancy although she was not a virgin. However, I did find that her lungs were over-distended and she had thickened bronchial walls with some blockages of the small air passages by viscous mucus. That looks rather like the white of an egg, Mr Pluke. And asthmatics can die suddenly, Mr Pluke, from a violent shock or even excitement. So in my opinion that is the cause of her death. In other words, she died naturally, but there is no sign of heart disease nor any indication of a blockage or circulatory problems. A rare cause of death, Mr Pluke. She just stopped living, Mr Pluke, she died of natural causes.'

'Natural causes?' Pluke shouted. 'But that's impossible ... I mean, Mr Taylor, the finding of the body where it was, and in such circumstances, nude, hidden, and now her car burnt out ... and the shooting of the man who found her body ... someone has done this to her, Mr Taylor. It cannot be natural causes. Surely, she was killed?'

'Perhaps someone *thinks* he has killed her, Mr Pluke, and then was panicked into disposing of the body in that way. Tell me what you know about the girl.'

Pluke obliged with an outline of her modelling activities and the pathologist listened intently.

When Pluke had finished, the pathologist said, 'I think she was in the bath, for reasons best known to herself, with water in it too I might add. Perhaps a man was with her and perhaps he did, or was about to do, something exciting to her or with her, with her consent. Maybe she was violently excited, or maybe she just panicked, Mr

Pluke. Whatever happened might have been part of the filming or maybe it was something else, but I think she died at that point. She did not drown, I can tell you that, there was no water in her lungs, but I cannot help further, except to say the brown fibre found in her toe nail is consistent with those found on domestic blankets. I cannot be more specific. All I can say is that you do not have a murder enquiry on your hands, Mr Pluke. A mystery perhaps, but not a murder. It cannot be murder. She died naturally. That is my conclusion and I might add that, because of the difficulty in establishing the cause of death, it is supported by two of my colleagues.'

'I'm sure there were two people involved ...' began Pluke.

'Involved in what, Mr Pluke? If she died naturally, there is no crime, is there? No reason for your investigation?'

Pluke paused for a long time to ponder that remark, then said, 'You'll be letting me have your usual written report?'

'I will, Mr Pluke. Good-evening.' And the telephone died. Pluke sat and looked at it for a moment, trying to come to terms with what he had heard, but found it hard to believe. Surely the pathologists were wrong? This death had all the elements of a murder, a *crime passionnel* perhaps, but murder none the less, so how could any pathologist, in spite of the findings, suggest there had been no offence?

There was a knock on the door and Inspector Horsley walked in. 'They said it was the path lab calling.' He stood before Pluke, eager to know the result of the examination. 'Any joy, Montague?'

'Sit down, Mr Horsley.'

Horsley sat.

'You're not going to believe this,' began Pluke when Horsley was comfortable.

'Try me,' invited Horsley.

After a pause, Pluke said, 'It's no crime.'

'No crime?' puzzled Horsley. 'What do you mean?'

'She died of natural causes,' said Pluke. 'Taylor, supported by two of his colleagues, confirms she died of natural causes, the cause of her death being linked to her asthmatic condition.'

'I don't believe that!' cried Horsley. 'And that pathologist knows the circumstances of the discovery of her body? Naked? In that fake burial chamber?'

'He knows everything, Mr Horsley, but he did say it was a fairly rare cause of death. He has tried all the tests — no drugs or poisons have been traced in her body. She died a natural death, that's all there is to it. Sudden and shocking perhaps, but completely natural due to her asthmatic condition.'

'Well, in my view, she died in very unnatural circumstances, Montague. What we need is a second opinion.'

'He was the second opinion, Mr Horsley, and he got two supporting opinions from his colleagues. Imagine trying to prosecute someone for murder if four pathologists state the death was from natural causes!'

'So, what do we do now?' asked Horsley, deflated by the news.

'I'll have to report to Jack Hart. He'll wind up the enquiry.'

'There's no time like the present,' said Horsley.

Montague lifted the handset to call his boss, Detective Superintendent Jack Hart, at Force Headquarters.

He was still in his office and listened with interest. 'Fine, great news, Montague,' he oozed. 'End of enquiry, eh? No murder, therefore no murder enquiry. The Chief'll be delighted — that's one less major enquiry to run away with his precious funds and no undetected murders to fret about in the annual statistics. Close down, Montague, terminate the enquiry, disband the detectives and close the Incident Room. Organise a press conference for tomorrow morning to tell the public and start wrapping everything up.'

'But there's that other death, sir, in Fossford, it was a murder ...'

'That's not your problem, Montague. Pass any files you have

collected to Boddy and Sole and let them sort it out.'

'But we were getting close to a possible ring of pornographic-film-makers, sir, our enquiries were beginning to bear fruit ...'

'That's not the sort of enquiry that demands a full murder Incident Room and teams of detectives, Montague. That's for the Porn Squad. Tell them what you have discovered, let them see the files and get them to sort it out.'

'But the body, sir, the girl who was found in the Druids' Circle, she did not die a natural death ...'

'I thought the forensic pathologist said she had?'

'Well, it was a natural death, sir, but in very unnatural circumstances.'

'That doesn't make it murder, Montague. The death itself was natural, irrespective of what happened to the body afterwards. What we might be left with is a minor offence under the Burial Laws or something similar. Tell the duty inspector about that aspect of things, then have a word with the coroner about these findings and get him to authorise burial. And that's it, Montague. It's over. No murder. That's good news for our crime stats.' And Hart replaced the telephone.

'What's he say?' demanded Horsley.

'We're to close down. He says I must tell the coroner and close down the enquiry because it's no longer a murder investigation,' said Montague with some sorrow.

'What a shame, I was beginning to enjoy this, Montague. I thought we were on the trail of her killer ...'

'Somebody was involved in that death, Mr Horsley, and in my view it was totally unnatural; whatever happened to that girl was not natural, her body was hidden and her car destroyed.'

'But if it's not murder, our role is over, Montague.'

'The town will not like it. This is a clean-living town full of decent people who wouldn't want dirty films being made surreptitiously in their midst. If a girl dies like that within our boundaries, we should be able to track down those responsible, murder or no murder.'

'The porn business can be dealt with by the Porn Squad,' said Horsley. 'The question of an unburied body at the Druids' Circle can be left to the town sergeant, as can the problem of the unauthorised taking of the car and its firing. That's assuming of course that the body was taken to the Druids' Circle after death. We don't know that for sure, do we, Montague? She might have died there, in the nude, without anyone else being present or involved. People do frolic nude in woods and glades, for reasons best known to themselves. And on top of that, the countryside is full of rubbish which includes burnt-out cars taken by joy-riders and the like, this one's no different. But if there is no murder, we need not hang on to her body, which means the girl can have a decent burial once the coroner gives the go-ahead. She deserves that, at least.'

'In isolation, those matters are each of relatively little importance, I will agree with you on that,' said Montague. 'But placed together they create something infinitely more sinister.'

'Montague? You are not reading more in to this sequence of events than necessary, are you? Look at it this way — let us say the girl died in the chamber of the Druids' Circle. She went in there, lay down and died, leaving her clothes in the car. Some yobbo comes along and nicks the car, as they do, used it for a joy ride and burnt it afterwards — like they do. Yobbo and death are not linked in any way. Nasty coincidences, no more than that. I agree it's not very nice, but it is still not murder. She died from natural causes, Montague. That is beyond dispute.'

'The man who found the body was murdered, let us not forget.' Montague spoke solemnly.

'Another nasty coincidence. We have no proof that his death is linked to hers, have we? If he hadn't found the body, someone else would have done.'

'I do feel there are links between the deaths. Certain similarities ...'

'Forget it, Montague, it's over. I'm sorry if you were hoping to solve the crime of the century, but this is not the time. Shall I break the news to the teams?'

'Yes. Call them in. I'll explain.' But Montague Pluke was unhappy about this development.

'And you will explain to your sergeant?'

'Yes, in due course. I have sent Detective Sergeant Wain home, he had a very exhausting night.'

'So I understand!' breathed Horsley who had heard of Wain's exploits. He got up to leave the tiny office. 'You know, Montague, I was looking forward to seeing this enquiry through to its conclusion. You were making a decent job of it.'

'I have not finished yet,' said Montague with determination.

'Not finished. What do you mean?'

'Any murder enquiry turns up a lot of dirt in any town or village; we discover the undercurrent of life, Mr Horsley, and our investigations to date have shown there is a filthy underbelly to Crickledale. Sordid things have clearly been going on right under our noses ...'

'But if we do not get complaints, then it does not concern us. And we have not had complaints, have we?'

'As a law enforcement officer, I think it does matter and it does concern us.'

'We are not the keepers of public morals, Montague,' Horsley reminded him. 'Sin and crime are not necessarily the same thing.'

'Someone helped to remove that girl's body from No. 15 Padgett Grove in the belief she had been murdered, I am convinced of that,' Montague said. 'And if those persons believed they had murdered her, then, in my eyes, that is tantamount to murder. It was murder in their minds.'

'Or accidental death followed by panic?'

'The answer lies in Crickledale, Mr Horsley, and it is linked to the death of Stephen Winton who was involved in our case. I am going to find the answer, whether or not the Chief allows this investigation to proceed.'

'I hope you find the answers you want, Montague,' said Horsley, rising to his feet. 'Right, I'll set about recalling the officers. A briefing in, say, an hour?'

'Yes, that will be very suitable,' sighed Montague Pluke.

*

Detective Superintendent Jack Hart rang Detective Inspector Boddy at Fossford and said, 'John, the woman in the Crickledale enquiry died naturally. So it's no murder out here in the sticks. How's that affect things at your end?'

'Our only known link between Winton and the Crickledale death was his finding of the body. And if that body was not murdered, there might not be a connection between his death and the events at the Druids' Circle.'

'Can we dismiss any likely links then?'

'Not according to your man Pluke. He thinks Winton was involved in her death.'

'But if her death was not murder, then how is that relevant?'

'Pluke insists that someone else was involved with her death, but in spite of that, I do need information from Crickledale, sir. There could still be a link between Winton and that girl, and with her death and his death, and with the filming of pornographic acts. We found a lot of pornographic photographs and negatives in his flat; he'd taken them for magazines. We found acceptance notes and statements of accounts for them. Some might contain pictures of your dead girl and her friends.'

'Fine, so there could still be a link? We'll co-operate with your lads, but I've stood down our Incident Room at Crickledale. No murder means no investigation, and no expenditure. Liaise with Pluke; he'll give you every assistance to examine our files and he'll tell you if any of the girls in Winton's pictures is our deceased.'

'Thanks, sir.'

*

That same evening, the coroner for Crickledale and District ordered the release of the body of Tracy Bretton and asked that the relatives be informed that the death was natural. It meant that her funeral could proceed. Detective Inspector Pluke pushed a note through Wayne Wain's letter-box to announce these developments, because there was no response to his knocking. Wayne was in a deep and refreshing sleep.

Tomorrow would be Saturday which, along with Sunday, were Pluke's usual scheduled rest days. Under normal circumstances, he would have taken them off, but not during a murder enquiry; as things stood, he would have to go in to the office to wind up the enquiry. Wayne Wain, however, could have the weekend off, so Pluke included that in his note. He said he would see Wain on Monday morning in the office.

Somewhat disappointed by events, Montague Pluke left for home, raising his panama to the ladies of the town *en route* and bidding good-evenings to everyone he encountered. It was not a very pleasant walk, he felt; the air was oppressive and the atmosphere sticky. Thunder was still a threat but had not yet arrived; the air was thick with thunderbugs and replete with an ominous feeling. He found that his shirt collar was sticking to his neck and that he was perspiring. As he walked briskly homewards, he realised that the skies were blackening and dark clouds were moving from the west. Rain — and a storm — was clearly due. It was with some relief that he entered the house, where he planted a kiss on the cheek of his loving wife who asked, 'Had a nice day, dear?'

'Not really,' he replied, hanging up his panama and coat.

'Well never mind, it's the Local History Society meeting tonight and you are speaking to them, remember!'

'Yes, of course.'

'Perhaps something about the murder enquiry? I know our members would love to hear from someone on the inside of a major investigation, Montague.'

'You know I cannot divulge professional matters to the public, Millicent. I might tell them about that series of Yorkshire civic horse troughs. Did you know that several have Roman numerals carved on the front? Fascinating troughs, lots of riveting information for a thrilling lecture, Millicent.'

'As you say, dear, I know you do not like talking about police work.'

'One needs to get away from the pressures of office, Millicent,' said Montague Pluke. 'Now, we might have to consider taking the car, it looks the picture of rain outside.'

'It was forecast, dear,' she said. 'Heavy showers with thunder in places. I hope it doesn't prevent our members turning out to listen to you.'

The thunder started to rumble as Montague was settling down for his meal and he looked out of the window. The rain began to beat down with all the ferocity that a sudden storm could produce and within seconds the road outside had the appearance of a river. And then the lightning flashed, to be followed by another roll of thunder.

'Thunder on a Friday means the death of a great man,' said Montague to Millicent.

*

Millicent wondered whether she should tell Montague of the gossip about events at Cyril's and May's bungalow, and about the demands of Mrs Councillor Farrell, but decided that he was not in a very good mood at the moment. Perhaps he would mellow by this evening?

But she did wonder whether Crickledale had any great men, and whether one of them was about to die. Unless it was an omen about the Prime Minister.

which they knew was about. And if please, it was perhaps about the famous Marater,

Chapter 15

Due to the unsettling news from the forensic pathologist, Montague Pluke's concentration was not one hundred per cent upon the subject of his lecture. Somehow, tonight's discourse on 'The Civic Horse Troughs of Yorkshire' was not as riveting as it should have been, because his mind persisted in wandering towards the Druids' Circle and its naked mystery. The puzzle which embraced the turmoil of the girl's last hours would not eradicate itself from his brain and compelled him to struggle with his talk in an attempt to make it fascinating. As he forged ahead, he gained a distinct feeling that his audience was not particularly interested in civic horse troughs, a shame because tonight's attendance was greater than usual in spite of the weather. Montague attributed this to his own drawing power, but in fact numbers were high because several wives had insisted upon being accompanied by their husbands due to fears about the rampant murderer/rapist who was at large in the Crickledale district.

Montague lumbered among the lighter gems of his subject in a vain hope of creating some sparks of interest. He explained how, in Roman times, the civic leaders of the invaders had commissioned ornately carved stone troughs to be installed outside their palaces for the sole use of their horses. Horses belonging to lesser mortals were not allowed to drink from that water. Troughs were plentiful in the market squares of Roman villages, then known as the forum, but few had survived.

During the first century AD, there had been a particularly fine specimen at Verulamium, now known as St Albans, but no trace remained and perhaps the most noteworthy was a Roman stone trough at Habitancum which bore a carved figure thought to be that of Vercingetorix, the Gallic leader defeated by Julius Caesar.

Another trough of note in more modern times was that which Queen Victoria had ordered; it was a specially made cast-iron edifice with a triple bowl and brass fittings. It bore the royal insignia and had been placed near the gates of Buckingham Palace for the refreshment of her horses and only her horses. Common horses could not enjoy the royal water and in fact, one of the royal coach horses would never pass that trough without halting for a swift intake of a gallon or two. Others of renown included the Byzantine trough of Birmingham, an elegant five-holer known as the Quinquetrough of Killiecrankie, the Italian-style horse trough outside the medieval town hall in Bradford, and one of Dutch design near Hull docks.

'Thus the humble horse trough embodies all that is great in the history of our splendid country. It is, in fact, a permanent record of the development of Great Britain,' was Montague's finale, and he accepted the polite applause of his audience with his customary grace. He announced he had a selection of his photographs if anyone wished to inspect them — they were laid out on a table behind him, each endorsed with details of the trough portrayed. He'd also brought copies of his book which was for sale, autographed, at the discount price of £3.50. Finally, when he said he was prepared to answer any questions, one gentleman raised his hand and asked, 'Have you arrested that bloke what killed that lass, Mr Pluke?' It was Jim Bealey speaking from the back row.

'Well, Mr Bealey, this is hardly the place to ask that question, particularly as it is not linked to the history of civic horse troughs …' he began but was immediately interrupted by the chairman of the meeting.

'Crickledonians would like to know whether you've caught him or are likely to catch him, Mr Pluke,' said the chairman, Arthur Norris. 'There is much concern in the town, I might add. Great and deep concern in fact. We appreciate there are matters of professional secrecy in a major investigation of this kind, but the townspeople are very alarmed and worried. I mean to say, if there's a maniac murderer and rapist at loose among us, nobody's safe, our wives, daughters and girlfriends are at risk, Mr Pluke. That's why some menfolk have come tonight, to protect our women.'

This diversion was most irregular and Montague Pluke was uncertain how to frame his response. The fact that Tracy Bretton had died from natural causes had not yet been made public and he felt it was unfair to reveal that to the Local History Society before any official announcement was made. The police and the public should be first to know, not the Local History Society. The formal announcement was due in the morning, at the press conference and so, after a moment's thought, he adopted a truly diplomatic response. 'Mr Norris, we are conducting thorough enquiries and have made very sound progress. I shall make an important official announcement tomorrow morning.'

'Aye, that's mebbe so, but have you arrested anybody?' persisted Mr Bealey.

'No, we cannot arrest anyone until all the facts have been gathered and assessed,' countered Pluke. 'We need evidence before we can arrest a suspect. We need to be sure we have arrested the right person. In any murder investigation there are many suspects, most of whom are eventually eliminated from the enquiry. It's a long process, one that's very delicate. We cannot proceed to arrest those who we feel are guilty unless we have very firm evidence of their guilt to present to a court of law.'

'There's that bloke in Fossford an' all,' continued Bealey. 'Him that was murdered. I heard it on the news. And he found that lass at the Circle. Two dead, eh? Two with links with yon circle of old stones.

So how many more, Mr Pluke? How many more must die before they catch the bloke who's doing it? As ratepayers, we need to feel safe in our beds. Well, council tax payers. Anyroad, they should bring back hanging, that's what I say.'

'All I can suggest is that we all wait until tomorrow's announcement.' Pluke found himself sweating as the audience began to grow restless in their concern about the harrowing events in Crickledale. He felt he had to quell any disturbance before it developed into a full-blown riot. 'Now, any questions about horse troughs? Are you sure how, when and why the first drainage holes were incorporated in troughs made from stone?'

'You'd have been better talking about them murders, Mr Pluke,' said Bealey, rising from his seat to leave the premises. 'It would have done us all more good.'

'Well, if there are no more questions …?' The chairman stood up. 'I will ask Mrs Gurden to propose a vote of thanks to our esteemed speaker, Mr Montague Pluke.'

'I think he ought to do summat about those goings-on on the cricket field,' muttered a woman from one of the centre rows. She managed to voice her complaint in a moment of utter silence as the applause faded, before Mrs Gurden, her back as troublesome as ever, could struggle to her feet to proffer the formal vote of thanks. And even though she had not intended her comment to be broadcast to the audience, Pluke heard it.

'Not more thefts from the pavilion, Mrs Holtby?' he asked her before the chairman could formally bring the meeting to a close, simultaneously recalling one of his major investigative triumphs.

'Thefts, Mr Pluke?' There was a note of provocation in her voice. 'Nowt so simple as that. No, this is sordid stuff, immoral behaviour, carnal goings-on. Not the sort of behaviour you expect on the cricket pitch of a town like Crickledale, even in modern times. Indecent exposure if you ask me, all of them folks cavorting about in their birthday suits up and down between the wickets and in and out of the pavilion at full moon … nudists, I reckon, from a caravan rally or summat. Your men should be stopping all that sort of thing. It's not decent, allowing that sort of thing in Crickledale, especially before a cup match.'

'We have had no complaints …' began Pluke, wishing to explain that the police could not take action unless there was a formal complaint.

'I should think not, all of them fellers ogling those young women, husbands of folks who ought to know better. You'd not expect fellers to complain about nude women cavorting on their cricket pitch, would you?'

'Well, er, some might …'

'That sort o' thing would fill the spectators' gallery in no time if it happened in daylight. By, I don't know, things is changing and not for the better if you ask me.'

'I note your concern, Mrs Holtby, but which men were ogling them?'

'Them that lives around the cricket field for a start. I know all about it, my Stan told me … disgusting it is. Was. Behaviour like that. Naked as the day they were born, some of them women. And being filmed an' all.'

'Filmed?' questioned Pluke.

'Aye, some had cameras and lights.'

'Well, all I can say is that if we get a complaint from the cricket club, or even from a member of the public, we shall investigate the problem.' Pluke was proud of the diplomatic streak he was displaying right now 'And I assure you, Mrs Holtby and everyone else, that once the Crickledale police do get a formal complaint of improper conduct on our cricket pitch, it will be investigated with the full weight of the law. I might add, however, that the cricket club and its grounds are private property and the police do not have complete jurisdiction over all the events which occur there. There are certain practices, some of which might involve consenting adults, which may occur in private without penalty, but which may become illegal if they were in a public place, like being nude in certain circumstances, whether or not there are consenting adults.'

As Montague waffled on, everyone looked at Mrs Holtby, wondering if she would dare to state formally that she would make a complaint about the matter, but she shook her head.

'Will you make an official complaint, Mrs Holtby?' Pluke directed the question specifically to her.

'Nay, Mr Pluke, not me. You won't get me having my name put down in police records. Besides, I never saw nowt, it's just what I heard.'

'Well.' Pluke smiled. 'I suggest that whose who are concerned should have a word with someone in authority at the cricket club or perhaps a householder in one of the houses which overlook the ground, and ask a responsible person to make a formal complaint to us at the police station. The matter will then be investigated, taking into account all that happened and, of course, basing any action upon the criminal law relating to that particular subject.'

That solid statement seemed to have the desired effect because there were no more questions, no more comments — and no formal complaint about frolics on the field between the stumps, near short leg or close to silly mid-on. Christine Gurden thanked Mr Pluke for his fascinating account of Yorkshire horse troughs and said that his revelations would make her excursions on to the moors and into the dales much more interesting in the future. She had no idea that Roman horses were so particular in their drinking habits or that there was so much to know about horse troughs. She was particularly interested to hear that an early horse trough in Scarborough had once been supplied with the original spa water. By drinking it, the horses of the time had produced superb shining coats and could gallop all day on one fill-up. It worked some wonders for humans too.

Following her remarks, the gathering dispersed. As the people returned to their homes, Montague gathered up his notes and photographs, thanked the officials for their hospitality and walked away with Millicent on his arm.

'You were so good, Montague,' she oozed. 'You spoke with such authority and your knowledge is astonishing. I was so proud of you.'

'Thank you, my dear.' He smiled in the darkness as they moved steadily through the deserted streets of Crickledale. 'But I felt the minds of most of the members were upon the murder and not upon the subject of my discourse.'

'That is not surprising, it is big news, Montague. There is concern in the town. I know you hate to talk about your work, but these crimes have upset a lot of people. Women dare not go out alone at night — you saw how many had husbands with them at the meeting.'

'I wish someone would make complaints to us if they are worried about events and goings-on in the town. There has been no complaint about those people prancing about on the cricket pitch. How can we undertake our duties if people do not keep us informed? How can we protect the public if we do not know what they need protecting against?'

'They probably don't want to bother you, with you being so busy keeping crime down. I mean, frolicking naked on the cricket pitch is hardly a criminal matter, dear, and from what I heard, some of those who witnessed it thought it was hilarious, not the sort of thing to complain about to a hard-worked police force.' She wondered what some of the men must have looked like and what position the stumps were in at the time of the frolicsome cavortings.

'You knew about it?' He sounded shocked.

'Well, yes, we ladies do keep informed of things that happen in the town, you know. Our meetings are important for that reason, we do keep up to date.'

'But you did not mention it to me, Millicent!' And he sounded shocked and hurt.

'You always insist on keeping your police duties quite apart from your domestic life, Montague, so I did not feel I should trespass upon your off-duty time. I do not like to worry you with such things when you are relaxing after a hard day's work.'

'Well, there could be exceptions in exceptional circumstances ...'

She could not miss this opportunity. 'Montague, I would like to mention that there is a lot of concern about May's and Cyril's house, all that activity in recent times, and that murder of the girl, and whether she is their niece ...'

'What activity precisely?' he pressed her.

'Well, Mrs Peat from No. 14 saw all sorts ...'

'Saw all sorts?'

'A nude man, and parties and things ...'

'My God, what is happening in Crickledale?' he burst out. 'People witnessing all manner of doubtful activities with never a word to the police ... really, Millicent, I am most disturbed at this lack of co-operation from the public. How can we do our job in such circumstances? These are matters of grave importance ...'

'One of your detectives did come to take a statement from her, Montague. Now, you must not get too excited, dear, people do gossip and none of us wants to trouble you in your off-duty times ... I know they were making fun about the cricket field, it was hardly a matter of great concern ...'

'But it could be linked to the murders, Millicent ...'

'You can't be serious, Montague?' she cried.

'I am very serious, Millicent.' He spoke strongly. 'I am most interested in the references to photographing the antics on the cricket field. Since beginning this investigation — this very trying investigation — I have come to believe there is a great deal of photography of naked people going on in Crickledale.'

'Oh, Montague, how dreadful!' She hoped she sounded shocked and not intrigued.

'I truly believe so. I am not speaking out of place when I say that Cyril's and May's house might have been used for that purpose, without their knowledge I might add, and I believe it may be occurring in the surrounding countryside.' He felt he could tell her a little of the background to his enquiry. 'After all, the beautiful landscape around us is idyllic and lends itself to romantic thoughts and unwise freedoms. If this sort of thing is happening, then I, as custodian of the Queen's Peace in Crickledale, should know who is involved. And I don't. All I know is that a lovely girl has died, who is not the niece of May or Cyril.'

'No?'

'No, she was house-sitting for them. That is all, and using it as a set for filming — and I believe some local people are involved, Millicent. I need to know who they are.'

'Maybe you should speak to the Camera Club?' she suggested. Millicent had never heard Montague speak about his work at such length. She hoped he would continue. This was much more interesting than horse troughs. He even smiled when she mentioned the Camera Club.

'Now that's a good idea,' he agreed as they reached their front door. 'Yes, Millicent, that is a very good idea indeed.'

And he walked into his comfortable home with a smile on his face.

*

Because the natural cause of Tracy's death had not been released to the press, all the Saturday morning papers carried front-page articles about the progress of the murder investigation of Crickledale. The bizarre circumstances surrounding Tracy's death had ensured maximum publicity combined with speculative reporting, even though it was noticeably devoid of facts and truths.

The tabloid stories had dreamt up tales of black masses, witchcraft, sun worship, multiple orgies and pornographic film-making. There were hints of Bacchanalian revels in wooded glades or terpsichorean sprees beside crystal-clear moorland streams.

The tales were guaranteed to attract tourists to the places mentioned — already an ice-cream van had been noticed near the entrance to the Druids' Circle, according to local intelligence. In addition, Crickledale Estate was contemplating a gate across the road to the Druids' Circle, plus a turnstile, and were considering an increased fee. £1 did not seem adequate for such a famous place and huge crowds were expected during forthcoming weekends.

Most of the accounts now incorporated the Druids' Circle along with ribald stories of goings-on rumoured to have taken place there. It was mainly rubbish, but it did get the townspeople talking — and that is what the CID required. But it was too late now. There had been no murder. There was no such crime to solve in Crickledale.

None the less, there were things to conclude in the office and on that Saturday morning Pluke's walk through the town took far longer than usual. Greater numbers of Crickledonians stopped him to ask about progress — and in all cases he said there was to be an announcement later that morning. Although it was a Saturday, the town seemed extraordinarily busy, even at this early hour, and after much raising of his panama and bidding of good-morning, he arrived at the office half an hour later than usual. He went through his normal arrival routine, tidied his desk, checked the correspondence, then noticed that Wayne Wain had also come to work. That was dedication and it would be noted in Wayne's personal record. But why had he come in if the investigation was over?

Wayne was in the Control Room, checking the night's inventory of minor crime and Mrs Plumpton was at work too, even though it was her normal day off. Pluke felt so proud of his team as she followed him into his office.

'Anything of interest before we finalise things?' he asked her.

'Yes, Mr Pluke, there's a circular from Fossford about the murder of Stephen Winton.'

'About time too!' he muttered. 'What's it say?'

'It links him with the finding of Tracy's body but does not ask for any special enquiries in Crickledale,' she answered.

'Our officers are not required to work on their behalf, Mrs Plumpton, particularly as we have no crime to solve. A team of detectives will come from Fossford to make enquiries in Crickledale,' he informed her. 'And they will want access to the information we have assembled to see whether any firm links can be established. I have no objection to that; in fact, I welcome it, especially if it helps to bring the murderer to justice. Please give them every co-operation. I would have hoped I would have received similar co-operation from them, had our enquiry become protracted.'

Followed by Wayne Wain, Pluke then made his way to the Incident Room where the formal closure of the investigation would be done at 10 a.m.; it would be followed by debriefing of the teams and completion of any outstanding paperwork. Horsley could have done that task in Pluke's absence, but now that Pluke had arrived, he agreed to take the appropriate action.

From a personal point of view, he was upset because it meant he had no justification in arranging in-depth enquiries into the lives of several Crickledale citizens, such as the Dunwoodys, Ephraim Holliday, the Crowthers and even Ron Brown alias Marcel Boussicourt from Teesside. Likewise, he could hardly justify a searching investigation of the Camera Club or any of the other Crickledale institutions. In many ways that would be a shame.

'So who will take the news conference?' asked Inspector Horsley, bringing Pluke's mind back to the facts of the case.

'It will have to be me,' said Pluke removing his panama and coat as he settled in to the morning duties. 'As officer in charge of the former investigation, I must explain the situation.'

And so the time came for the news conference. The press had been told, during their routine calls to the Control Room, that Detective Inspector Pluke was going to make a very important statement this morning, and this had been interpreted by many as news of an arrest or some other highly significant break-through. Accordingly, a lot of journalists and photographers arrived. The large turn-out had been assembled in the lecture room at the police station and Mrs Plumpton had had the bright idea of using some of the surplus milk, sugar and coffee to supply them with drinks. This added to the importance of the occasion. For the police to give journalists refreshments at a news conference was indeed a major development and heralded news of some magnitude — at least in the minds of the waiting journalists.

There was a loud hubbub of conversation as Montague Pluke led in his team, which comprised Inspector Horsley and Detective Sergeant Wayne Wain. They made for three chairs positioned behind a trestle table upon which someone had placed a white cloth, a carafe of water and three glasses, another sign of the importance of this occasion.

'Is it a multiple killer you're after?' shouted a journalist from their midst before they were seated.

'Arrest of local councillor after death orgy in ancient druids' stone circle,' called another, trying to pre-empt tomorrow's headlines,

'Naked Model in Druid Death Drama,' cried another, quoting the heading in one of today's tabloids.

There was a mood of cheerfulness among the journalists, as some photographers took pictures of Montague and his colleagues as they settled in their pre-arranged seats. A triple-headed news conference was indeed a rarity.

'Gentlemen,' shouted Montague. 'Ladies and gentlemen,' he repeated upon seeing several female reporters, and he rapped the table with a gavel conveniently placed by Mrs Plumpton. They lapsed into a respectful silence.

'My name is Detective Inspector Montague Pluke of Crickledale CID.' He introduced himself, then his colleagues. 'I wish to thank you all for the coverage you have already given to our quest for information surrounding the death of Tracy Bretton,' he began. 'I need not elaborate upon the facts already known to you — your papers have covered the story in their individual ways and the coverage has produced a lot of valuable information for my officers. But' — and he paused for effect — 'when her body was examined by a forensic scientist yesterday — having earlier been examined by a local pathologist who could not determine the cause of death — he concluded that Tracy's death was from natural causes.'

Montague paused at this point, but the importance of his words was overlooked momentarily as the reporters wrote down or taped his words. And then, seconds later, the reality of the situation dawned upon them. Pandemonium broke loose, as they all began to ask questions at the same time. Montague, relishing his moment of power, held up a hand to quell the noise and they lapsed into silence once again.

'For those who missed the importance of that announcement,' he repeated, 'I stated that Tracy Bretton died from natural causes.' He paused again. 'She was not murdered. The investigation is therefore concluded. There was no crime.'

One of the journalists, a large, solidly built man, stood up and spoke for the others. 'But Mr Pluke, if my memory serves me right, and bearing in mind this is not the first news conference, may I remind you that your earlier statements led us to believe that the body was found naked at the Druids' Circle with no apparent means of getting there. Added to that, you told us that the deceased girl's car was fired on the moors and, from our own investigation, we know there has been a lot of porn-film-making in this town, and that she was a porn model … and now the man who found her is dead, murdered, in Fossford … and you say there is no crime?'

'I am saying that Tracy Bretton was not murdered. That is a statement of fact. She died from natural causes,' emphasised Montague. 'That is the opinion of not one, but four pathologists. All experts, I might add. I might also add that it was not the result that I foresaw.'

'But she was naked … dumped …'

'I am aware of that. I am vividly aware of all the surrounding factors, gentlemen, but facts are facts,' Montague said loudly. 'Whatever the circumstances of Tracy's arrival at the Druids' Circle, she died from natural causes. Whatever happened to her mortal remains after death, she was not murdered. This investigation will therefore close as of this moment.'

'But you will be trying to find out what happened, surely?' pleaded the same large reporter. 'And there is the Fossford murder, surely associated with this one?'

'Fossford police are making their own enquiries into that death, albeit without the death of Tracy Bretton being categorised as murder. We shall help them with their enquiries if they ask. Officers from Crickledale police will make enquiries about the burnt-out car — don't forget she might have driven it to the moor herself and disposed of it in that way — and there will be enquiries about the possibility of an offence in contravention of the Burial Laws so far as the body is concerned. However, we cannot rule out the fact she might have lain down and died in that cave without the aid of any other person. And that is not a criminal offence. But because the girl was not the victim of murder, this investigation is over. The coroner has ordered that the body be returned to the relatives for burial. The case is closed.'

Sensing they would receive no further enlightenment from Montague Pluke, the journalists rushed from the meeting to file their first copy or to catch any local news bulletins. But if Montague Pluke thought that announcement would end the press coverage of the death of Tracy Bretton, he was sadly mistaken. It prompted the reporters to decide to find out for themselves what had really happened. Having phoned in their headline news to the effect that Tracy Bretton was a murder victim who had not been murdered, they turned their attention to the known facts. The finder of her body had been murdered, her car had been burnt to a cinder on remote moorland and her body had been dumped naked in the burial chamber of a fake Druids' Circle — but she had not been murdered. All these factors combined to deepen the mystery of the Druids' Circle and to ensure that it became part of Crickledale folklore.

*

After dismissing the detectives, Montague Pluke thanked Inspector Horsley for his meticulous supervision of the Incident Room, to which Horsley replied he hoped they would work together again; he had enjoyed the experience, even though the enquiry had had such a premature and unsatisfactory finale. The closing down of the Incident Room would be completed by lunchtime, and so everyone could have the Saturday afternoon off duty, a rare bonus for a detective.

Montague Pluke went home. Millicent had his lunch ready and he settled down with her to explain the situation, before enjoying his lamb chops with new potatoes and peas. She was sad about the news and unhappy for Montague.

Being already prominent in Crickledale, she had hoped she might become known as the wife of the man who solved Crickledale's first murder enquiry and arrested a vicious killer. But it was not to be.

'I think we should get out of the house,' said Millicent after lunch. 'After all, it is Saturday and you do need a break. I think a walk would be nice.'

'And I agree, Millicent,' sighed Montague. 'To go hunting for horse troughs in the fresh moorland air would be most invigorating.'

'You always said you had never been to Trattledale,' she reminded him. 'That deserted valley.'

'It was going to be turned into a reservoir,' Montague recalled. 'It's full of deserted farms and cottages, ruined buildings galore, but access has been closed to the public for years.'

'That's right, well, there was an article in the *Gazette* about it,' she said. 'Yesterday's edition. I know you haven't had time to read it, but those plans have been abandoned now that the Water Authority has been privatised, and the National Park Authority is trying to get money from the National Lottery to repair all those tumbledown houses. They're going to revive the dale, Montague, they're even talking of turning them into a theme park or a holiday complex ...'

'Have you got the paper handy?' he asked.

'I kept it for you.' She went across to the magazine rack in the lounge and returned with the *Gazette*, open at the page in question.

It showed a view of upper Trattledale with a hamlet comprising a ruined farmstead, outbuildings and several cottages. There were other similar ruins in the dale. Of those in the photograph, most had their roofs missing, several had walls missing too, and in every case the ruins were overgrown with vegetation. It was a picture of dereliction and desertion, the result of the dale being cleared of its resident population in readiness for the flooding which had never happened.

'I know we have never been there and I thought we might visit the dale, to seek more horse troughs, before those plans are put into action. I mean, Montague, there could be abandoned horse troughs galore up there and if the place is going to be renovated, they might be disposed of, lost for ever, unless you record them.'

'I intended making a visit years ago,' he mused. 'Then it was placed out of bounds to the public. When the Authority bought the land, they closed all the roads and cordoned off the dale.'

He quietly studied the report, examined the photographs and said, 'Yes, I think I would like to visit Trattledale. I will enjoy a break from police work.'

'I'll get the car out while you get ready then,' she offered.

He found his map of the moors, made sure he had his notebook and camera in his pocket, and then, as Millicent was locking the garage doors, picked up the newspaper to re-examine the report and to have another look at the photograph of the ruins.

It was then he noticed a crow upon the roof of one of the derelict buildings.

Chapter 16

Montague Pluke recognised the hamlet in the picture. It was called Little Larrock and was situated deep in Trattledale. Years ago, this long-dead community had comprised a ruined nunnery, a flour mill, several farms and a handful of cottages. It had featured in some early topographical books and its subsequent fate had spawned articles in the local press and magazines, as well as the occasional feature on radio or television. As time went by, however, doubtless exacerbated by its 'No Entry' signs and lack of vehicular access, it had gradually ceased to be of interest and the place had become derelict in readiness for its transformation into a reservoir. But that had never happened and the dale had developed into a wilderness, a haven for wildlife.

Now that the Water Authority had abandoned its scheme, access was again permitted, with hikers and tourists visiting the ruins and exploring the neglected paths. There was a haunting beauty about the place, a hint of moorland mystery and romance. It was firmly back on the tourist trail.

Larrock was an old local word meaning skylark, a bird which frequented this isolated region. Reclining in a slightly elevated part of Trattledale, the hamlet featured in folk stories of Yorkshire because, years ago, a man had died while building one of the houses. That would have occurred some hundred and eighty years ago, but the story lingered because of a superstition linked to such an accident. It was thought that if a person died while working upon a new building, that building would always be an unhappy one and that other deaths would occur on the premises.

As a matter of local history, Montague Pluke had researched that death — the name of the deceased did not come readily to mind, but there was no doubt it had been accidental. There was no question of murder or suicide, but the house in question — the one on the extreme right of his picture — had endured a long history of sadness. Illness, bad fortune and problems with livestock and children had all come to residents of Laverock Cottage. The latest sadness, of course, had been the plan to turn the entire dale into a reservoir and thus drown the houses and fields, but in spite of the good news, it would require a lot of hard work before people could return to live there.

All the buildings were in ruins. No one could afford the cash to rebuild them and there would be problems of drainage and power supplies, but newspaper reports hinted there were those who felt that the dale's old spell of bad fortune had come to an end. Montague Pluke feared otherwise. He knew that someone else would die in Laverock Cottage. The legend of Laverock Cottage had not come to an end. That was the message from the crow. So when had the picture been taken, he wondered? The article had appeared yesterday and the paper would require an up-to-date illustration, so it was highly feasible that the photograph had been taken during this past week.

A new picture, in other words.

'I think we should be careful if we plan to explore those old ruins,' he suddenly said to Millicent, without explaining why.

'Yes, of course, dear,' was her response, knowing he was always careful whenever and wherever he went exploring. He had a constant awareness of the dangers of falling rocks, stones, tiles and hay-bales, especially on the thirteenth of the month. Today was not the thirteenth, yet she did not question his judgement or scoff at his caution.

Having exercised due care along their route, they arrived at the ruined hamlet shortly before three o-clock that Saturday afternoon. Millicent parked the car upon what had once been the stone floor of an outbuilding; it was covered with thistles and other plants which had found sustenance in cracks and tiny holes. Around the floor upon which she had parked every wall had gone, every vestige of windows and doors had vanished and only an occasional blue roofing slate lay among the nettles and briars. But the solid base provided a most useful parking place.

Montague, his heavy coat looking incongruous in the sultry sunshine, carried his panama in his hand as he peered at the surrounding buildings in their varying states of ruin. He was seeking the crow, but it was not here today. A few smaller birds did flit among the stones — he noticed a yellowhammer, a linnet, siskin and a family of long-tailed tits. A kestrel hovered in the distance, the smaller birds having not apparently noticed it, and as Montague began to move away from the parking base, a stoat scuttled into the undergrowth ahead of him. A wildlife haven, he thought. How marvellous. The influx of tourists would soon destroy that.

'I'm going to examine that house over there.' He pointed to his left. 'That's the one that was in the paper, Laverock Cottage.'

'Be careful,' she said, not mocking his earlier concern but noticing the precarious condition of some of the walls.

Montague wandered off, simultaneously scanning the landscape for indications of long-forgotten horse troughs and at the same time keeping an eye on the stonework around him. Certainly, much of it did look unsafe. Weeds and miniature trees were growing from cracks; a pair of jackdaws flew from an old chimney breast as Millicent followed his slow progress.

'I think this was a farm cottage,' he called to her. 'Scullery, two rooms downstairs, outhouses … and that one over there.' He pointed. 'That would be the farmhouse, the owner's place. I'll bet there is a horse trough or two hereabouts … there must have been

…'

'Maybe a developer has taken them away,' she suggested. 'And sold them in a garden centre?'

'They'd need some hefty lifting gear to do that, and the roads to this place aren't particularly good,' he observed.

'We got here all right,' Millicent retorted. 'And we don't have a four-wheel cross-country vehicle.'

'Yes, but we couldn't take a horse trough without some help, not that we would, of course,' he countered. 'Now, this would be what we would call the lounge of the cottage. They called it the house. Scullery at the back, house here, where they ate, sat by the fire and lived. Two little bedrooms at ground level and a pile of stones in the corner of what used to be one of them.'

The stones were like an elongated cairn; instead of tumbling from the walls at random to form an untidy mess along the ground, these had been carefully assembled in a fairly symmetrical pile about three feet (one metre) high. The pile was slightly more than six feet (two metres) long and would be about four foot six inches (one and a half metres) wide. Thus it was oblong in shape and stood upon the grassed floor in the corner of the former bedroom. Montague noted that it was orientated east to west.

'Someone's arranged the stones like this,' he said, noting that some had moss on their southern edge. 'Neatly arranged, aren't they? Probably stored for future use.'

'There's a funny smell,' Millicent said, her nose twitching.

'A dead animal,' he said, then sniffed the air. She was right. There was a smell and it was the scent of death — and it was coming from this pile of stones. He thought of that crow.

'Millicent, I am going to examine these stones,' said Montague, and for this he removed his voluminous overcoat. He hung it, and his panama hat, on a piece of stick protruding from a standing wall.

'What on earth for, dearest? You'll get filthy dirty, there's no water out here to wash your hands ...' Millicent had seen him do this before. 'There's not a trough under there, is there?'

On many occasions she had watched him scrape away dirt and remove huge stones with his bare hands, especially if he thought there was a horse trough hidden beneath.

At such times he seemed oblivious to the dirt he inevitably transferred on to his hands and clothing. Today was such an occasion. Montague did not respond as he began to lift away stone after stone, each the size of one used in the building of houses and dry-stone walls. Starting at the eastern end, he tossed them into the nettles nearby. And then he found the foot. A human foot. A man's foot, clad in a smart, highly polished black shoe ... he moved several more stones and quickly realised that this pile had been used to conceal a corpse. Did it contain a great man?

He recalled the lore of the thunderstorm, and said to Millicent, 'Millicent, I fear I have discovered human remains, fairly recently dead, I would say, judging by the condition of the leg and clothing. Buried under this pile of stone, and he didn't get under here either by himself or by accident. He is dead, the smell says so, there's no way any human body could survive the crushing weight of these stones. And he didn't crawl in there by himself.'

As if to reinforce his opinion, he shouted at the still form but won no response, then reached down to touch the leg. Baring the skin, he found it was cold, dead ...

'Oh, Montague, what is going on around here, I ask you?' She remained calm as she always was. 'People will think this is the murder centre of England ...'

'No one has said it is murder, Millicent. It might be an unauthorised burial. Now take the car, find a telephone and ring the Control Room at Crickledale Police Station. Tell them where I am and that I have found human remains of recent origin and tell them that a doctor, the Scenes of Crime department and the usual call-out personnel are required. Tell them the death is definitely suspicious. I shall wait here until they arrive. You'll come back for me?'

Millicent bravely did as she was asked and roared away in their private car, chugging through the narrow lanes in search of a telephone, while Montague began to inspect his immediate surroundings. Ferns grew from many of the walls, these once being encouraged as a protection against thunder and lightning, but the most prolific plant hereabouts was the elder. Thickets of elder trees grew around these ruins, these berry-bearers once being planted to keep away evil spirits and to drive away warts, sore throats and fits. They were used as a deterrent against lightning too — this place was riddled with superstitious reminders. But they had not prevented the crow from settling upon the roof of this ruined cottage. That alone suggested the man had died here.

Taking his notebook and his camera from his pocket, he began to make notes about this discovery, drawing a rough sketch of the scene showing the direction in which the corpse lay, its relationship to the walls of the ruin, the width of the burial mound of stones (by pacing it) and an estimate of the height. If the size of the burial mound was relevant, it must conceal a very large person. He noted the man's shoe was good-quality black leather and his trouser leg was black and of good-quality material too, rather like an evening suit. The sock on display was also black. The remainder was still covered up and Montague was tempted to remove the stones, but desisted, knowing that the scene must be left as nearly as possible in its original state.

As with the Druids' Circle death, he wondered whether the body had been brought here and dumped, or whether the victim, presumably male, had been lured here and killed on the spot. Or was this merely a strange burial? All were possibilities and quite feasible — he and Millicent had had no difficulty arriving and a determined killer could easily despatch a victim in these remote surrounds, either by hitting him on the head with a stone, or by shooting, or strangling …

As he wandered around, taking photographs and making notes, he realised this was an ideal place for death, remote, quiet, devoid of witnesses. So who would know of its existence? It was quite possible, of course, that the article in the newspaper had generated a lot of new interest, as it had done for Montague, but that had appeared only yesterday.

Until the body had been extracted from its cairn-like burial mound and identified, there was little more he could do. Millicent returned after fifteen minutes or so to announce that the police of Crickledale were *en route*.

'Shouldn't we be taking those stones off him?' she asked, as Montague wandered around with his hands behind his back, peering at interesting things.

'No,' he said with firmness. 'We must leave the scene exactly as it is, that's the only positive way of securing a complete investigation from a scientific point of view.'

'But he might be alive, Montague …'

'No, dearest, he's very dead. Dead as can be. Certifiably dead.'

'Who can it be, I wonder?' was her next question.

'Someone of importance,' he answered, thinking of the thunder and the quality of the black shoe. 'A large man, too, I would suggest. A great man, perhaps? But I cannot hazard a guess at this stage, for we have not received any reports of missing persons in this locality, Millicent. At least, there was none when I left the office this morning.'

And so they waited, with Millicent struggling to recall a conversation she'd heard at one of her social functions. Hadn't someone passed a comment to the effect that a certain person had not been seen in his usual haunts? It had been a fleeting comment, one which would not normally have meant anything, but now, in retrospect, it might be important. She would try to recall who had said it, and what they had said. She took to wandering around the ruins, like Montague with her hands behind her back, as she fought to recall the words and then, as the Pluke pair perambulated, the first policeman arrived. It was a uniformed constable in a small beat car and he recognised Montague, inspected the protruding foot and said, 'I'll secure the scene, sir, I was sent to confirm that there was a body here …'

'There is a body, Constable, and it is dead; not only that, it is dead in circumstances of some suspicion, as I am sure was made clear to the Control Room.'

'I am just doing what I was told, sir …'

'Well, you have seen the object to which my wife referred, so perhaps you would now radio Control Room and get Sergeant Cockfield pronounced Cofield to call out the support services? I mean the services one normally expects when there is a suspicious death! And get the Task Force out to remove this pile of stones, under my supervision, and have Detective Sergeant Tabler liaise with me here at the scene, at the earliest opportunity.'

'Yes, sir,' responded the constable, hurrying to his car.

'My word, Montague, you are impressive when you are in charge!' Millicent beamed. 'Does this mean you are on duty now?'

'Yes I am.' And he thrust out his chest, never before having had Millicent so close at hand while conducting an investigation.

'How exciting,' she oozed, with pride in her voice. 'You are so forceful when you are on duty, Montague.'

'One has one's responsibilities, Millicent.' He smiled. 'One is trained, throughout one's career, to cope with sudden and unexpected events. Now, I am afraid I must let you go. I shall be here for some considerable time, so I suggest you return home. I exhort you to keep this to yourself for the time being, but I am afraid there is nothing you can do here. I will be transported home in due course, but I might be late.'

'Can't I be of some assistance?' she almost pleaded. 'I would love to help you.'

'This is no longer a horse-trough-hunting expedition, Millicent. It is the scene of a suspicious death and all unauthorised persons must vacate or avoid the area. I must ask you to leave and take the car with you, there can be no exceptions in such an important case. I shall contact you later. I must now establish another Incident Room at Crickledale, but I fear the Chief Constable will not like it. He will begin worrying about money again, but is money more important than justice, Millicent?'

'Of course not, dearest. Well, seeing you are so determined to get rid of me, I will leave.' And she politely left the scene with a final wave from her car as she departed.

Half an hour later, the police doctor from Crickledale arrived, examined the leg and said the fellow was dead. He did not carry out a full examination because all the vital bits of the corpse were still beneath the stones. He was followed quickly by Scenes of Crime teams, the Task Force, Detective Sergeant Tabler, the Force Photographer and other back-up services. Montague gathered them around and outlined his discovery and how he had made it. Photographs were taken, with instructions to show the protruding leg, and when all the experts had studied the cairn, Montague gave word for it to be dismantled. Stone by stone, the Task Force began their work, with each stone being examined before being set aside in an orderly fashion. It did not escape anyone's notice that any one of those stones could have been the murder weapon — and what better place to conceal it than a miniature mountain of similar pieces?

A video film was made as the pile decreased and eventually the body of a large man was uncovered. From his standpoint, Montague could not see his face, but the fellow was very well dressed in what looked like an expensive dark suit.

The doctor came forward, examined the body and said, 'Good God, see who it is? Yes, I can confirm he's dead, but cannot certify the cause of death. You'll need a postmortem, Mr Pluke. Poor old Moses ...'

'Moses Nettlewren?' gasped Pluke, coming forward to examine the chubby features of the Clerk to the Crickledale Magistrates.

'I fear so,' said the doctor. 'And shot in the head by the look of it.' He pointed to a blood-encrusted hole in the side of Moses' head just below the hairline on the temple. 'I would guess that is the cause of death, Mr Pluke, but you will need confirmation.'

'Poor old Moses ...' Pluke felt a sense of shock and dismay at the realisation that one of the men with whom he had worked so closely had been murdered. The weapon was not in evidence, but no suicide could have shot himself in the head and then heaped those boulders upon himself. This was murder, most definitely. 'Poor, poor Moses. What on earth has he done to deserve this?'

Detective Sergeant Tabler had come to his side now. 'He was close to the wheels of justice, sir. Maybe a villain had it in for poor old Moses. We shall need to examine court records now, over the years, to see if Moses was instrumental in having someone put in prison. But who's going to tell his mother?'

'She is a friend of my wife, Sergeant, such a nice lady and very good with pastry, I am assured. My wife was here when I found the body ...'

'That's two murdered bodies you have found, sir, in a very short space of time,' commented Sergeant Tabler. 'I trust you now regard yourself as a prime suspect?'

'I do understand the implications, Sergeant, and I shall be willing to co-operate with the investigating officers. I know the routine, so I shall now ask the duty sergeant to inform Mrs Nettlewren. Poor old Gertrude ...'

Leaving the experts to conclude their work at the scene, Montague

Pluke adjourned to Tabler's car to make his preliminary report.

'Detective Inspector Pluke to Control,' he said into the handset of the radio. 'I confirm that we have a murder investigation on our hands.' And he gave the precise location. 'Full turn-out please. Establish an Incident Room at Crickledale Police Station, inform CID, the Chief Constable and the Divisional Commander. Do not inform the press yet — I will arrange a news conference for this evening at six at Crickledale Police Station. The deceased has not been formally identified, but I know him to be Mr Moses Nettlewren, the Magistrates' Clerk for Crickledale. Please arrange for a sympathetic officer to visit his mother to break the news.'

And so a real murder investigation, led by Detective Inspector Montague Pluke, got under way in Crickledale.

Chapter 17

The setting up of the new Incident Room occupied Detective Inspector Montague Pluke and his team during the remainder of that Saturday afternoon and into the evening. He recruited the same personnel he had deployed for the Tracy Bretton death, except for Wayne Wain, who could not be contacted because he was not at his usual place of abode. Messages had been left for his return — Pluke needed his assistance.

Although the preliminaries were undertaken that evening, with Pluke and his teams working into the late hours of Saturday night, the investigation of the death of Moses Nettlewren began in earnest on Sunday. Montague considered Sunday a moderately good day for the beginning of a new enterprise, even though it was widely considered a day of rest. There were certain exceptions to the day-of-rest syndrome, of course, such as ministers of religion who were performing their duties and senior police officers who were conducting murder investigations. It was also a good day for setting eggs under a broody hen, but not very suitable for picking hazelnuts or cutting one's hair or nails. Furthermore, there was an old belief which indicated it was unwise to make plans for the future on a Sunday.

For that reason, he decided not to make the initial stages of this investigation too formalised — there were comparisons he needed to make with the Tracy Bretton and Stephen Winton cases, so he decided to postpone any detailed plans until tomorrow. It was a fact, of course, that Monday was an excellent day for starting new enterprises and certain things like married life, so detailed plans made on a Monday in the light of what transpired on Sunday should benefit the investigation.

As he walked through the town that Sunday morning with the streets almost deserted save for a scattering of dog walkers, joggers and churchgoers, he mused upon the findings gleaned since the death of Moses. Moses Nettlewren had been formally identified by his bewildered and tearful mother, after which his huge body had been removed to the hospital mortuary; the initial PM, hastily conducted late last night, had confirmed that death was from a bullet wound in the brain. Forensic examination of his clothes and of the scene would be undertaken today while house-to-house enquiries had already started.

One problem with house-to-house enquiries near the scene was that there weren't many houses in Trattledale. There were several farms and cottages along the lanes leading into the dale, however, any one of which might contain an observant person who had seen cars or people driving around the time of Moses Nettlewren's death. That, according to the pathologist, had probably occurred on Friday afternoon or Friday evening. Already, Moses' movements and contacts at the material times were being checked, in an attempt to determine when and where he had last been seen alive, and by whom. Montague himself had seen Moses on Friday morning during his walk to work and it had been ascertained last night that Moses had been at work during the day on Friday. He had left the office at 4.30 p.m. as was his usual practice and his behaviour had been perfectly normal at that time. His secretary had expressed her opinion that he was going straight home — he did so every Friday as a rule, calling at the fish and chip shop *en route* to get tea for himself and his mother.

However, he had not called at the fish and chip shop that night, enquiries had already ascertained, and he had not been seen since leaving his office. His car was at home, in the garage, so he had not used that to drive out to Trattledale. He had clearly been transported by another person, so surely someone must have seen him during that journey?

Of major importance was the fact that the bullet in Moses Nettlewren's head had been compared with the one found in the head of Stephen Winton and the ballistics expert, persuaded to undertake the examination on a Saturday night instead of having an evening on the patio with his barbecue, had confirmed they had come from the same weapon. In all probability, that was a .22 pistol or revolver rather than a .22 rifle, something fired at fairly close range.

That diagnosis tallied with the shooting of Stephen Winton. Montague had instigated a check upon all local holders of firearms certificates by which the possession or use of .22 weapons was authorised. There were hundreds, unfortunately, some seventy of whom lived in or near Crickledale. Quite a lot of the Crickledale certificate holders belonged to Crickledale Rifle and Pistol Club — indeed the club itself held a quantity of firearms used in competitions by its members — and all certificate holders would be visited and questioned about their movements or the whereabouts of their guns. Interviewing them all would be a lengthy task.

As Montague walked through the town, raising his panama to the ladies and bidding his good-mornings to everyone *en route*, he was sure that the person who had killed Moses Nettlewren had also killed Stephen Winton, and that the person who had killed Stephen Winton was identical with the individual who thought he had killed Tracy Bretton.

This led Montague to conclude that a mass murderer was at large in Crickledale and he was firmly of the belief that the Fossford murder had occurred because of Winton's links with Crickledale. Those links, he knew, were rather more than photographing follies.

The scenario, as Montague saw it, suggested that a Crickledale killer had ventured into Fossford to despatch Winton; it was not a Fossford killer who had trekked into the Crickledale countryside to commit these foul deeds. That a Crickledonian should commit such a crime was almost unthinkable, but Montague knew that senior police officers often had to think the unthinkable and accept the unacceptable.

Having been late home last night, after supervising the establishment of the Incident Room and instigating the initial enquiries, Montague had not slept very well, even though his head had been facing south. Persons who sleep with their heads to the north, he knew, could not expect a long life, so he avoided that and made sure Millicent did likewise. The wisest thing was to sleep with one's head to the west — that was a sure way of attracting good fortune, and the term 'good fortune' embraced a host of possibilities, money, health and happiness being just a few.

His lack of sleep had arisen because the facts of the three cases, as he knew them, had churned around in his mind without respite and he had been unable to switch off his brain; he had tried to count sheep but that had produced no useful effect, other than the knowledge that the meeting of a flock of sheep on the road was regarded as a sign of good luck, even if you were late for a train or bus or other appointment.

In spite of his efforts to dismiss them, the cast of possible culprits had continued to march through his restless mind, even into the early hours. In spite of his wakeful night, one pleasing factor was that the Chief Constable had telephoned him last night at home. Furthermore, the call had been made in person from the restaurant where the Chief had been having a meal with the County Treasurer and he had said, 'Detective Inspector Pluke, you must catch this killer! This kind of thing is very bad for the image of the county … so get to work. Spare no expense this time … do you hear?'

'Yes, sir.' Montague had wondered if the Chief had had too many brandies. Normally, he told his officers not to spend money.

'I am dining with John Fortune, he's the County Treasurer you know, and he says we must catch this fellow because people will start moving out of the county in droves if they think there is a killer at large, and a bad reputation of that kind could cause small businesses not to base themselves within our boundaries … that would cost him a lot in council taxes, you see …'

'Yes, sir,' Montague had said.

If that was the good news, it had not helped ease Montague into blissful slumbers, even though he had looked under the bed and taken care not to leave his hat lying on the covers.

With Millicent slumbering at peace, he had pondered the puzzle of the three deaths and the more he had turned over the facts and clues in his mind, the more certain he was that he now knew the identity of the villain. The answer was there if one knew where to look — and Montague felt sure he did know where to look. Shocking though that first realisation was, Montague knew that it was his task, his duty no less, to bring that person to justice even if it did offend organisations like the Ladies' Tea Circle, the Local History Society, the Crickledale Ladies' Cricket Club or the Crickledale Church Flower Rota Group. As the senior law enforcement officer in Crickledale, Montague's responsibility was to uphold the law without fear or favour and in spite of friendships.

But, in those long and restless moments in bed, Montague had decided not to reveal his suspicions to anyone — after all, his beliefs were little more than surmise at this stage and he had no real facts to support his hypothesis; certainly, there was not enough evidence to justify an arrest or to arraign the suspect before a court of law. *Knowing* that a person was guilty was easy — proving that same guilt was often immensely difficult. These days, the Crown Prosecution Service wanted incontrovertible evidence before they would sanction a prosecution and so Montague knew that his main task now was either to gather the evidence necessary to secure a conviction or failing that, to persuade his suspect to make a confession or otherwise reveal his or her culpability. Montague was aware that whatever path he chose, he would need all his experience, knowledge and, he knew, just a little touch of guile. Montague Pluke was going to catch his first killer.

It was with these somewhat disturbing thoughts in his mind that he entered his office at 8.50 a.m. that Sunday morning. Perspiring slightly, he hung his panama on the hat stand and removed his cumbersome greatcoat before checking his in-tray. Nothing had arrived since last night, not surprising because there was no mail on the Sabbath, so he hurried down to the Incident Room. Already many of the officers had assembled and Mrs Plumpton, his flowing secretary in her red cascade of a dress, was organising coffee. For a Sunday morning, she seemed remarkably cheerful — but there again, she was inordinately cheerful every morning.

Wayne Wain was there too, Montague was pleased to see.

Relieved to note the sergeant's presence, Montague hailed Wayne and drew him into his tiny Incident Room office. 'I am very pleased to see you, Wayne,' he began.

'Sorry I was away, sir, I went racing yesterday afternoon at Redcar, with a friend from West Hartlepool. I won, sir — I put a tenner on Calling Lady. Thanks for that.'

'You are thanking me, Wayne? I am not a betting man.'

'It's the things you say, sir — but what about this murder? It is a murder this time, is it?'

'It is indeed, Wayne, and a nasty one into the bargain,' said Pluke. 'I fear we might have a serial killer in our midst. You know the details?'

'Yes, sir, I came as fast as I could once I heard about it. I have familiarised myself with the details — poor old Nettlewren. I was not idle last night, by the way. I managed to get some videos made by that man Ron, sir, films made in houses here in Crickledale. I got seven of them, part of a series based upon this locality. They're using the Nine Sights of Crickledale, sir, as locations. They intend doing two more to complete the set of nine.'

'You acquired those even though the old investigation has been halted? That is dedication, Wayne. We are of like minds so far as the death of Tracy Bretton is concerned. It remains very suspicious in my troubled mind. Now, do you think the videos will reveal the locations of any of the premises?'

'I think some of the scenes will reveal the identity of our suspects, sir. It seems the film company made extensive use of amateur actors. Extras, sir. People from the area who took part in the orgies just for the fun of it. And, of course, it might be possible to identify some of the interiors of the houses, assuming one has been there.'

'Then we had better view the films, Wayne.'

'They are of the kind that would offend delicate sensibilities, sir …'

'When there is duty to be done, Wayne, a police officer cannot be offended. We are not supposed to have sensibilities. So shall we examine the films after the news conference?'

'If you wish, sir,' agreed Wayne Wain, thinking that frequent instances of fast-forwarding might spare Montague's blushes.

Prior to the news conference, Montague conducted the first conference of detectives and after outlining the facts and allocating the teams their actions, he told them he was able to pay overtime with the Chief Constable's consent. This produced a short cheer. Then he added, 'I have asked for all the officers who were on the Druids' Circle enquiry to be drafted on to this investigation. I want the same brains to work on this one. I want the information that you gathered and assessed during the enquiries into Tracy Bretton's death to be considered alongside the Moses Nettlewren enquiry and likewise we must be aware constantly of the circumstances of Stephen Winton's death. Liaison with Fossford police becomes even more important. The same weapon was used to kill both Moses and Winton, never forget, and it has not been found. We must operate as if the weapon is still in the hands of the killer.'

'But ours wasn't a murder, sir,' pointed out someone from the body of the hall. 'She died of natural causes.'

'For the purposes of this investigation, Detective Constable Johnson, I want that enquiry to be treated as a murder, even though it wasn't a crime. In my view, in everything but the final technical cause of death, it was murder. I am convinced that a man thinks he killed Tracy — and her death, I am equally convinced, is linked to the death of Stephen Winton. I fully realise we shall never convict anyone of the murder of Tracy Bretton, but her untimely death, induced as I believe it was, may lead us to the killer of Stephen Winton and Moses Nettlewren.'

'Point taken, sir,' capitulated Johnson.

'I would like you all to concentrate upon the movements of the people of this town,' Pluke said. 'Those detectives on house-to-house are probably best able to check on that. Take the material times of each death — the Fossford one included — and try to ascertain if anyone was missing from their usual haunts upon each of those three occasions. There has to be a common factor. Our guilty person will be someone who possesses or who has the use of a .22 firearm of some kind — try Rifle and Pistol Club members, and the club itself. Our villain had ammunition which he must have purchased or acquired somewhere — and I must warn you of the dangers of approaching someone who might kill again. Our suspect has killed twice and thinks he — or she — has killed three times. One more death is of little consequence to him or her. Our suspect is also someone who has access to transport — each death has involved a trip out of Crickledale: one to the Druids' Circle, one to Fossford and one to Trattledale.

'There is also evidence that houses in this town have been used for the making of pornographic films, possibly without the knowledge of their owners so it might be wise for our house-to-house teams to ask each householder if he or she has ever been away from home and left the premises in the care of house-sitters. Have we someone in town who is acting as an agent for that sort of thing? How does the film company know of the unoccupied houses? The man who runs it is not saying — he says his girls find the houses. If we produce the name of a local suspect, then he, or she, must be subjected to interrogation to determine his or her movements in relation to those empty and available homes. Is he, or she, known to the householders in question, for example? Has he called there under any pretext?'

Montague Pluke spent some time outlining his ideas, careful at this stage not to categorise any of his themes as plans. Plans would come later — once the background information had been collected and analysed. Plans would be determined on Monday, which was a good day to start planning.

Having addressed his detectives, he dismissed them to go about their important duties and turned his attention to the press. They were already waiting in the reception area, news of the latest killing having attracted a large contingent of reporters and photographers representing newspapers, radio and television. The story would feature strongly in Monday's papers and news bulletins — a perfect beginning to the week for Montague Pluke. Settling them in the conference room, he provided them with the name of the deceased, the fact that he had died from gunshot wounds and that his body had been found hidden beneath a pile of stones in Trattledale. He appealed for sightings of Moses Nettlewren since Friday when he had finished work and was asked whether the murder of the eminent Magistrates' Clerk could be linked to that of Mr Stephen Winton in Fossford and the mysterious death of Tracy Bretton.

Pluke, being diplomatic and without yet referring to the links already established through the .22 bullets, said, 'We are examining that possibility and I am in contact with Fossford police. To date, we have not established any connection between the three persons, but enquiries are continuing.'

'Is an arrest imminent?' asked one reporter.

Pluke knew the reason for this question — if an arrest had been made or was imminent, then it would curtail the extent of the reported news item. Too much pre-trial publicity of the wrong kind could prejudice the fair hearing of an accused, so the press were restricted in what they could print before a trial. But if there was no arrest, or no immediate likelihood of one, they could speculate and carry out their own investigations. In this case, Pluke felt that speculation and wide publicity might help in his own campaign to flush out the accused, so he said, 'There has been no arrest, and none is imminent.'

Thus he knew the media would produce some lurid and fanciful pieces about deaths in ancient ruins and druids' circles, along with the inevitable links with witchcraft and peculiar practices. The market town of Crickledale would become famous, he knew, but it might generate a lot of gossip which in turn could produce a useful flow of information from the public. Publicity of any kind, good or bad, would mean that some of the local businesses would benefit. He could envisage that little shop in Stumpgate selling miniature druids' circles and reproductions of Trattledale Mill, although Montague did wonder if there was a market for miniature Crickledale horse troughs.

After the reporters had got their stories and the photographers their pictures of Montague standing beside a police car with a radio handset in his hand and looking business-like, Montague adjourned to one of the cells where Wayne Wain had installed a TV set at the end of a long lead.

After explaining that this place was one of the few truly dark rooms in the police station which was secure, Wain said the videos were each of half an hour's duration, and each hair-raising to the uninitiated. It is perhaps fair to say that Montague's hair did stand on end. Having once, albeit accidentally, seen Millicent in the bath, he had no idea that pieces of the female anatomy were able to perform such unusual and effective things to pieces of the male anatomy and found himself wondering why he had never learned or experienced such apparent delights.

'You can see from the titles how they have used seven of the Nine Sights, sir — *Dirty* Devil's *Bridge*, *Kinky Keep*, *Bondage beneath the Bells*, *Cupid in the Crypt*, *Bosoms in the Bath*, *Throbbing Thomas in the Tower* and *Desire with the Druids*. They'll probably finish up with something like *Naughtiness at the Nunnery* and *Virgins in the Vaults*.'

'Is all that from your rather overworked imagination, Wayne?'

'No, sir, from enquiries I have made. Right, sir, now I'll slow this sequence down. See? Isn't that Samuel Purslane ...'

'The newsagent, you mean?' said Montague, staring hard. 'Yes, by jove it is ... and what on earth is he doing with that flower vase? And that's Nathaniel Nethersage, isn't it? That man with the leather shop? Secretary of the Rifle and Pistol Club? Good heavens, Wayne, that's that chap who sells life insurance ... what's his name ... isn't he chairman of the Camera Club?'

'John George Dewberry, sir.'

'That's him, and what on earth's he doing with that rifle? And, oh dear, Wayne. That's Moses, isn't it? What a big fellow, eh? You can really appreciate his size when he has no clothes on. You know, Wayne, I'm surprised he never got married ... he would have made some woman happy, I am sure, and now he's gone. Wasted. My word, and there's that girl we met in Hartlepool ...'

'Sharon Pellow, sir.'

'Goodness gracious, Wayne, she is energetic, isn't she? Did she learn that from riding horses, I wonder?'

'She has been very co-operative with me, sir, in my enquiries I mean. It was she who gave me these tapes ... she's on them all, you see, a present from Ron but useful to us, I would suggest.'

'Very useful indeed, Wayne.' And so the viewing continued with Montague Pluke growing hot under his collar and perspiring in the coolness of the cell. Wayne, however, was revelling in the open and undisguised display of Sharon's assets and skills.

When the viewing was over, Pluke wiped his brow, asked for a drink of water and said, 'Those films are part of a series, you said, Wayne?'

'Yes, sir. They intended to make one film set in each of the tourist attractions around Crickledale. Seven are complete — the seven we have viewed. It was Ron's intention to make two more to complete the set. *Naughtiness at the Nunnery* and *Virgins in the Vaults* were the planned ones.'

'Using places in and around our fair town?'

'I fear so, sir. *Desire with the Druids* was the last one ...'

'Wayne, I saw several gentlemen in those films, people of Crickledale whom one would never dream of taking part in such things ... filthy things, really, but quite interesting in their own way, if only from an athletic point of view.'

'Two of the people in the videos are dead, sir,' Wayne had to point out. 'Tracy is one, Moses Nettlewren the other.'

'What are you saying, Wayne?' asked Montague Pluke, still visualising that scene with Sharon and the lampshade.

'I wondered how many more of the people in these films are going to die, sir.'

'A silencing routine, you mean, Wayne? Someone killing witnesses?'

'Yes, sir, something like that. I wondered if some of the people — not all, but some — will know the identity of the killer, sir. Like Moses Nettlewren.'

'And Sharon, Wayne? What about your friend, Sharon?'

'I have quizzed her, sir, she has no idea who it might be. And I have made sure she keeps out of harm's way.'

'Does this mean we have to view more of these films, Wayne?'

'I fear so, sir.'

'The things I must do for my country, Wayne.' There was a slight hint of keenness in Montague's voice. 'But Winton is not depicted in the one we have just viewed.'

'No, sir, I think he was taking photographs. He did stills, sir, for magazines.'

'Ah, so we must identify the other menfolk who are performing and rush to their rescue, Wayne, before they get shot?'

'I think so, sir.'

'But our killer could strike at any time, in any place, at any minute, Wayne ...'

'Precisely, sir.'

Chapter 18

'Purslane, Nethersage and Dewberry. I think all three are at risk, Wayne, but I believe we must find Samuel Purslane first.'

'Purslane, sir? The newsagent?' Detective Sergeant Wayne Wain puzzled over Pluke's choice. 'He's not our man, is he?'

'He is not our killer, I am sure of that, but I fear he could be the next victim, Wayne, unless we find him very soon, Come along, no time to waste.'

'But why, sir ... why Purslane?'

'On Friday morning I saw a black beetle crawling across his shoe, Wayne. A black beetle running over someone's shoe is an omen of death, yet, oddly enough, it is unlucky to kill a black beetle. Purslane did not kill it — I saw him flick it away with a newspaper and thus he retained the good fortune implied by that move. But one cannot ignore the underlying threat of evil, Wayne, which in this case is the fact that the beetle *did* crawl across his boot. It is a serious omen, Wayne, and I fear that unless we prevent it, he could die — either that, or someone closely connected with him could die.'

'Oh, blimey, he's at it again,' muttered Wayne Wain beneath his breath as he hurried to locate the official car. If he told any of his mates he'd worried about the life of a grown man because a black beetle had crawled over his shoe ...

Purslane's paper shop opened on the morning of the Sabbath to dispense the Sunday papers, but closed during the afternoon. Consequently it was closed when Pluke and Wain arrived. 'Where to now, sir?' asked Wain anxiously.

'His house, Wayne.'

Pluke's local knowledge took them directly to the semi-detached house of Mr and Mrs Purslane. Mrs Purslane, a pretty forty-year-old in tight-fitting shorts and a T-shirt, was in the garden enjoying the heat of the day while tending her borders and removing weeds. She looked up and smiled as the police car eased to a halt. Wayne Wain thought she was gorgeous; how on earth her husband could make those awful films, which involved having congress with other women, was beyond him ... did she know what he got up to? pondered Wain.

'I'd like to have a chat with Samuel, Mrs Purslane,' said Pluke without any sign of urgency, for he did not wish to alarm this cheated woman unduly.

'He's gone off with some friends, Mr Pluke,' she said. 'Twitching.'

'Twitching?' puzzled Wayne Wain.

'Rushing off and looking for rare birds,' interpreted Pluke, not noticing the *double entendre*.

But Wayne Wain understood the message. 'Where did he go?' he asked with just a hint of concern.

'I don't know. When he got home, he said they'd rung him at his shop this morning to say there was a melon-breasted cocotte in Priory Woods, just arrived from France, they'd told him, a very rare sighting. They're usually seen on the Mediterranean beaches, so they said.'

'Did he describe it as a French bird?' asked Pluke.

'Yes, that might have been what he said. A French bird.'

'Did they collect him from home?' asked Pluke.

'No, he went by himself, Mr Pluke. Only a few minutes ago, you've just missed him.'

'Did he take his own car?' continued Pluke.

'No, he said somebody would pick him up at the War Memorial, so he went off with his binoculars and camera. He said he'd be back for supper unless it meant chasing the bird a long way. Is it something important, Mr Pluke?'

'I would like to have words with him as soon as possible,' was all Pluke felt inclined to say in the circumstances. 'If he does come home, ask him to call the office, would you? Just to let me know he's back? They'll radio me if I am out of my office and I have no objection to him ringing me at home.'

'Yes, all right.' Mrs Purslane smiled, bending to deal with a *sanicula europaea*, her actions prompting palpitations in all sorts of private places within Wayne Wain's anatomy, particularly around the region of his groin. She was a handsome woman, was Mrs Purslane, mature yet fascinating, and she made a fantastic job of giving shape to her shorts.

'Shall we try Priory Wood?' suggested Wayne Wain.

'Most definitely, but how does one, with limited resources, search a large wood for someone who does not wish to be found? It is high summer, remember, with the floor of the wood thick with vegetation and cover. So, in order to have more information before me in advance of our visit to the wood, Wayne, I would like to call on George Dunwoody,' announced Pluke.

'Dunwoody, sir? Have we time?'

'My knowledge of the geography of the wood and the layout of the priory it contains leads me to conclude that we do have a little time, Wayne, but apart from that, I wish to see whether he is involved in this expedition. You see, Dunwoody is my chief suspect and I fear he might have abducted Samuel with a view to executing him.'

'Dunwoody, sir? Good God! Why him?'

'I believe he wishes to silence anyone who knows that he killed Tracy Bretton.'

'I thought she died naturally, sir?'

'She did, but I am sure that Dunwoody thinks he killed her, which is why he panicked and killed Stephen Winton — who knew what had happened — and then, for like reasons, he had to dispose of Moses ...'

'Good God, sir! All them? I can't see how you think it could be Dunwoody, sir.'

Already, Wayne was speeding the car towards the Dunwoody bungalow at No. 11a Padgett Grove and as they rushed through the quiet Sunday streets, Pluke said, 'Winton was evil, Wayne, I could sense his evil during our very first visit to the Druids' Circle. In his wake, there was a perception of evil, Wayne, rather as some people leave behind the scent of perfume or tobacco, but in this case infinitely more subtle and not even as tangible as an aura. I could sense it, however, and it was confirmed by a flight of swifts as we carried out our inspection. And we now know about his previous convictions. But Winton was not the killer, Wayne.

'The killer of Tracy Bretton is very superstitious. Of that I am positive. In both the Crowther bungalow and Stephen Winton's flat, all the mirrors were covered up with towels or sweaters or something similar. I am sure you recall that, and I am sure the Scenes of Crime teams have recorded that MO. Those mirror covers were not put there to dry, Wayne, as most police officers might think. They were put there by someone highly superstitious who believes that if a person catches sight of a reflection of himself in a mirror while there is a dead body in the room, that person will die soon afterwards. It's an old belief, Wayne, one which is still extant in some places, and that provided me with my main clue.

'Another one concerns the position of each of the dead bodies. It's a longstanding belief that it is unlucky to walk past a murdered body, especially when it is lying on the ground. Our killer placed all his victims so that he need not walk past them: they were all in corners; and at the hospital, Tracy was in a filing cabinet on the wall. He did not have to walk past her either. The positions of the bodies therefore provided another clue.

'A further one came from the glove that was found in the woods near the Druids' Circle. It was in good condition and we had every reason to believe it was dropped by the killer. I believe it was — and who wears black gloves in summer? Undertakers and their assistants, Wayne. Smart men in black suits carrying coffins. Or those helping them, as Dunwoody does. But why did he not pick it up? I will explain. There is an old notion that if you drop a glove, you should never pick it up because it would bring bad fortune — you let someone else pick it up because that brings good fortune. But the killer, in the midst of disposing of the body, would hardly want to attract bad fortune, so he took the calculated risk of the glove not being found or identified and therefore left it where it fell. I am sure he felt that an anonymous black glove, with no means of identification, would not be regarded as important — but we know that any clue is important, Wayne. And we know that a local supplier stocks gloves of an identical kind.

'Now, to continue. You may recall that when I mentioned to Dunwoody about the girl's body being transported to the Druids' Circle, he commented that the route taken might become a public right of way, even though it traverses private premises. Well, Wayne, that is an old superstition too, and the basis of the many so-called corpse roads which cross our countryside.'

'And I suppose he had all the opportunities, sir, being a freelance taxi driver and man-of-all-parts. But you continue to refer to the *killer* of the girl found at the Druids' Circle, sir, while we know that Tracy died naturally.'

'I have already said I believe that Dunwoody thought he had killed the girl, and his subsequent behaviour is a direct result of that. Remember, I did tell him that I was hunting a murderer, and I did that quite deliberately. He has gone berserk since then ...'

'You're not saying your actions are responsible for these deaths, sir?'

'Of course not. He was responsible for those deaths, not me. And who knows what goes through a killer's mind? My task is to keep this town as free from crime and criminals as I can. Now, back to the Dunwoody theory — we know that he has the means of travelling out of town to all sorts of places while no one considers his movements odd, whatever time of the night or day they occur.

'I saw his taxi in town in the early hours following the night Winton was killed. His landlady heard a car engine left running an hour or so prior to that. And taxis do stand outside houses with their engines running. Taxis were also seen outside No. 15 Padgett Grove during filming sessions and what better way for the film-makers to move around a location individually than by local taxi? It is a system widely used by the television and film industry. Was it one taxi seen several times, or several taxis? If Dunwoody was hired regularly by the pornographic film-makers, he would know their routines, their locations, the personalities involved, the houses they used … And I think the message about the French bird was a secret way of telling Samuel that a willing woman had been found and that his presence was required for filming. It was a ploy, of course, but one that convinced him that his attendance was needed. A melon-breasted cocotte is just another way of describing a high-class prostitute … a cocotte is the French for prostitute, you see, Wayne, and we all know what melon breasts are like … even I know that — and the term "French bird" is often used to describe any bird that is unusual in any way … like a white blackbird or even a hen blackbird, which is brown …'

'Hang on, sir, you're ahead of me, a long way ahead. What makes you think Dunwoody is superstitious? Covered-up mirrors, fallen gloves and an old notion of corpse roads are not totally convincing reasons.'

'Very true, Wayne. Apart from the things I have mentioned, he has numbered his house 11a instead of 13 for one thing,' said Pluke.

'He deals with his boiled-egg shells by crushing them in exactly the same way our ancestors did when trying to avoid witches; he touches wood for good luck; he refuses to allow red and white flowers in the house, just as hospitals won't allow them inside the wards ... he's superstitious all right, Wayne. And remember how the girl's body was laid, feet together to prevent the egress of evil spirits, while poor old Moses Nettlewren was laid with his head towards the rising sun. And another thing, Wayne, why were such elaborate steps taken to conceal the body of Moses Nettlewren? It was, I believe, because there was a very likely chance that, in such a remote place, he would lie unburied on a Sunday. If a funeral is postponed for any reason, it means others in the vicinity will die within a week, or certainly within three months, and this is especially the case if a body remains unburied over a Sunday. So our superstitious killer, thinking of his own skin, made sure Moses was buried beneath that heap of stones before the arrival of Sunday.'

They were now approaching Padgett Grove and Wayne drove into the drive of No. 11a. There was no sign of activity at the house, but Pluke knocked on the kitchen door and soon Ada Dunwoody appeared.

'Oh, hello, Mr Pluke. I thought for a moment it was May and Cyril coming to say they were back after their holiday.'

'Is Mr Dunwoody around?' asked Pluke.

'No, he's had to do a run, a taxi run. Some bird-watching fanatics ...'

'Where to? Did he say?'

'No, he just said he had to meet somebody at the War Memorial and off he went ...'

'How long ago?'

She glanced at her watch. 'Not long, Mr Pluke, ten minutes, no longer.'

'Thanks,' said Pluke, shouting at Wayne, 'War Memorial, Wayne.

It's him!'

'Mr Pluke, what is it?' called Ada as the detective in the funny coat ran towards his car. But she got no reply and when they reached the War Memorial there was no sign of Samuel Purslane or of George Dunwoody and his taxi.

'Shouldn't we circulate a description for all mobiles to keep observations, sir?' suggested Wayne Wain.

'Yes, we shall require their support, Wayne. Place them on the alert, will you, by radio, but stress that they must keep away from all routes into Priory Wood until I order otherwise. I do not want Dunwoody to know we're on to him, Wayne. A surfeit of rushing police officers might precipitate some illogical actions on his part and put Purslane at a greater risk. Remember, Dunwoody has used a gun and I am sure he is still in possession of one.'

'He's not on our list of firearms holders, sir, I checked,' stated Wayne Wain.

'No, he's not. But one of the men used for making those films was the secretary of the Crickledale Rifle and Pistol Club, Wayne, and a rifle was used in at least one of the films. I am sure he was, shall we say, persuaded to let the film people use weapons from the club armoury — and then allow himself to be rewarded by favours from attractive girls — and it would not surprise me at all to learn that Dunwoody, who taxied such people around, was able to acquire such a firearm — even that very one — nor that, if we examine the club's records right now, we should find one .22 weapon missing, but we have no time at this moment.'

'But, sir, where do we begin? There's a lot of countryside out there …'

'The priory in Priory Wood … Mrs Purslane mentioned Priory Wood. Remember the two films yet to be made? *Naughtiness in the Nunnery* and *Virgins in the Vaults* or something like that, you said. If the film-makers are planning two more films at the remaining two of Crickledale's Nine Sights, one must have surely been planned at the old nunnery in Trattledale, Wayne. That being so, consider how easy it must have been for our killer to persuade poor old Moses Nettlewren that he was required there for a filming session, with all the pleasures that promised him, and how easy it would have been to take him there by taxi to be shot. So that Sight has now been used — by the killer, that is.'

'Point taken, sir, and Priory Woods?'

'Our superstitious killer will not want a body unburied on a Sunday, so he has decided to kill him and place him in a ready-made grave, Wayne. A vault. You know and I know that there are vaults at the old priory. I have, in the course of my historical researches, examined the vaults in some detail, Wayne, without finding a horse trough, I might add. So what on earth did the monks' horses drink from? However, I believe Purslane has been tricked into travelling there by taxi, to meet his death and be buried there ...'

'But it's Sunday, sir, the place will be overrun with tourists?'

'Precisely, Wayne,' said Pluke without elaboration. 'So we must take due cognisance of that fact.'

With Wayne Wain exercising all his driving skills, they were hurtling towards the old priory in the woods. It was an eight-mile journey, during which Wayne radioed to Control to alert the support services to order them to stand by for a call for assistance with a firearms unit.

'I do not, repeat not, want the teams to join me yet,' Pluke ordered, taking the handset from his sergeant to address Control. 'But be prepared for my call and stand by to rendezvous with me immediately — you could muster close to the priory — because I want Purslane to survive.'

'And I want to survive ...' muttered Wayne Wain as he guided the fast-moving car with all his expertise towards the villainous vaults.

Chapter 19

'The Crickledale vaults', said Detective Inspector Montague Pluke as Detective Sergeant Wain eased to a halt in the car-park of Priory Woods, 'are unique in this country, Wayne. Their design is based on the nave of St Ambrogio at Milan, which was one of the earliest completely ribbed vaults and dates from the eleventh century. The local vaults extend over a huge area, far larger than the ground floor of York Minster, although only a tiny portion is open to the public. The Norman design, which you can see in some of our abbeys, was based on this style ...'

'Are you saying these vaults date from Norman times, sir?'

'No, Wayne, our vaults are copies of those in Milan which means they are later, but they are most unusual, more so because they are on the North York Moors. Our vaults are believed to have been built in the fourteenth century and the records show that a certain Erasmus Pluke helped with the construction. He was a lay worker at the priory, the prior being Father Jerome from Rome, hence the Italian connection. But, in this case, the Crickledale vaults are of further interest because they are underground and used for the storage of coffins and contents — did you realise that the body of St Teilo of Penally is said to be buried here? I am sure our Welsh friends do not know that. Now, Wayne, the vaults in our cathedrals and abbeys are above ground and do not contain coffins, which makes ours of such importance and interest.'

'So where will Dunwoody be?' Wayne was getting anxious. Pluke seemed to be acting as if he was on a walking tour rather than in pursuit of an alleged armed murderer.

'We are about to enter via the tourists' gate,' said Pluke, who was now standing beside their vehicle. 'You pay, Wayne, and recover the money through expenses. We will descend the staircase into the vaults ...'

'Sir, we need to plan carefully ... Dunwoody must know we are on to him.'

'I am sure he does not, Wayne. I am sure he has never given that a thought.'

'But we do need back-up, sir! Dunwoody is thought to be armed.'

'He will not enter the vaults via this route, Wayne. He would never bring his intended victim into the vaults through the entrance used by the general public, that would be rank stupidity; besides, it means he would meet others on the staircase, and it is very unlucky to cross on the stairs. Dunwoody will use the other entrance, Wayne, the one that is never used by tourists or paying visitors to the vaults. It lies at the northern boundary, Wayne, an extra drive of some six or seven miles, followed by a long walk across three fields. It is well off the beaten track.'

'I had no idea there was another entrance, sir.'

'Few people do know, Wayne. But I know, being interested in local history, and so do many of the local people, especially boys who have played here for generations, getting into mischief, like Dunwoody ... the door has never been locked either. There is simply a massive wooden door studded with metal, which is almost hidden behind centuries of thickening vegetation.'

'So what is our plan, sir?'

'We shall enter the vaults by the tourist route, Wayne, then await the arrival of our suspect. And I shall take the precaution of being accompanied by an armed officer. Now, do these radios work from underground?' Pluke held up a personal radio set for Wayne to examine.

'Yes, they even work underwater, sir.'

'That is very useful if the fish pond above the vaults is ever replenished, Wayne. Now, where are our back-up teams?'

Using his own personal radio, Wayne Wain contacted Sergeant Cockfield pronounced Cofield in the Control Room and was told that the support services, including an armed response unit, had assembled and were awaiting Pluke's instructions. Two units were within two minutes' drive of the priory. Without using a map as his reference, Pluke then issued orders to Sergeant Cockfield pronounced Cofield and instructed one unit of two officers to proceed to a specified map reference which he provided from memory, to report sightings of Dunwoody's taxi but not to approach it and then to prepare to enter the vaults upon the command of Pluke. That unit comprised one armed constable and one unarmed. A second team, of like composition, was to report to the main entrance of the vaults, there to rendezvous with Pluke and Wain. Pluke said he would close the place to the public, but only when his quarry had entered. Of the remaining supporting officers, numbering a dozen, half were to rendezvous at the main car-park to deal with any eventuality that might arise, with the other half at the northern entrance to do likewise.

'Now, let us proceed,' said Pluke to his sergeant as he strode from the car-park towards the turnstile.

'Shouldn't our officers pick him off before he gets here, sir?'

'Left to his own devices, he will not kill Purslane until he is inside the vaults, Wayne. It's a question of disposal of the body you see, and of his own beliefs. He needs to be sure he has disposed of the corpse, so he must kill Purslane deep inside the vaults. If we harass him and make our presence known before he gets into the vaults, though, he might be panicked into killing Purslane and even others ... I cannot risk that. Terrible though it might sound, we might have to sacrifice Purslane in order to save further lives, Wayne.'

'So the map reference you have just given is the rear approach?'

'Yes, by the time our officers arrive at that point, Dunwoody will have departed for the long walk across the fields. His car will be there ... that will be a sign that we know for certain what he is about to do.'

'You seem very sure about things, sir.'

'I know Dunwoody, Wayne, and I know how he will react. Local knowledge you see, it's very important in a police officer. And I know my way around these vaults — as indeed does he. Do you know that it is unlucky to step across a grave?'

'I heard my mother say that a long time ago when we went to put flowers on my granny's grave ...'

'Now, Wayne, the floor of the vaults, in both the public and private portions, is full of graves. The walls of the vault, however, contain lead coffins, stacked high on shelves rather like a wine cellar and dating back centuries. None the less, there are one or two empty places, Wayne. Very handy for leaving a corpse. As you'd find in a church, there are graves in the floor which are covered with huge stone and marble memorials laid flat upon them. There is a route between them, Wayne. It's almost like a maze, but Dunwoody will take that route. He will not want to step over a grave. But because it is unlucky to pass a dead body which is lying on the ground, he will take his victim to the deepest part of the vaults, so that he can kill him and return the way he came, without passing the corpse he has just created. I do not think he will be giving deep thought to his plans: his reactions will be instinctive, due to his beliefs. It is dark down there and that section is not, and never has been, open to the public. He will know that the chances of anyone finding the corpse are remote in the extreme; he could even lock the door, I suppose, to keep wanderers out. If children found a body down there, I wonder if they would report it?'

'But can we get into that enclosed part of the vaults, sir?'

'Indeed we can, Wayne, and we can do it from the public area. I know the way, I have used it many times in my research, and I shall take one of the firearms officers. First, though, we must close the vaults to the general public; Dunwoody will never know what is going on at this end, he is too far away.'

Calmly, Montague Pluke asked the man at the turnstile to close the vaults until further notice, due to a vital police operation within them, and to clear the place of those visitors already there. As this was happening, PC Dave Horne of the firearms response unit (FRU) arrived, complete with a rifle that looked like a machine-gun, and was briefed by Pluke. He was clad in a smart navy-blue uniform sweater and beret. A radio check with his colleague, PC Kev Hatfield, revealed that Dunwoody's taxi had been observed; it was parked empty at the edge of the priory grounds on the northern boundary, adjacent to a footpath which led across several meadows.

'There is no time to lose,' said Pluke, leading the way.

Leaving a uniformed member of the support team to prevent anyone entering the vaults via the public route, Montague Pluke led his team of two into the well-lit depths, his actions being observed by the assembled tourists. Word would soon spread that something sinister was happening in the vaults. Leading into the depths was a modern stone staircase with a metal rail at each side and another running down the middle to provide both an Up and a Down route. Pluke walked on to the first step, leading with his right foot, and opted for the right-hand route. All the visitors had now left, Wayne Wain noting that no one was ascending to thwart the good fortune that his boss would require. The interior below ground was brightly illuminated and the visitors' route around the vaults, with a variety of lead, oak and stone coffins on view, was marked with chromium-plated rails and arrows pointing 'This Way. Please Keep to the Official Route. Do Not Touch the Exhibits.'

'The section to which we are heading will be in darkness,' Pluke told Wayne and Dave. 'I have a torch.'

'Are you sure you know what you are doing, sir?' asked Dave Horne with just a hint of nervousness, producing a torch of his own from the kit he carried on his belt. It was like a miner's light.

He clipped it around his head, the lead reaching down to the battery in his kit.

'Completely,' said Pluke, upon which Wain nodded his head briefly to the constable, to indicate his own faith in Montague Pluke. 'We shall reach a point in the other section, PC Horne, where we can conceal ourselves. Dunwoody will bring his victim to a position from which he will intend to carry out his execution — I know precisely where that will be because his choice is limited to that place. We will announce our presence and you will order him to lay down his arms and submit to arrest. If he runs away, your colleague will be outside, also armed. The secret door into the vaults will be standing open — Dunwoody will make sure he leaves it open. It is a custom at the moment of death to throw open the door, you see, and Dunwoody will make sure that is done, so that the soul of his victim is able to depart without hindrance. Wayne, perhaps you will radio for the support units at Dunwoody's car to move across the fields towards the rear entrance.' And he provided the map reference. 'But ask them not to make a noise and not to enter the vaults. Their duty is to arrest Dunwoody if he attempts to flee, bearing in mind he is armed. He will exit via the route he used for entry. If, on the other hand, he does attempt to flee or hide below ground, then we shall shout "Ten Nine, Ten Nine" upon our radio sets and at that signal they should enter the vaults, albeit in the knowledge that they are likely to confront an armed intruder. Otherwise, radio silence will be enforced. Now, let us proceed.'

Following Pluke, Wayne Wain radioed his instructions to the outside teams. Then Pluke halted, placed a finger upon his lips to indicate the need for silence and stepped over the chromium rail.

He appeared to be walking into a dark comer, but produced his miniature torch and shone it on the ground for his companions. It could now be seen in the dim light that the corner was shaped like a double 'Z' and that there was an exit.

After a trek of some fifteen paces, Pluke halted. 'We are now in the disused section of the vaults,' he whispered. 'These are far more extensive than the public area; we need to move to a position which is some fifty paces from here. Keep very quiet and listen for the sound of Dunwoody's approach. We shall hear him long before he becomes aware of our presence ...'

In total silence and in darkness broken only by the beam from Pluke's tiny torch, they moved through the high ranks of ancient coffins until Pluke halted.

'PC Horne, for reasons I explained earlier to Detective Sergeant Wain,' whispered Pluke, 'Dunwoody will come to this point.' And he shone his beam on to the floor. 'He will want to kill his victim so that the body either falls, or is easily moved, into that space directly ahead.' And he shone his torch on to the bare stone floor; it was a narrow gap between the tiers of coffins and the rock wall of the vault. There was just room for an adult human to be laid there. 'The chances of anyone finding the deceased before his body turns to dust are remote in the extreme,' continued Pluke. 'The perfect hiding place for a corpse, in other words, especially if it is covered in some way ...' And he switched off his torch.

'Purslane would never come here voluntarily,' muttered Wayne Wain in the darkness, thinking of the supposed birdwatching expedition.

'At this stage, he will be at gunpoint, Wayne,' Pluke reminded him. 'Now, PC Horne, your role is vital, so where do you wish to position yourself?'

PC Horne, highly trained, used his own powerful light to examine the inlet routes and other factors, before determining a suitable position. 'I'll be fine here, sir. I can protect the victim, cover the assailant and watch the exit route ...'

And then they heard noises. Voices. Footsteps. A harsh, domineering voice echoing in the distant darkness. Each switched off his light.

'Total silence, total darkness,' whispered Pluke. 'Radio silence.'

At first, the words were indistinct but soon they could hear a male voice ordering, 'Keep going ... down there ... no fooling about, Sam ... I'm right behind you with the gun ...'

'But George, I don't understand ...'

'You don't have to, not any more. You know too much, you have got to go, Sam, sorry but I can't risk you being alive ...'

'But we're in this together, for God's sake.'

'The filming, the dealing, the fun, yes, but not the girl ...'

'The girl as well, George, one secret's like any other ...'

'I don't want locking up, Sam, I can avoid it ...'

'But I can keep your secret ... and that photographer and poor old Moses ... I won't talk, I daren't talk, we're too deep in all this, all of us.'

'I can't risk it, not now the girl's dead ... come along, move ...'

'But my wife ...'

'She'll think you have run off with a French bird.' And Dunwoody laughed. 'Nobody will find you down here, Sam, not for a few centuries, anyway.'

The voices came nearer and nearer, growing louder and louder as murderer and potential victim came closer to the dark and deep recess where the three policemen had concealed themselves. Dunwoody had a powerful torch which was now reflecting from the ceiling and exposed walls, casting weird shadows as, from time to time, it lighted on a white skull or a bone dragged on to the floor by a visiting animal. From the way it waved about, Pluke deduced it was hand-held.

'Act as you think necessary,' whispered Pluke to PC Horne, adding almost as an afterthought, 'We want them both alive. Dunwoody is the man with the gun.'

*

'Stand there, Sam,' said Dunwoody, his torch shining into the face of his one-time friend. 'In that gap ...'

In the reflected light of Dunwoody's torch Pluke noticed that Dunwoody now had it in the same hand that held the stock of his rifle. It was clutched against the stock, pointing at the sights. Blinded by the light, the hapless Purslane obeyed and the watchers saw him stand blinking in the place which might soon be his final resting place, then Pluke whispered, 'Now, PC Horne.'

In a trice, the brilliant light from Horne's head bathed Dunwoody as the policeman bellowed, 'Police. Halt. Drop your gun ... this is the police and we are armed ...'

But Dunwoody reacted instantly. He turned and ran back along the route, his bobbing light weaving between the rows of coffins. Then he halted, rested his rifle on a lead coffin and turned, shouting, 'One move, any of you, and you're dead.'

'Can you hit his torch?' Pluke asked Horne. 'Can you extinguish his light?'

'I'll try, sir.'

'Give me one moment.' And he called, 'George Dunwoody. This is Detective Inspector Montague Pluke. You are under arrest for the murders of Stephen Winton and Moses Nettlewren ...'

'Catch me first.' And there was a crack as the first of his shots whizzed into the darkness somewhere above their heads and thumped into the solid rock; PC Horne took careful aim and squeezed his trigger. It was an easy shot at a fairly close distance. It smashed into the torch, extinguishing its light and hurtling the remains from Dunwoody's hand, breaking two fingers in the process. His rifle clattered to the floor in the darkness.

'Nice shot,' said Wayne Wain. 'Brilliant, in fact. Mr Dunwoody, you are surrounded, armed officers are outside and inside the vaults.'

'I didn't intend to kill her ...' He was weeping now. 'God knows I didn't ... she just died on me ... in the bath, they were all there watching, taking photos, filming ...'

'I know,' said Pluke.

*

'I thought you might like to see where it all started,' said Pluke to Millicent the following Sunday. So they drove out to the Druids' Circle where Millicent parked the car and locked it. Pluke showed her the old horse trough which he had found and they strolled towards the Circle, now busy with visitors. He led her to the underground chamber and said, 'She was in there, round the corner.'

'Show me.' Millicent smiled. 'I am very interested in how you solved this crime.'

Taking his faithful little torch from his pocket, he led her into the smelly place and shone the light upon the stone shelf upon which Tracy's body had lain.

'She was lying there, naked,' he said in hushed tones.

'It's a double-bowled horse trough,' she said. 'Lying on its side ... see? And you never noticed, Montague.'

Other Montgue Pluke books

A well-pressed shroud - March 200(

Superstitious Death - 1998

A Full Churchyard - Aug. 2014

Prize Murder

Garland for a Dead Maiden

The Curse of the Golden Trough.